OBSCENE GESTURES OF AN INVISIBLE HAND

Financial Doom and the Death of Culture – The Lighter Side

a novel by

Jeffrey J. Trester

OBSCENE GESTURES OF AN INVISIBLE HAND

Financial Doom and the Death of Culture – The Lighter Side

OBSCENE GESTURES OF AN INVISIBLE HAND

Financial Doom and the Death of Culture – The Lighter Side

Contents:

AUTHOR'S NOTE

I would like to thank the two people who made my vision for the cover of this book a reality, they being Charles S. Carrano, who took the cover photograph and did the layout, and Francine G. Trester, who did the cover design. Just goes to show you how much you can accomplish when you have a gifted sister and brother-in-law. I'd also like to express my gratitude to Malena Santomero, who gave generously of her time and talent to proofread my manuscript. Last but not least, thank you to my parents, Seymour and Patricia A. Trester, for raising me, educating me and generally putting up with me all these years.

...he intends only his own gain, and he is in this, as in many other cases, led by an invisible hand to promote an end which was no part of his intention.

-Adam Smith, *The Wealth of Nations*, 1776

Chapter 1: In the Temple of Mammon

There are people in New York who move fortunes around the world, yet still take the bus to work.

Jack Kline was one of these. It was 6:30 in the morning, and he stood at Fifth Avenue and Seventy-ninth Street, dreading the arrival of the bus that would take him to midtown. Twenty other young professionals stood with him, huddled under umbrellas, protecting themselves from a freak icy November rain.

This is not where I'm supposed to be. He'd never imagined himself in the job he had now. It felt unnatural, and that feeling of strangeness seemed to permeate everything. The street, the city, even the people around him seemed alien. He glanced at the faces surrounding him and saw exhaustion, tension, and barely concealed hostility. Some kid under the bus stop shelter was taking out his aggression on a hand-held video game that sounded like a dog's squeak toy being passed through a fax machine. The freezing rain came down a little harder.

"It's a beautiful day in the neighborhood," Jack whispered under his condensing breath. This scene was not what he needed. He was tired, and this was a morning he needed to be sharp, focused. He knew he might have a shot today, one he'd waited for with excruciating patience, and he didn't want to blow it because of transit stress.

The bus came and he stepped aboard, swiping a pass card through the reader. Looking down the aisle he saw the mix of Upper Manhattan working class and Upper East Side financial types who'd boarded on the way down Fifth.

He slid into a seat behind a well-dressed thirtyish couple, attachés at their feet. Matching wedding bands graced their hands, and the woman gently cradled a bundle in a blanket. Maybe the strangeness was all in his head. Here was a perfectly normal married couple, happily chatting as they took their baby to work with them. Perhaps they even worked together, the rug rat playing on the floor. Jack's groggy mind was cheered by the image.

Just then, the woman adjusted the bundle so Jack could observe the face of its contents. To his horror, he gazed upon a visage covered in scales, with large, glassy, inhuman eyes. He let out an audible gasp before his sleep-deprived brain realized he was looking not at the demon baby from some low budget horror flick, but at a large fish packed in ice.

The woman turned around, startled by Jack's outburst. Jack smiled apologetically, and, feeling the need to say something, volunteered, "Er ... that's quite a...cod...you have there."

"Actually, it's a sturgeon," she replied coldly, seeming offended.

Jack had broken the first rule of New York mass transit: never invite the attention of anyone around you, especially if they're toting deceased marine life. Yet he had to ask,

"Do you often transport fish this way?"

At that her husband, apparently taking the question as some kind of come-on, jerked his head around and snapped,

"Hey, this is my woman and my seafood. Mind your own damn business."

"Uh, no problem."

Jack got off the bus at Fifty-seventh Street.

"Now forget what just happened," he whispered. "Got to focus this morning. You can do it. Mind over Manhattan..."

He took a few steps and stopped.

Fucking city's got me talking to myself.

Jack was a Vice President of Sales and Trading at Stone & Co., an investment bank. It was not what he'd intended to be. He'd been educated as a theoretical physicist, gone to college at MIT and spent four more years there to get a Ph.D. He'd graduated just in time for the collapse of the academic job market. With people talking about cutting Medicaid, there was little congressional enthusiasm for spending billions on accelerators to find subatomic particles known only to Jack and a few hundred others. Research budgets were slashed. Thousands of newly minted scientists found only poverty in the groves of academe, if there were any place for them at all.

Jack had published a string of papers in prestigious journals, and when his professors described him, words like "brilliant" inevitably came up. But the brilliant were leaving physics, especially those of ambition and the flexibility of mind to do something else. Had he endured the postdoctoral appointments and assistant professorships, if he'd spent his youth begging for grants and kissing senior faculty posterior, if he'd done all this he'd have probably won tenure eventually. Somewhere along the way, all that supplication, the struggle just to secure a position of poverty, lost its appeal.

As a result, Jack found himself looking for a new career, and he found it on Wall Street. The mathematical skills he'd acquired were valued there. Hoards of physicists, mathematicians and computer scientists, exiles from the ivory tower, had already descended on the Street. There they applied their knowledge to the increasingly technical world of finance. Unlocking the secrets of the universe, well, that and fifty cents will get you a cup of coffee. But show someone a way to make all that pointy-headed stuff turn a buck and, hey, you've got something there.

Stone & Co. had its offices on Sixth Avenue and Fifty-fourth, in one of the dozens of nondescript towers that lined the avenue like so many glass and steel Kleenex boxes stood on end. These uninspired geometric forms were New York's cathedrals of commerce, its temples of Mammon. Much of Wall Street was actually in midtown, much more since that September day when great towers were replaced in the mind with the numerals they'd resembled. People convinced they speak for heaven often bring hell to Earth. For those on the Street who had lived it, life had stopped as they'd grieved and struggled. But in the end they had returned to their dealing and trading, because these things had to be done, and because those who did these things did not know what else to do.

Jack entered the building and rode the elevator up to the fifty-fifth floor, the home of Stone's sales and trading department.

Stone & Co. was a partnership. The large investment banks were now publicly traded companies. Private partnerships like Stone were denied the capital that could be raised by going public. This kept them small, unable to compete with the Merrills or Morgans in leading blue chip underwritings. Instead, they specialized in "boutique" businesses – M&A advice, merchant banking, money management, proprietary trading. This last, gambling with the firm's own money, was what Jack now did for a living.

It was 6:50 a.m. and there weren't many people on the floor yet, just some foreign bond guys seeing how Europe was doing and chewing over the Asia closes. Jack sat down at his trading desk and flipped on the flat-panel displays of his Bloomberg financial data terminals, his eyes on the markets. He squinted at the foreign trading summaries. The symbols in front of him refused to make sense – it was too early for greed, and he was still upset by the bus incident.

He looked at his reflection in the terminal screen, a sandy-haired, thirty-three-year-old with the kind of fair-complected face that, in a dark bar, could still get him carded. He stretched a wiry six-foot frame in his swivel chair. His was an athleticism that comes to some small, bespectacled, bookish kids when they get older, in time to protect against arteriolosclerosis but not the fists of playground bullies. Running and regular visits to the gym had so far staved off what his colleagues termed "body by trading floor"; the end result of sitting at a computer all day while unlimited amounts of food are delivered to you on the firm's dime.

What the fuck's happened to me? Only a few years ago he saw himself as one of the elect of science, attempting to divine the hidden structure of the cosmos. Now his main concern was surviving the bus ride to Midtown. For truly great minds, even mass transit could be an intellectually stimulating experience. Einstein had sat on a streetcar at the age of sixteen and imagined what it would be like to ride on a wave of light, a daydream that led him to the theory of special relativity. What insight had *he* gleaned on his daily forty-block sojourn - the importance of avoiding commuters bearing fish?

As a proprietary trader at Stone, Jack's job was to make trades using the firm's own capital, placing bets on the movements of financial markets based on the output of complex mathematical models he developed to help him figure the odds. The firm referred to such activities with terms like "risk-controlled arbitrage" and "informed speculation," lending them an aura of prudence and sophistication. Jack was more inclined to view his current career as the answer to the question, "What if a bookie knew calculus?"

He tried to concentrate again, punching up a graph of the kyat. This was the currency of Myanmar, the nation also known as Burma. The kyat had fallen overnight, snapping a five-session winning streak that had raised the currency 4% versus the dollar. For weeks Jack had been contemplating the possibility of a serious correction in the kyat, a sharp drop in its exchange rate. This could be the beginning of what he'd been waiting for. In an instant, he was fully awake, analyzing how this latest movement affected the output of his models.

By now it was 7:15 and the floor was beginning to fill up. Jack didn't have to look up from his screens to know this; in fact, he didn't even have to hear their voices to know the traders had arrived. He could feel them through the floor. The trading room was filled with computers, quote terminals, telephones and fax machines, and all of these were hooked up to the rest of the world through an impossible tangle of cables and power lines. To avoid having traders constantly tripping over this electrical spaghetti, a false wooden floor was constructed above the wires, which emerged only through holes under the trading desks. The result was that the traders did business on a constantly vibrating surface, and the more of them on the floor, the greater the oscillations. Thus, the traders were, quite literally, always on shaky ground.

Jack felt a hand on his shoulder. He looked up and saw Mike Hubert, one of Stone's foreign exchange traders, standing over him. Universally known as Hubie, he was a short, rotund man with a shock of jet-black hair and heavy eyebrows. His eyelids were never more than half open, giving him the appearance of continuous exhaustion. Fifteen years ago he'd started as a trading clerk, spending his nights earning an MBA from NYU. He'd bounced from firm to firm, and for a time been a rising star on a trading desk run by the man who was now Secretary of the Treasury. Now thirty-six and with a brain like a calculator, he'd have risen far higher than his current position as a V.P. at Stone, but for one peculiar trait: Hubie had no visceral appreciation for the relative significance of different sized gains and losses. To him, a ten-dollar gain and a ten-million-dollar gain were equivalent on some basic moral plane. You either won or you lost, period. That was all that mattered to him. Unfortunately, this was not the attitude of either the other traders or of management. At Stone he was thought some kind of idiot savant, incredibly useful but not to be trusted with decision-making power. As a result, Hubie's main responsibility was placing large trades for proprietary traders like Jack. Hubie had a special gift for placing trades of any size without "moving the market," or causing the price to change, and was thus both highly prized and well compensated. This arrangement was fine with him, because at least as far as Jack could tell, Hubie's interest in trading was actually quite modest, especially compared to his concern over the difficulty of his commute from Long Island. Obsession was more like it, and he gave Jack a report on his morning travail at the start of each day. After this morning's bus ride, Jack didn't really feel up to it. He was relieved when Hubie started talking politics instead.

"Hey Jack, you hear what our President just announced? He's proposing a budget package with huge cuts in services. He's just gonna gut them. Like they're not pathetic enough already. Unbelievable."

"You're kidding…" Jack was surprised – he considered the current administration profligate spenders. Bonds should rally on such news, but his screen told him that market was flat.

"Yeah. And you know they'll hike fares anyway!" Hubie was near apoplectic.

"Hike what?"

"Fares. Like the Long Island Rail Road isn't the world's biggest rolling rip-off already."

"You're saying the White House is planning to hike fares on the LIRR?"

"What the fuck are you talking about, Kline?"

"You said the President of the United States would submit a budget proposal…"

"Not him. *Our* president. The president of the Mass Transit Authority."

"*Our* president?"

"Look, it's not that I don't give a shit about what goes on inside the Beltway or the board rooms around here, but I care about policy that effects *my life*, and I'm on that train every damn day. The MTA couldn't impact my life more if they ran a track up my ass. Being a New Yorker, a Presbyterian, an American, a freaking mammal – most of the time, that's just abstraction. I'm a *commuter*. That's real, and that makes the MTA's president *my* president, whether I like it or not."

Like most of the traders, Jack liked Hubie a great deal. He knew his upset was genuine. "Look, if commuting gets to you that much, why don't you just move back to the city?"

"Are you insane? The only thing worse than getting in and out of this town is moving around inside it. If it's not cab drivers wanted by Interpol, then it's some psycho on the subway or bus. You don't know what those maniacs are carrying. A machete, an Uzi..."

"A sturgeon," Jack muttered.

"What?"

"Nothing. Never mind."

"Hey, Kline, you're looking a little green. You alright?"

"Yeah. I'm just going to go wash up before the trading meeting. I'll see you there."

Early in his career, Jack had learned the importance of getting to the men's lavatory well before the morning trading conference. During that meeting, fifty or so senior capital markets personnel sat around a table discussing the latest tumult in the market, all the while inhaling coffee and sugared breakfast foods in an often vain attempt to increase alertness. These mood-altering diuretics and laxatives mixed with tension to produce a frantic stampede to the bathroom at the conference's conclusion. That migration, coupled with the less-than-reserved manner of most traders, invariably led to an atmosphere in this chamber not dissimilar to that of the primate house of the Bronx Zoo.

He used the facilities and went to the sink, pouring blessedly ice-cold water over his face. Stepping in front of a full-length mirror, he smoothed the creases in his Hugo Boss suit and straightened his Robert Talbot tie. He'd decided a crepe tie would go better with his suit, then felt a flush of the unreal. He was a million light-years from where he thought he'd be. A doctorate at twenty-six, several published papers on cosmology... and for what? A succession of twenty-thousand-dollar-a-year post-doctoral fellowships, years of fighting for tenure, maybe even unemployment? That would not be his reward for a youth full of the kind of peer persecution only a premature interest in quantum mechanics could bring. That's the thing about getting your teeth kicked in when you're young; the taste of blood never really leaves your mouth.

When they canceled the Supercollider, it was the last straw. As far as Jack was concerned, theory without experiment wasn't science, and theorizing without getting paid wasn't a life.

He knew Wall Street had learned to prize the analytical skills he possessed, and a call to a headhunter got him a job at Stone. He'd already taken some economics at MIT, and he persuaded his superiors to let him take the train down to Philadelphia, where he took a few of the Wharton School's finance Ph.D. courses. There he learned option pricing, swap design and interest rate modeling, methods that had made the Street the province of math people like himself.

That was the beauty of it. Guys like him had created a financial world so complex only they could understand it. Grasping the subtleties of the new financial engineering required advanced mathematics. The increasingly global economy produced myriad interrelationships best studied with methods taken from the sciences. Even staid old pursuits like stock picking required the analyst to comprehend innovations in computers, the Internet, genetics, advanced materials, and dozens of other fields best understood by refugees from science. The geeks had inherited the earth. It was a hell of a franchise.

Now he was making a small fortune using his knowledge to help Stone & Co. make a large one. He placed the firm's bets in the casino of global markets. His job might be less than profound, but it was more than a living, which in turn was more than he could say for physics.

He walked down the hall and entered the conference room, actually a glass-walled structure on a raised platform, containing only a large table and chairs. A fish tank for human piranhas. Through the wall you could look out over the entire trading floor. Jack could also see in as he approached. He was late and the room was full, the more senior traders seated, others standing.

Peter Torelli, the fifty-seven-year-old senior partner and capital markets chief, was already going around the room getting the traders' view of the markets, querying with his usual "So what's cheap?" A large man, broad-shouldered and barrel-chested, he ran a meaty hand through salt-and-pepper hair, his silver, bushy eyebrows in constant arch. He was questioning Carl Rich, the head mortgage trader, whose habit of taking off his toupee in the middle of the day was a source of endless amusement on the floor. Several of the traders had nicknamed the rug Ben, after the large, intelligent rat in the movie "Willard." He was answering Pete's question with "Ginnie-Mae Nine and a Halves" when Jack walked in.

"Nice of you to join us, Jack. Care to share any of the great ideas you undoubtedly came up with during the sabbatical you just took?" Pete was not a guy who normally trusted the new breed of mathematical traders. He was a legend from the old school, a product of CUNY and an era when tough, smart working-class ethnic kids used trading as a back door onto Wall Street. Trading had been considered *déclassé* in those days, secondary to the relationship-based activities of investment banking. That time was long gone, and trading had become the domain of M.B.A.s and Ph.D.s from the finest schools. The very tail that wagged the dog. Stone & Co. had been slow to catch on to this trend, but its partners saw the whopping profits high-tech trading had brought their competitors. They pressured the senior partner to start hiring "quants," as the new traders were called. Pete resisted; he saw a bunch of kids blindly following some algebraic witchcraft and taking insane risks. Jack had been his compromise, seemingly conservative enough to tolerate, so he brought him on board.

Jack sat down, composing himself for a moment before making his pitch. "Well, uh...right now I'm looking at shorting the kyat". This meant he was contemplating borrowing Myanmarese currency the firm didn't own, selling it, and, later, buying it back at what would hopefully be a lower price. Thus, when the firm returned the kyat to those who lent it, Stone would pocket the difference between the sales and repurchase prices. "It just broke twenty-six and a half to the buck, and I think it's ready to drop."

The traders had seen this before, in emerging markets from Mexico to Thailand. In the present case, the "Myanmar miracle" had started three-and-a-half years earlier when the country shook off the usual (crazy) military dictatorship and installed a (somewhat) democratic, (quasi-) capitalist regime, with the usual corruption and cronyism. All the same, it was a huge improvement over the prior junta of lunatics, who had renamed the nation Myanmar and then insured the name change would be the only innovation the country would ever experience under their rule. The change in government ushered in a burst of growth and the inevitable flood of foreign investment. Now growth had given way to unproductive consumption, investment to speculation.

"Myanmar's been running a chronic trade deficit for the last three years, financed by foreign investment. Those flows are drying up in the face of inflation and lower growth prospects, at least in the short term. This, in turn, has put pressure on the kyat and the Yangon exchange; the index of Myanmarese stocks, is already down 8% over the last two weeks."

"Christ, who can even keep these places straight?" interjected Carl Rich. "Now we're worrying about the Yangon exchange? Where the hell's Yangon?"

"It used to be called Rangoon."

"Oh, well, just so it's not some backwater..."

Jack looked around the room and saw that, with the exception of Hubie, who was paring his nails, all eyes were on him. Others might find the soliloquy he was giving dull enough to wilt plants, but not traders. They sensed profit potential in his logic. This was how the game was played: figure out how some change - political, economic, technological - would in turn change other factors. Then determine what effects those changes would trigger, and so on in an expanding web of consequence until you found some reaction from which cash could be extracted. He recalled Hesse's imagined land of scholars who played "the glass bead game," in which they searched for relationships between various concepts in art, music, philosophy, and science. They played to discover and celebrate the elegant underlying connectedness of ideas, and did so to the exclusion of worldly pursuits, even the creation of new ideas themselves. The traders turned this on its head. They too searched for the underlying connections between many concepts, but their lines of reasoning always led to a central, very terrestrial idea, which was that they should have more money. They sought lucre, not light.

"How big a decline are we talking about?" asked Ted Harris. Ted was a sharp, burly redhead with the kind of gut peculiar to ex-football players who eschewed sit-ups. He was also Jack's best friend on the floor. A former aerospace engineer out of Stanford with a Harvard M.B.A., he'd made partner the prior year, "one year shy of thirty-five," as he was fond of boasting, and was now busy setting up Stone's new merchant banking fund.

"Well, this isn't Mexico. The underlying Myanmarese economy is still strong. A devaluation of 10% should be enough to make Myanmar's exports more competitive and restore the balance of trade. Of course, in a panic, you never know."

"And our downside?" barked Pete.

"Maybe if the hedge funds get cold feet and the Bank of Myanmar tightens aggressively, you could see the kyat pop 5%, but I don't think it would last."

A reedy voice from the back of the room interjected: "The kyat isn't a very liquid currency." The traders turned to Nate Henkel, the firm's risk control officer. He leaned his slight frame against a glass wall. "You could have trouble covering your short if the market turns against you." Nate's job was to monitor the firm's various risk exposures and make sure management, i.e. Pete, was cognizant of them. Because his activities amounted to reining in the traders' behavior, and since he himself was not a profit center, Nate was treated on the floor with the kind of deference normally reserved for sixth-grade substitute teachers.

"Spoken like the swashbuckling CPA you are, Nate," Ted laughed. "The real risk here is we discover a sudden absence of balls."

"Nate, how do you audit for that?" asked Carl. Nate rolled eyes that at times like this looked older than his forty-two years.

Caroline Stewart, the chief of the bond desk and traditionally Nate's main defender, counterattacked on his behalf: "Ted, how many times do I have to tell you those are not hedging instruments?"

Caroline fancied herself the Dorothy Parker of the trading floor, but no one was going to confuse this group with the Algonquin Roundtable. Jack wondered how much her sense of humor had changed since her days studying literature at Yale. Not that it mattered – a Wharton M.B.A. and bond-trading prowess had allowed her to make partner with Ted, and she was a year younger than the merchant banker she now constantly sparred with. It had occurred to Jack that Caroline and Ted created a hostile work environment for each other to the point where they could probably sue one another and the firm. He figured they owned so much of the place, however, that they'd just wind up exchanging their considerable fortunes, less attorney's fees.

"This is the kind of trade we want to do here," Ted continued, "No exposure, no reward. Hubie, you can handle the kyat, right?"

Without looking up from the contemplation of his fingernails, Hubie replied, "If Jack wants, we can do it in the interbank market. I'll get our guys in Hong Kong to handle it overnight. No sweat."

Jack could see Pete wasn't sold on the trade. "Hasn't Myanmar's central bank successfully defended the kyat up to this point? What's to stop them now?"

"The Bank of Myanmar could raise rates to bolster its currency," Jack countered, "but that would cause a severe recession, and the government doesn't want that with an election coming up. So instead, the Bank has been buying up kyat to support the currency. This would eventually have the same effect as raising rates, so they've 'sterilized' those trades..."

Carl interrupted, "What do you mean 'sterilized'?"

"It means they've been buying up their short-term debt to keep interest rates low..."

Ted grinned. "I didn't think anything in this unclean business was sterilized. Not even our Ms. Stewart."

Caroline slowly rotated a pen she habitually kept in her blond ponytail's barrette. "I can think of some people who should be." She glanced at Ted, and laughter began to rise again.

"*Anyway...*" Jack sighed, trying to ignore the locker room atmosphere, "The Bank's strategy worked fine for the last year and a half, but now they're running out of dollars to make the purchases. Their reserves are low enough that a large bout of institutional kyat selling could exhaust them, if the Bank tries to intervene."

"Still, the kyat's been under pressure for a while," Pete noted, "How do you know it's gonna take a dive now?"

"Well, my model indicates..."

"Oh, the *Model...*" Pete's tone immediately provoked smiles around the room. They all knew his thoughts on models, particularly ones he didn't understand. Many a firm had blown up betting on such so-called "rocket science."

Pete leaned forward. "You want to tell us what's inside that black box again, Jack?"

They'd all heard Jack try to explain his method before, but the traders got a kick out of hearing him struggle to be understood.

"Well, basically, I think I've found a way to map technical trading ranges to strange attractors in phase space..."

Amused murmurs were already going around the room, and Caroline spoke up. "Uh, Jack, any chance you could translate that from the original geek?"

"Look, sometimes a mechanical system, like a pendulum, say, will move in a limited range of positions and velocities, but won't exactly repeat its motions. That's sort of what's called a strange attractor. Anyway, at times you see something similar in the financial markets. A stock or bond or currency will float around in a range of prices and rates of return. What technical analysts call a trading range. My model treats those ranges as strange attractors, and that helps me calculate certain things, like the odds of an economic shock kicking a currency out of its trading range, as I think may be about to happen with the kyat."

Silence.

"I mean, theoretically."

"Oh. Well, now I feel much better," groaned Ned.

As the traders laughed, Carl bellowed, "Yeah, Jack. Go ahead. Bet the ranch."

Jack looked over at Ted, whom he counted on at moments like this. "Look folks, the Doc here may be a little obscure, but his kung fu's been pretty strong lately..."

Pete nodded, smiling. Jack had been right more than half the time, and that was often enough not to be ignored. "O.K., Mr. Wizard. You wanna go short, go short. You can let your profits run, but make sure we're stopped out at a 10% loss." He glanced at Nate. "And keep the position down to a few tens of millions."

The meeting broke up around eight o'clock and Jack headed back to his desk. Turning to the screen of the laptop computer on which he developed and maintained his models, he began to input parameters from the prior night's trading into his program.

Jack smiled. Much of this theory had originally been developed for the sheer mathematical beauty of it. It turned out the demand for mathematical beauty was a little light just then, as many of his friends from grad school could attest. The demand for accurate market calls, on the other hand...

He spent most of the rest of the day sitting at his screens, looking at the output of his model and thinking about the kyat. His program strongly indicated the currency was ready to drop. His pulse quickened as he focused in on the vulnerability. As was his habit, he took off and half-folded his wire-rimmed glasses, holding them as one would a pipe, gnawing at the earpiece. By 3:40 in the afternoon he'd made up his mind. He would go short that night. He was about to give his instructions to Hubie when Ted Harris walked over to his desk with the kind of smile on his face children get after they've placed a tack on someone's seat.

"Jack, this thing with smoking your specs - is this just an oral fixation or is there a deeper subtext? Perhaps some kind of phallic, homoerotic thing?"

"Ted, sometimes glasses are just glasses. But if merchant banking doesn't work out I'm sure you'd have a bright future in psychoanalysis - you've got the psycho part down anyway."

"And I could pick up a hell of a clientele right in this room." He pointed in the direction of Carl Rich. "Case in point: Ginnie's are in the shitter, and Carl's about to blow his top again. Check it out."

Carl was not having a good trading day. His position in the mortgage-backed bonds known as Ginnie Maes was collapsing under the weight of market fears. Carl wasn't the only trader on the floor who took his losses badly. He was, however, the only one in the habit of pulling off his toupee and striking his trading screens with it in frustration. This was a phenomenon much looked forward to by the others on the floor, especially Ted, who could spot all the warning signs: increased cursing, flushed cheeks, throbbing temple veins. And indeed, as Jack looked over at Carl sitting at the fixed-income desk, all indications were that an eruption was imminent.

"Goddamn Morgan just had to come out with a high fucking prepayment forecast," Carl growled.

"Ginnie's down another two ticks," intoned Caroline, who, while normally the closest thing to a voice of reason on the floor, was not above egging Carl on at a moment like this.

"I'm getting killed on the negative convexity here!" Carl was almost whining, and his fingers were already buried in his hairpiece.

"Looks like we just dropped another three," cried Ted across the floor, having punched up the Ginne Mac quotes on Jack's screen.

That was it. "Fuck it!" Carl shouted, and in a single smooth motion he whipped the toupee off his head and snapped it against the side of his laptop computer, nearly knocking it off his desk.

Laughter now volleyed across the floor. Ted was beside himself, but managed to speak. "Now, Carl, don't take it so hard. It's only money."

"Oh yeah it's money - money out of *my* P and L, out of *my bonus!*" Carl hit the side of his Reuters terminal, but this time he balled his fist around the toupee and struck with such force that the machine was sent flying off his trading desk and on to the floor, taking with it his flat-screen Bloomberg, phone bank and his laptop computer. Sparks flew from the pile of electronics and a column of blue smoke began to rise. Startled, Carl lost his grip on the hairpiece, which fell on top of the short-circuiting equipment and instantly burst into flames.

The stunned traders stared at the now blazing pyre of silicon, blown display screens and synthetic hair. "Well, somebody get a damn fire extinguisher!" yelled Pete, standing up from his seat, but a trading clerk had already grabbed one off the wall and was attempting to operate it. Ted began a bad imitation of the Hindenburg radio broadcast: "Its flaming terrible... it's the worst catastrophe in the history of mankind... Oh, the humanity!" The laughter resumed. As Caroline led Carl off the floor, some traders put their hands on his back, but a trading floor is not known for its oversupply of empathy. An acrid smell rolled through the room.

"Poor Ben," someone lamented.

Another trader called out "Christ, what is that stink?"

"Could be roadkill," shouted Ted. "I always suspected that rug was just something Rich ran over one night."

Jack knew his concentration was failing in the face of this madness, and he forced his mind to return to his screens, escaping into his math. His model was based on a branch of mathematics known as nonlinear dynamics; sometimes called complexity or chaos theory. The idea was that the future evolution of almost anything – be it a pendulum, a storm, or an economy - has some degree of sensitivity to history, to past conditions. If that thing's future were very sensitive to its past, then that thing was said to be highly chaotic. For example, the weather was said to be chaotic if the beat of a butterfly's wing in Brazil could, three weeks hence, be the difference between a sunny day and a hurricane over Bermuda. Indeed, systems like that were said to be subject to "butterfly effects." It was idea, like time warps or gene splicing, so chewed over by pop culture that one could forget it was something more than a premise for bad science fiction. But Jack knew it could be very real, especially in his world.

Jack believed that the markets' sensitivity to current events varied; sometimes they were chaotic, sometimes stable, often in between. Generally, he had no idea how turbulent the market would be. But he had developed a program, which, very occasionally, indicated to him when the market was likely to respond to events in a volatile but *highly predictable* fashion. Then the market's behavior might be complex, but not chaotic, and assuming Jack understood the factors affecting the market correctly, this predictability presented the opportunity to make money. Serious money. It was no sure thing; his model was wrong a lot. It was right just often enough to get the odds in his favor once in a while. It was then that he made his largest bets. He was like a blackjack card counter making his big wager on the one hand in which recall of past deals made it possible to guess the next card out of the shoe with a good chance of being right. And now was one of those times.

Jack had had enough of this place for the day, and he got up and made his way to Hubie, who was remarkably nonplused by the conflagration a few yards away. He was watching the fire containment efforts while speaking intensely into his headset: "So I'm telling you, I know the schedule says the train leaves at 6:18, but it never gets out before 6:25, and if your foot hits that platform one second earlier, you're just wasting your time! That's how they steal our lives, minute by wasted minute!" Hubie parsed time the way a diamond cutter cleaves stones.

"Hubie..." Jack tried to interrupt.

Hubie held up his hand, shouting into the phone: "Help? Nothing can help. It doesn't matter if you're the Pope or the fucking Treasury secretary. No power on earth can fix the MTA. Do you want to be played for a fool? Do you want to let the bastards win?" Hubie was speaking into one of his trading lines, which was recorded so there'd be no "misunderstandings," which meant no one could back out of a losing trade after the fact. It was that kind of business. Jack mused that Hubie's tape must have been about five percent trades and ninety-five percent anti-MTA tirade.

"Look, Hubie, I know how you feel about mass transit, but there's this matter of a kyat trade?"

"What? Oh, just a moment," Hubie said to the caller as he looked up at Jack.

"Hubie, I want you to short forty million dollars worth of Myanmarese kyat tonight. Stop us out at a 10% loss, and, let's say, a 40% gain - not that we'll get there but just in case I don't want to have the winnings truncated."

Hubie was still trying to hear the caller as he listened to Jack, "No, the 6:50 isn't better...you can't escape that easily. How much kyat?"

"Forty million," Jack said again, watching the trading assistant spray Carl's flaming debris with carbon dioxide. This place made no sense to him anymore, and a trader's sarcasm spilled out of him. "Screw it, Hubie, at this point I'd just as soon short four hundred million. Go for broke one last time and get the fuck out of here before I turn into a maniac like that." He gestured toward the now nearly extinguished fire. "I'm gone, man. Take care of this for me, will you?"

Hubie kept talking on the phone as he scribbled an order on a trade ticket. "That's what I'm trying to tell you...it's some kind of conspiracy...wait a sec." Hubie looked up again. "Uh, sure, Jack. Got it right here. No problem."

As he turned from Hubie, Jack bumped into Ted, who'd been watching the physicist try to interrupt the trader's rants while the last embers of Carl's toupee were extinguished.

Ted smiled. "Just another day in the land of misfit toys."

"Yeah, and I'm one of 'em. Just not cut out for this stuff, man, not like you."

"Hey, I could take that personally," he laughed, pulling Jack aside. "You think I'm cut out for this? I went to Stanford to learn how to build spaceships. Then they declared peace with the Ruskies. I don't have to tell you what happened to the space program."

"They do still send up probes."

"Yeah, like that Mars rover. So long as you can build the prototype in your garage, and get some grad students to fly it in exchange for food, you've got yourself a mission."

Jack nodded. "I guess people are a lot less into going where no man's gone before when they're not racing enemies to that new frontier."

"Like they say: 'Success is not enough; failure of your neighbors is also very important.' You know, when I was a kid my whole room was filled models of the Saturn V. I sat in front of the TV watching that thing take off, and those guys walking on the moon." He shook his head. "I mean, Jack, they actually walked on the *moon*.... Now people just want to watch movies about it. Anyway, don't see many blastoffs around here..."

"Unless of course you count Carl..."

Hubie's voice rose above the trading din, shouting into his phone something about "fucking fare hikes."

Ted rolled his eyes. "Although I do think we may have made contact with an alien life-form."

"You mean from a galaxy so far, far away its inhabitants think only about commuting?"

"Precisely. Look, it's not just us. Take Caroline – before she went to B-school, she spent two years interning at some pretentious old literary magazine. You know, what's it called?"

"The *Manhattanite*."

"Right. She was hoping to get discovered. I happen to know a few months ago she actually published a short story in one of those little indie journals you see crammed in the back of the racks at Borders. I figure they paid her maybe fifty bucks, tops. Somehow I think she needed more than that to close on her duplex on Sutton."

"Maybe the co-op board's full of big readers. How'd you find out about Caroline's story, anyway? You can't tell me you read that stuff."

"Let's just say I keep my eye on Ms. Stewart. Point is, what you're looking at here is what happens when a lot of brainpower that might be otherwise engaged turns to avarice as an outlet. You can't make it without money, but money alone can't replace what's missing. And since what's missing isn't available at any price, the void's never filled and the acquisitiveness just spirals out of control. Next thing you know..."

"Some guy not only flips his lid but uses it to assault a computer?"

"Well, I think in Carl's case superficial avarice is just a cover for deep-seated greed. You get the general idea, though."

"Funny, I never knew you were so into the space thing."

Ted looked over at what had been Carl's trading station. Three bond traders were playing catch with the charred remains of their colleague's hairpiece. "Yeah, Jack, like this would be the place to get misty over trips to the moon. Look, basically, people like you and Caroline and me, we're nerds. Being a nerd isn't about walking around with a calculator and pens in your shirt pocket. It's giving a shit about galaxies or poetry or anything else that won't make you a dime. And that's not cool here, not in this world. 'Cause if your mind's not on the money, you're weak; a mark waiting to be taken. So you don't let on and you never convey any sense of loss. If you're a nerd, you'd better be a stealth nerd. A little suppression of the higher mind's a small price to pay for getting rich. And nobody's gonna shed tears for a bunch of guys making as much money as we are." He smiled. "Anyway, I've got to get back to the troops before anyone else tries to burn the joint down." He put a hand on Jack's shoulder and shook him. "Hey, don't let it get to you. It's just the Street. Be cool – like me."

"Ted, you pop Rolaids from a Daffy Duck Pez dispenser."

"And isn't it marvelous how I've kept my sense of whimsy?"

It was 4:15 and Jack walked over to Pete. Stone's chief was talking to some other firm's trader on the phone, and Jack could tell he was leading up to a trademark Torelli blow-off.

"Yeah…yeah, absolutely…your pricing's dead on…I don't know why I didn't see it your way before…Hey, Stevie, its been a long day and I'm older than I used to be, so just let me ask…did I forget to tell you to go fuck yourself?"

Jack interrupted. "Listen, Pete, Hubie's putting on my trade and I'm not feeling so great. If it's all the same with you, I'm gonna split. I'll take my laptop so I can monitor how we're doing from home."

Pete nodded. "I know how you feel. You see that furball burn? Really makes you think. You know he won't try minoxidil. Says he doesn't want a monkey on his head."

"Well, it'd be more like a Chia Pet. Guess losing money and hair at the same time does cruel things to a man. I'll see you tomorrow."

In his apartment on Seventy-ninth Street, Jack leaned against the closing door and shut his eyes, listening to the latch lock. It was the most pleasant sound he'd heard all day.

Fucking job.

Not that home was so great. He opened his eyes and looked around the one-bedroom, Upper East Side, high-rise apartment he'd lived in since coming to Wall Street. The place looked like an Ikea display, containing only a desk and chair, futon bed, a ficus plant and a small kitchen set. And bookcases – tall and filled with the volumes of his past scholarship. He could buy a larger place, but he didn't have much to put in it. Besides, with the tight Manhattan real estate market, even with his kind of money he'd end up in some flashy but cheaply constructed postwar tower or in a prewar with a mediocre view. Neither seemed worth the seven figures it would cost him. Frustrating as hell.

He had not been brought up to be particularly concerned with "things." A Jewish kid from Long Island, the son of a mathematician and a classicist, he'd been raised in the life of the mind. The lack of remuneration inherent therein hadn't bothered him, at least not as he'd envisioned it. He'd thought he would be a professor like his parents, trading higher compensation for the greater freedom and intellectual stimulation of academia.

Jack placed his briefcase on his desk and removed his laptop. He establishied a high-speed Internet connection, with which he'd check the markets later that night to see if Hubie and the traders in Stone's Hong Kong office were having any trouble shorting the kyat. Sitting at his desk, he looked over at the shelves containing his physics texts and the eight spiral binders of his thesis notes. He had no idea where he'd gotten the strength to do all that work. These days it took a supreme exercise of will to haul himself into the office.

Sometimes, over the trading floor's lunatic din, he heard siren call of the beauty in his notebooks. When he thought of returning to the elegance of curved space-time and quantum equations that had unfurled a universe in his mind, it was then he recalled the exact moment he'd resolved to get out of science. He'd just completed his doctorate, and was visiting a friend of his who'd gotten his degree two years earlier and held a postdoctoral fellowship at a prominent university. The guy had four publications in the *Physical Review* and still couldn't get another two-year appointment. His funding had run out, and the department had evicted him from his office. After much pleading, they did give him some space to continue to make out job applications. A circular room in the attic of an old faux-Gothic tower adjacent to the physics building, declared unfit for occupation due to a lack of fire exits. Jack climbed with his friend to this perch, so poorly illuminated he couldn't see the high ceiling. As they stood inside, he had the sensation that something was moving over his head. Seconds later he heard a squeak as a score of shadows seemed to break free of the darkness above and circle the room before flying out the window.

Jack instantly hit the floor and, looking up at his remarkably calm colleague, shouted: "What the fuck was that?"

"Oh, just bats. They sleep in here at night but split whenever someone comes in. That's why I leave the window open. It's not a problem... I don't *think* they're rabid or anything."

That was it for Jack. It all came down to Adam Smith's metaphor for the irresistible force of the marketplace, his "Invisible Hand." Sacrifice to further the knowledge of mankind was one thing, but when you're being asked to share office space with leathery-winged, fanged, flying vermin, well, Jack figured that was the Invisible Hand's way of flipping you the bird. So he came to Stone & Co. His friend, with more invested in the field and maybe more idealism, held out longer. He spent nearly a year living with his sonar-guided friends before he took his present position in the technology practice of a large consulting firm.

The truth was, by the standards of the business, Jack had nothing to complain about. Stone was a good place to be. Small, but not sleepy, at least not anymore. Modest size guarded against layoffs in lean times, and the presence of new, younger partners like Ted Harris and Caroline Stewart had earned Stone respect on the Street. Ted had switched from pure investment banking to actual investing. He was now using his corporate finance expertise to set up a new fund designed to participate in buyouts of undervalued companies, and his reputation had attracted over a billion in investor capital. Caroline, under Pete Torelli's watchful gaze, had reinvigorated the firm's trading operations, increasing Stone's appetite for risk. And she'd helped persuade Pete to bring on board more sophisticated traders, including Jack.

The firm had record earnings last year and was well on its way to surpassing them. Jack's trading had been a significant part of the firm's recent success. Assuming he didn't screw up between now and the end of the year, he stood a good chance of a bonus that would bring his total compensation up around a million. Admission to the partnership in a year or so was a pretty good bet, more like a lock if trades like this kyat thing paid off.

The trading room's atmosphere was actually far more pleasant than the norm on the Street. It was a place tolerant enough to employ eccentrics like Hubie and Carl Rich. There was some truth in Ted's remark about the firm being a land of misfit toys. The small size and private ownership of the firm gave it a less vicious culture than that of many houses. A man might ignite his own hair (artificial or otherwise), but at least he was unlikely to set fire to yours. And, as Ted observed, he wasn't alone. There were other "stealth nerds" in the place.

Nevertheless, Jack's attitude toward his career grew increasingly hostile. It didn't bother him so much when he was in the thick of trading, when noise, calculation and adrenaline drowned out any introspective thought. It was when he returned to the quiet of his apartment, his cases of books surrounding him like some Neolithic stone circle, monuments to a lost faith...

What the hell am I doing?   Sure, he'd spared himself poverty, and, which was more, the indignity of penury amidst the prosperity of those he considered half as smart and hardworking as himself. The idea of the alternative galled him. Academic life, dependent on politicians and financiers for funding, at the mercy of the whim of others, held an impotence he'd come to detest. He wanted power, over his own fate if nothing else. Yet to discover the only way he could make the world reward him for his skills and knowledge was by engaging in activities he often found meaningless, even venal...

Economics itself was to Jack's mind a beautiful science: the human drama, all its aspiration and peril, writ in a mathematical poetry to rival that of his former field. It was his current application of those equations that troubled him. To true believers in the free market, the followers of Smith and Milton Friedman, self-interest was a high calling indeed. By their lights a *Homo economicus* facilitated that supreme endeavor, commerce: the means by which the Invisible Hand worked its will, creating and destroying like some treasure-driven Shiva, all the time pushing civilization forward. Besides, what was it Sophie Tucker said? "I have been poor and I have been rich, and please believe me, rich is better." Lately, though, such arguments left him cold. He couldn't help but feel there was more to life than pushing around a big pile of kyat.

Not that he was under the illusion that his prior life was devoid of self-interest. Jack smirked when he thought of the denizens of Cambridge, his former world. Most of the scholars, scientists, and artists he'd known were motivated as much by ego and ambition as any desire to advance knowledge or culture. Yet there had been the higher purpose as well, and he missed that.

Who gives a damn. He figured if the world didn't care enough about pursuing knowledge to give people a way to make a living at it, why should he sweat it? He owed the world nothing more than the world owed him, which was clearly zilch. So once he left science, he was on his own and out for himself.

There was something else, though. Something in that adrenaline when he was on the floor...

All good researchers have a little of the hunter in them. It's what combines with intelligence to inspire curiosity, to drive them in pursuing the unknown. Yet taken outside of that search, placed in the real world's jungle, that drive changed. You saw it in the empire builders of biotech and Silicon Valley. Or in the high-tech traders, swooping down on the Street for their prey. He could see it in himself, in the way he'd eyed the kyat today. The integrals blended with an innate feel for when the other guy would break. A killer instinct.

He gazed out the window over his desk. When he placed his face close to the pane, he was afforded an angle at which he could see the distant Art Deco crown of the Chrysler building. The sunset's reflection lit the spire like the flame of a torch in the sky.

At least I'm not hurting anyone.

His exhale condensed on the cold glass, obscuring his view, and he turned away.

After eating a sandwich for dinner, he spent an hour watching talking heads yell at each other on CNN. At 9:15 p.m. he hit the sack, setting his alarm for 11:00 p.m., when it would be 11:00 a.m. in Yangon. At that time he'd call Hubie, by then out on Long Island and working from home, to see if there was any problem with the Hong Kong desk putting on his trade. This was their usual procedure for large overnight transactions. For traders like them the market never really closed; it just orbited the earth with the daylight like some gigantic floating crap game.

Sleep wouldn't come; his mind rioted with the market's math. Black-Schoales option equations, purchasing power parities, his strange attractors. Theorems of greed and fear. So he did what he did most nights, groping in his mind for the old music, Einstein's and Schrödinger's and Feynman's. At last he wrapped his mind in their gossamer abstractions and drifted away.

Jack was awakened at 10:30 by the sound of other music. The occupant of the next apartment was a twenty-something graphic designer with whom Jack had never actually spoken. She was in the habit of coming home late and playing her stereo for an hour, her way of mellowing out, he supposed. Her tastes ran toward the disheveled, clinically depressed band 'Angst.' Their hollow-eyed, haunted appearance and desolate lyrics made Nirvana seem like the Chipmunks. She also enjoyed the bizarrely hair-dyed pop singer Æther, whose recent antics included covering herself in highly reflective body paint and simulating a sex act on stage with some kind of vegetable. The woman might look like dancing aluminum foil, but she'd parlayed this "performance art" into a two-hundred-million-dollar entertainment conglomerate. Jack could barely tolerate this stuff; his preferences ran more toward Bach. Worse, the thin post-war plaster walls allowed the low bass frequencies to resonate throughout his apartment to the point where the whole place seemed to throb. He lay on his mattress, thinking this must be what it would be like to live inside a toothache.

In the past he'd retaliate for this behavior by banging on the wall he shared with his neighbor, but he'd discovered it was more effective to wait until the next morning, when he awoke at 6:00, and then exact his revenge. His weapon was one of the "deal mementos" Ted was always giving him, a reproduction of a *Wall Street Journal* "tombstone" announcement of a Stone transaction, suspended in a Lucite obelisk. This one celebrated Stone's role in the merger of two software firms, not that Jack cared. He'd place this item inside a sock and slam it against the wall with all his might, sending a deafening concussion through to the still-somnolent music lover. This quotidian tit for tat would sometimes go on for weeks, the kind of demented application of game theory endemic to Manhattan apartment living. At least it gave a cathartic purpose to Ted's otherwise useless pieces of plastic.

There was no point in trying to get back to sleep now, so he stayed up watching the kyat on his screen. The price hadn't changed much since that afternoon. When 11:00 rolled around he placed his call.

"So Hubie, my man, what's it look like?"

"Well, you're keeping me up tonight. So far the Hong Kong desk's put on a little over half of the trade. The market's thin and I don't want to move the price, so I'm going slow and spreading the trade around. It looks O.K., though. We're still around twenty-six and a half and we'll have the whole thing done before the Asia closes."

"Need me for anything?"

"Naw. Go back to sleep. One of us should be conscious in the morning."

"O.K., then. I'll see you tomorrow. Oh, and don't forget the stops."

"Hey, who are you talking to here?"

"I know, Hubie. You're flawless. Goodnight," he paused "and have a good trip in tomorrow."

"Don't ask the impossible, Jack. I'll see you in the morning."

Chapter 2: The Touch of the Valkyrie

He awoke the next morning, his mind blank but for the vague memory of a dream involving a fish wearing a flaming hairpiece and complaining about transit fares. He looked at his watch:

7:31 a.m.

Oh *shit!*   Between his neighbor's musical interlude and his discussion with Hubie, he'd forgotten to set his alarm. By now the morning trading meeting was already underway.

Jack took a two-minute shower, pulled on his pants and ran to his desk. He delayed shoving his laptop into his briefcase just long enough to punch up a quote on the kyat.

It stood at 52.08 to the dollar, down 49% overnight.

The trader stood blinking at his screen, his wet hair dripping into his eyes. Down 49%. It had to be some kind of glitch in the system, he thought. He punched up an Asian financial news summary:

"...In the final three hours of trading, the Myanmarese kyat collapsed in its largest one-day loss in history... foreign investment firms and hedge funds were the biggest sellers, with traders citing rumors that a major American investment bank had precipitated the panic with the sale of over ten billion kyat...The index of Yangon shares followed suit, falling 27%..."

Jack let out a sound that was part gasp, part laugh, and his hands started to shake. He couldn't believe his luck. He'd gone short expecting a correction, not a collapse. And just hours later Goldman, Morgan or some other behemoth decides to dump about four hundred million dollars' worth of kyat, and the next thing you know the currency craters. If Hubie put the trade on right, they'd be stopped out by now. That would put his profit on the short sale at over 48% of forty million. That was sixteen million dollars. *In one night!*

He had a feeling Peter Torelli would be able to get over him missing the trading meeting. He finished dressing, packed his computer and was halfway out the door when he remembered last night's serenade. Grabbing a sweat sock out of a drawer, he stuffed the deal memento into it and ran towards the wall he shared with his neighbor, screaming:

"Sixteen fucking million!"

He did a half twist-jump as he whipped the weighted sock against the wall with such force that it dented the plaster.

Jack flew out into the icy air and hailed a cab, jumping in the back and panting "Sixth and Fifty-fourth" as they drove west on Seventy-ninth. Against his collar he could feel his pulse pounding in his carotids. He was high. Nothing like the rush of making vast fortunes in a matter of hours, especially when a serious fraction of that money was sure to find its way into your bonus. Any ruminations on his *raison d'être* were banished from his mind; he was too focused on the couple of million *raisons* he figured were coming his way.

The cab swerved as it turned down Fifth, and Jack reached between the seat cushions for a safety belt. He came up with nothing but a used tissue of indeterminate age. "Way to start to the morning," he muttered, repelled by the thought that he'd just randomly plugged into the biosphere of New York.

"No seat belts, huh?" he said to the cabby.

"Oh, they're back there somewhere," the driver replied, his Brooklyn accent thick as an egg cream. "Probably worth putting it on, too. Back in October, just before Halloween, this guy I know picks up a fare carrying a big-ass pumpkin. Anyway, my guy stops short and the pumpkin cracks the partition."

"Yeah?"

"Yup. Left a spider web right in the Plexiglas. And ya know, a pumpkin's not that different from a human skull, when you're talkin' your high speed collisions."

"I guess." Jack wasn't really listening, his mind shuttling between the crushed kyat and the possibility that he might now have the Ebola virus crawling over his right hand.

"Actually, we've got the glass up on the garage wall. Sort of a trophy."

Jack snapped out of it. "How badly was the guy hurt?"

"Oh, he walked away. My pal always wears a seatbelt."

"I meant the passenger."

"Oh. He was strapped in too. Pretty upset though – I heard he was suing. Emotional trauma, dry cleaning, loss of pumpkin..."

Jack wondered if one peaceful trip downtown was too much to ask. He began to feel a high degree of empathy with Hubie.

Ten blocks to his destination and traffic was moving slowly. He thought of the tissue he'd touched, imagining he could feel microbes forming a conga line up his arm, and decided to assess any potential contagion.

"Any sick passengers back here lately?"

"You mean you can still smell it?"

Jack decided he didn't want to know. He jumped out of the cab and tossed six-fifty though the window for a six-dollar fare. "Sorry it can't be more," he shouted, "but I need the change to make a quick call to the Centers for Disease Control." Without waiting for a reply, he turned and headed into the building.

He bounded across the polished floor of the lobby so fast he almost slipped. It was all he could do to contain himself as the elevator silently lifted him to the fifty-fifth floor. He stepped out and almost ran to the trading room, but then, remembering the biohazard he'd touched, stopped off in the lavatory. He spent two minutes washing up to his elbows, hard enough to take off a layer of skin. Then he headed out onto the floor.

It was already 8:10. The trading meeting should have ended, yet the floor's population seemed strangely sparse. No Pete, Ted, or Caroline. In fact, none of the partners who normally graced the trading desks were anywhere in sight.

He did, however, see Hubie in front of his screen eating a muffin.

"Hey, if it isn't the man of the hour. And late for his hour I might add," called Hubie. "Congrats." A couple of traders gave Jack a smattering of applause, yet it seemed oddly muted.

"Are we stopped out?" asked Jack, almost hyperventilating. "Why didn't you call me?"

"Why should two of us lose sleep? Your instructions were clear enough. We started covering the short when the kyat dropped 40%, just like you said. Our position was so big I needed to spread my purchases out – I didn't want to risk driving the price back up even a little." Hubie laughed. "Not that there was much of a chance of that. Actually, we ended up covering a lot of it at even lower prices, because the fucker wouldn't stop dropping. Still, I stayed up all night closing out your damn position. You owe me dinner, man." Hubie saw Jack looked flushed "You O.K.? Tough time coming in?"

Jack took the seat next to Hubie. "It's nothing - had a little trouble in a cab."

"So, call the Taxi and Limousine Commission!" cried Hubie, instantly indignant. He pulled out his wallet. "I've got their number right here..."

Jack smiled. "I'm sure you do, Hubie, but that's alright. I think this one may be more of a job for the Department of Health." He looked around. "So where the hell is everyone?"

"Well, the partners all hung around after the morning prayer meeting, talking about you. Torelli was pretty upset."

"Why would he be upset over us making north of sixteen million dollars?"

"Gee, for a Ph.D. your multiplication's a little off, but then I guess you just got up. We're up over a hundred and sixty million."

Jack just stared at Hubie as he went on.

"Closer to a hundred and eighty million, actually. Torelli's got his Jockeys in a knot over you raising that trade to four hundred million at the end of the day. You know, exceeding his trading limit. Kept yelling about how you said you'd keep it to a few tens of millions. I told the guy forty tens was still a few. I mean, who the hell knows what a few is, anyway? And you had a winner, so what's the problem? Ted was with me..."

"I said...you..." Jack trailed off, suddenly remembering his parting crack about upping the trade to four hundred million as Hubie ranted on about the MTA yesterday afternoon...

Oh God, Hubie wasn't listening! He was so busy complaining about the LIRR that when he heard him say four hundred million *the little maniac actually took him seriously!* Jack knew the magnitude of a trade was next to meaningless for Hubie, a blind spot actually exacerbated by his talent for executing large transactions without moving the market

There were stories of screw ups like this. Once, some trading clerk at the Cotton Exchange's orange juice pit had made a remark about the juice in a vending machine having frozen solid. The traders misinterpreted this to mean a freeze in Florida had ruined the crop, and they sent the futures through the roof. Another time, a trading floor assistant had misread a hand signal and executed a trade in S&P futures so large it briefly disrupted the stock market.

The effects of those errors had been short term, but what if someone made a mistake like that in a thin currency market, like that of the kyat, at just the wrong time...

Now it made sense. Jack's stomach turned over as he grasped the meaning of the Bridge story he'd read in his apartment. *Stone* had been the American bank that had crushed the kyat. He must not have been the only trader anticipating a decline. The hedge funds and the other investment banks must have been preparing to short at the same time he had, and when Stone dropped the bomb they must have followed suit.

Without saying another word to Hubie, Jack spun around in his chair and punched up the kyat's five-day trading history on a Bloomberg. He saw the orange line of the graph make a nearly ninety-degree turn down in late-afternoon Asian trading. The scenario began to take shape in his mind. The market had gotten wind of Hubie's trades late in the session. The other banks and hedge funds were already primed to sell. Then they saw a house like Stone, a *conservative* house, which *never* made huge bets, suddenly short the hell out of the kyat. Everyone figured Stone knew something. The other players decided to jump on the bandwagon and test the resolve of the Bank of Myanmar. As Jack had earlier ascertained, Myanmar's central bankers didn't have the reserves to buy up all that currency, and they weren't willing to raise rates in a sluggish economy ahead of an election. So they simply let the currency float undefended.

And the kyat was delivered into the hands of her enemies.

It hadn't been the forecast of Jack's model; the orderly correction, the rational decline to a more stable level. Calculation had given way to panic, complexity to chaos.

Jack looked back at Hubie. He was smiling under his sleepy eyes. He had absolutely no idea he'd done anything wrong. He honestly believed Jack had told him to short that mountain of currency, and anyway they won, so to him there could be no objection.

Behind him he heard the voice of Carl Rich crying out, "Hey, we're on TV!" Jack was too engrossed in his revelation to marvel at Rich's reappearance on the floor a day after almost burning down the place. Besides, Stone tended to tolerate tantrums from its traders, so long as they stayed profitable. Carl stood on the scorched carpet behind the trading desk next to his own, which was covered by disconnected cables. As a technician attempted to install new terminals, the now rugless trader turned a television monitor around to face Hubie and Jack. A CNBC reporter spoke, a silhouette of Myanmar and the Stone logo (the firm's name with the letters covered in a green marble pattern) floating in a box behind him.

"...Market sources report that the currency's plunge began with a massive sale of kyat by the investment bank of Stone & Co. Sources say Stone recently moved into a variety of high-risk foreign exchange transactions under the direction of trader Jacob Kline..."

"A fucking star is born!" laughed Carl, his bare pate gleaming.

Jack walked back to his own desk, covered his face and tried to think. His cheeks felt hot and he was starting to sweat. Regardless of the profit, he knew Pete and Nate Henkel would be furious at him for putting that much of the firm's capital at risk. What if the kyat had gone the other way? Stone would have taken a huge hit, even with the 10% stop loss, assuming Hubie would have been able to execute it. It might not have brought down the firm *a la* Nick Lesson's destruction of Bearing Brothers, but it would have been a very bad scene, with Jack cast as the "rogue trader" of the month.

Now he had to figure out what to tell Pete. If he told the truth he might not be believed, and instead seen as squirming out of responsibility. His respect for Pete made him dread that, but it wasn't the deciding factor. He just couldn't blame Hubie, who in his confusion surely thought he'd followed Jack's instructions perfectly, and with the desired result. Jack looked over at the portly trader. He was hunched over his desk, surrounded by trading screens, shaking his head and mumbling to himself as he worried over a train schedule spread across a keyboard. No, Jack thought, he could not put it on Hubie. This job was Hubie's life. Given his idiosyncrasies, it was doubtful he'd be able to hold a position at some less-tolerant shop, or even land one if the circumstances of his getting blown out of Stone came out.

By contrast, it wasn't like Jack lived to trade, and anyway he felt pretty sure there were plenty of "swing for the fence" firms out there that would view his kyat trade as their kind of deal, even if Pete decided it wasn't his. There were no two ways about it. He was going to have to take the spear on this one if it came to it.

An odd feeling of calm came over him. Jack wondered at his curious indifference to his fate, especially given his level of excitement over the success of the trade a half hour before. It was the kind release that comes to one who knows his destiny is entirely out of his hands. Anyway, he guessed that deep down it just wasn't that big a deal to him. He leaned back in his chair and looked over at the conference room. Through its glass walls he could see the partners' impromptu meeting breaking up.

As they emerged, Jack felt twenty pairs of eyes focusing on him. He stood up and regarded them without expression. His gaze met Ted's, who let out with, "Rock and fucking roll! Way to trade...!" Pete cut him off.

"I'm still senior partner here, Ted, and I'll handle this." He turned to Jack. "Doctor Kline, if I could see you upstairs, please?"

Jack couldn't recall a previous occasion on which Pete had referred to him as "Doctor." He and Pete didn't speak as they took the elevator to the top floor. It was here, sixty stories above Sixth Avenue, that Stone's partners had their private offices. Pete's was almost never occupied; he spent most of the day on the floor. Indeed, the principal use Pete found for his paneled chamber was as a quiet space to can someone.

They entered the office and Jack closed the door behind him, not so much to protect his privacy as to make it easier for Pete to do what he had to do. The senior partner could be a pit bull, but Jack knew Pete truly hated to fire people and actually felt guilty for putting him through this.

The room had little personal in it except for a model of a sailboat. Jack vaguely recalled sailing was a hobby of Pete's. There was a mahogany conference table, a sofa, and a heavy oak desk whose surface was unoccupied except for a few papers and a couple of those ubiquitous Lucite deal trophies. Behind the desk was a matching cadenza, above which a pair of screens, the double display of a Bloomberg terminal, glowed with their rainbow of symbols and numbers. A large leather swivel chair stood behind the desk and two others were placed before it, but neither man sat down.

Pete leaned against the wall, eyebrows even more arched than the norm, clearly angry. When he spoke, however, the tone of his voice conveyed more exhaustion than fury.

"I want you to know, Jack, how hard it is for me to say what I've got to say..." He exhaled, shaking his head. "You know why I hired you, kid?"

"I assumed it was because of my analytical skills and..."

Pete interrupted. "I hired you because you seemed like the kind of guy who wasn't going to give me gas. After thirty-six years on a trading floor you start to measure risk control in terms of your level of intestinal disturbance. Between Ted, Caroline and our friend with the flaming toupee I've got more *agita* than a guy on the Cyclone who's just had a burrito. I figured someone like you had some sense, that maybe some of that scientific caution and academic integrity guys like you are supposed to have might come with you to the Street. Obviously I had my head up my ass. I thought I was hiring a gentleman and a scholar, and now I find out I got Atilla the Nerd."

Pete paused, then in a soft voice said, "Just tell me something. Why? You'd a made partner in a year or two anyway. I'd have nominated you myself. Why'd you bullshit me to my face?"

Jack had already concluded there was no point in trying to explain what happened, but he didn't want to lie either, so he went with a vacuous truth: "All I can say, Pete, is I found myself dealing with a more fluid situation than I expected."

"You realize this could have gone against us. Other traders could have seen your giant short and bought the kyat, pushing up the price until we had to buy back the kyat from them at a massive loss."

"Obviously that's not what happened. We never take positions like this – maybe the rest of the market figured we knew something if we were doing a trade this extreme. And maybe we did – the Bank of Myanmar was vulnerable, the other players must have realized it too after they got wind of our trade." The only problem, thought Jack, was he himself hadn't been anywhere near sure enough of his theory to knowingly do a trade of this size. "Anyway it worked out…I did what I did, and now I know you'll do what you have to do."

"That's all you gotta say?"

"I'm afraid so."

"Well then, as you've probably guessed I wanted your ass. Your pal Ted had different ideas. He was more concerned that Goldman or George Soros might try to hire you away from us. He and Caroline started shouting me down right in front of the traders. So after we had our frank exchange of views, I decided it was time to show him who runs this firm, so we had a partners' conference. Got everyone together, even got the guys in London and Hong Kong on the line, and put it to a vote. That sure as hell settled it."

"Look, Pete, I accept your decision…"

"I'm sure everyone will be thrilled to hear that, because as senior partner, I have been directed to inform you that you have been voted an invitation to join the partnership of Stone & Co., effective immediately."

Jack mouth went dry. "They…Pete, I didn't…"

"You'll forgive me if I don't congratulate you. And please don't give me that 'I had no idea this would happen' crap. You obviously thought you had a home run shorting the kyat and you decided there wasn't any point waiting around another year or so to make partner. Even if that meant putting the whole firm in jeopardy and rolling over me. The majority of the partnership is now either young maniacs like you or guys like me who should know better but just can't resist the chance of boosting their cash-out through your computer-aided lunacy."

"Pete, I'm sorry. Truly, I have only the highest respect..."

"Skip it, Doc," Pete snapped. "If there's one thing I don't need right now it's some punk condescending to me. The truth is you probably did me a favor. Right after that vote I decided to retire. I'll stick around for a little while to make everything look stable, but I want to start cashing out as soon as possible. Once Stone partners go limited, their capital is paid out over five years, and the way I see it, with you guys running the show it'll be a fucking miracle if you don't blow the place up in half that time. I'm heading back down to the floor now. Feel free to hang out here as long as you like. I won't be needing this office much longer. You and your little playmates can thumb wrestle for it or something." He walked out, closing the door behind him.

Jack stood alone in the room, his mind a blank. The only sound was the whir of the building's ventilation system expelling the cool, metallic-smelling air that was the atmosphere of most Manhattan office towers. He tried to summon the strength to go back to the trading floor, but the events of this day had evolved fast enough to rob him of his sense of reality. He felt as if his feet were frozen beneath him.

No rush of victory came to him – and not just because he felt bad about Pete. Although he did regret the older man's feelings of betrayal and the destruction of his primacy in the firm, Jack felt like someone who'd been close to an accident and wished he could have done something about it. After all, it's not like this had been his idea.

He told himself it was over. The kyat had collapsed, the short was covered, the trade done. He had to live with the consequences, which in the final analysis, weren't that bad. He'd won the lottery, for God's sake! The equity he'd receive in the firm upon being named a partner would make him an instant multimillionaire, at least on paper. Pete's disappointment was regrettable, but there was nothing he could do about it. As for his bonus, well, with a win of this size it was sure to be in the millions.

Yet there was something else...

He gazed out the window, whose northern exposure provided a breathtaking view of Central Park. Even now, as the yellow, orange and red pastels of autumn faded, the park's evergreens rendered the great rectangle verdant.

The fact was the trade had not gone according to plan. His model had predicted a relatively gentle correction in the value of the Myanmarese currency, not a massive collapse. That his sale could trigger such a plunge indicated the situation had been considerably more explosive, more chaotic than he'd realized. An unanticipated event of such magnitude might have equally unforeseen implications for the future.

He watched as a light snow began to fall, the crystals dancing in the updrafts over the park, little whirlwinds appearing and vanishing.

The financial world was like a great web of ever-changing interconnections, an endlessly complex lattice of trades and contracts between individuals, corporations, banks, and governments. The lattice was maintained on global computer networks, like veins of gold threading through the fabric of cyberspace. The web was transformed with every transaction between traders. When a cataclysmic event like a currency's collapse occurred, waves of consequence rippled through the structure of the web, making and destroying the fortunes of market participants.

As he looked out over the treetops of the park, his mind formed an image of the more tropical canopies of Myanmar, the spires of Buddhist temples rising above the rain forest. The twin Bloomberg screens were reflected in the window, two shifting bursts of color, and in his mind they became a butterfly, floating above the foliage, gently beating its wings...

A butterfly effect. The tiny disruption of an unstable system, with vast and unforeseeable repercussions. This time he'd been the butterfly, his ill-timed quip to Hubie the fateful twitch of his wing. Would the kyat have collapsed without his trade? Impossible to say, and no longer relevant, not unless he considered the one certainty he knew: that Burma's economy would now collapse. There would be untold misery beneath the Burmese canopies and in the spired cities he imagined.

He couldn't let himself think like that, no trader could. He had to see himself as reacting to the market, to events. Maybe getting a little ahead of the game, if he were smart or lucky enough, but certainly not making the rules. And anyway it had all been a mistake. Yet his thoughts darkened. It wasn't guilt, exactly, but a feeling of taint just from being part of the thing. And, he realized, the thing could get worse.

Now the waves of consequence would begin to emanate from the disruption he had set in motion. Generally, such waves dissipated with time as they spread across the globe. There was always the risk, however, that the shape of the web would guide the ripples to engender a greater disruption than the one that originally set them in motion. If some ephemeral fluke of the network's ever-changing topology focused the waves on a point of unusual vulnerability, then a new and greater chaos could be unleashed, and what were merely swells would become a tsunami.

He felt a chill in the office and a shiver went through him as he finally turned and headed out the door. When he got down to the trading floor Ted made a beeline for him, with Caroline and Hubie in tow.

"So how's it feel, partner? You *are* our partner, right? We've already had the PR office draft a press release...I'm not going to hear any crap about some call from Salomon..."

"I have no other plans, Ted."

"You should know, Jack," Caroline chimed in, "that you're looking at a compensation package of ten million. Normally you'd start with two but given what you've generated, it seems only right. Of course that vests over the next five years. We haven't divided up the bonus pool yet but you'll clear over two million in cash this year easy." She turned to Ted and laughed: "As will a few other people around here."

Jack looked over in the direction of Carl Rich's desk and noticed a shoebox dangling over the trader's head from a string attached to a ceiling light. He pointed and asked, "What the hell is that?"

"That's Carl's rug's casket," Hubie replied. "We figured we'd have Ben lie in state through the trading day and then bury him in the park by the reservoir."

"Ben always loved the park," Ted said wistfully, and Caroline rolled her eyes. "Afterward, we figured we'd go hit this steakhouse I know. They've got one of those smoking ban exemptions. We'll get a private room, buy out the wine list, fire up some cigars and generally celebrate you making us rich."

"Maybe I'll join you later," Jack replied. "Tell you the truth, right now I just want to get out of here. It's Friday, I don't have any open positions, and I really need to clear my head."

"Probably just as well," said Caroline. "Some CNN guy showed up here asking about you, and the *Journal* called. We just handed them the usual 'It's a natural result of the workings of the free market' statement, and sent 'em away. You don't need to talk to the press right now, and more might show up."

"I'll try to be inconspicuous as I slink away," Jack sighed.

Ted put his hand on Jack's shoulder. "I'll walk you out."

"Thanks."

"Hey, thanks for all the nice money. And don't worry about Pete. He'll get over it when he sees what this does to his bonus. Besides, I'm sure all the dinosaurs were upset right after that comet hit, but that's evolution for you."

"Well, that's how I like to think of myself," said Jack, slipping on his coat and scarf, "a globe-shattering catastrophe, striking without warning."

"That's what we like about you," said Caroline.

As they headed into the elevator Jack saw Jenny Murdoch, Stone's PR chief, bounding down the hallway toward them. As she called to them, her beaming smile and the bounce of her curly red mane telegraphed her enthusiasm. Jack moaned: "Oh no. Ted, my head's ringing. I can't take this right now."

"Perky, isn't she?"

"She makes the Laker girls look like candidates for Prozac."

She leapt through the elevator doors with such momentum she almost plowed into Ted. "Hey guys! Just fabulous, isn't it? But I better make sure you two get out O.K. There's press downstairs."

Jack had a sinking feeling. "Press?"

"Yeah. That's the great thing about wiping out a whole foreign economy. You generate *awesome buzz!*" Her cornflower blue eyes twinkled with delight. "It should be a feeding frenzy!"

"That's a *good* thing?"

"Damn straight!" She nodded her head so furiously her curls struck Jack in the face. "I mean, look at the hedge funds. Sure, they took a lot of heat the last time the emerging markets tanked, but you'd better believe the ones who'd gone short picked up a boatload of new clients. After this, people will be breaking our doors down just to throw money at us."

The elevator doors opened on a lower floor and Nate Henkel stepped in. Jack saw that the risk control officer's eyes didn't meet his, so he felt he had to explain: "Nate, about this kyat exposure; it was never my intention to..."

The car stopped on Nate's floor and he held up his hands as the doors opened. "Hey, you don't have to justify anything to me. I hear you're a partner now, so it's your money. I just work here."

When they got to the ground floor, Jack and Ted strode quickly through the lobby. Murdoch almost seemed to skip along side them as she read a press release to the men. Jack wasn't listening. He did notice a couple of reporters and a news cameraman, and he smiled at them in embarrassment. Someone snapped a flash photo, but the PR woman put herself between the partners and the press and began reading the statement. As they escaped otherwise un-harassed, Ted gave Jack a last slap on the back.

"Congratulations, man. You've arrived."

Jack glanced back at the reporters. "Yeah. I think that's what the Sioux said to Custer."

Jack walked up Sixth and headed east on Central Park South until he hit Fifth. He made his way up that avenue, walking on the park side of the street. It was difficult to keep his balance on the iced-over, hexagonal gray stones. The freezing air was redolent of street vendor pretzels, car exhaust, pine needles and hansom cab horse manure.

After a few blocks his head began to clear, and his thoughts turned back to the sense of foreboding he'd felt in Pete's office. Jack had never imagined himself to be in command of the market. He'd just thought he had a reasonable chance of anticipating its evolution and dealing with it in a rational manner. Figuring the odds, and placing his bets appropriately. The flow of events had proved beyond not only his control but also the ken of his divinations, and this disturbed him. Chance might favor him today, but that same randomness could crush him the next if his powers of prediction failed him.

And they were failing him now. Having not figured on a major collapse, he had no idea what further effects this catastrophe might have on international markets. Everything seemed shakier than he'd ever thought possible. He knew that an unstable financial system could not sustain a currency shock of this magnitude without spillover into other markets, other nations. His models, however, were far too primitive to say anything meaningful about what those repercussions might be. In fact, he wasn't even sure they worked on the limited scale to which he'd tried to apply them yesterday. All he had were vague conjectures. Maybe analogies about butterflies and hurricanes hadn't led him to a theory he could trade on after all. He felt very unprotected in his victory.

He looked over his left shoulder into the park. The wind was blowing drifts between trees whose boughs were dusted with a fine, perfectly white snow. He lost his dark ruminations in the beauty of the moment.

What the hell. Forget Pete, forget the markets, forget chaos. He'd won. It was an old saw on Wall Street that given a choice between smart and lucky, a trader should pick lucky every time. And guys spent careers dreaming of this kind of luck.

A tendency to look gift horses in the mouth was a hazard of his education. In college he'd heard a joke about three students, from Harvard, Yale and MIT, caught smuggling drugs in a foreign country that publicly executes for that offense by guillotine. When the Harvard guy's head is on the block, the executioner throws the lever and the blade fails to drop. The crowd cries "It's a miracle!" and he's released. The same scenario plays out when the Yalie is brought forward. When the MIT guy steps up to the block, he stares intently up at the machine and, after a moment, excitedly announces: "Hey, I think I know what's wrong with this thing!"

Well, Jack wasn't going to question the break he'd caught. Who deserved it more than he, anyway? He'd been anointed by fate, blessed by chance. It was like the touch of the Valkyrie, the wing-helmeted shield maidens of Norse lore, who, on flying mounts, rode the sky, selecting for glory warriors in battle. When in the field a combatant felt the killer angel's touch, he knew to fight without caution, for when struck down he would be raised up into the legions of Valhalla, placed high in the councils of the gods. Nothing like a Wagnerian parable to lend operatic drama to what was in the end a fortuitous fuck-up.

Looking over the treetops and across the park, he gazed at the elegant old towers of Central Park West. Speaking of opera, he'd always wanted to live near Lincoln Center. It was time he moved from his tiny place and his neighbor's evening concerts. Maybe he'd try CPW; the West Side always seemed more lively, and on that avenue he could have an aerie above the park worthy of the merchant prince he was, by the second, beginning to imagine himself. He might not be a "master of the universe," or even of the moment, but he was this day fortune's child. As for any further consequences of the events that had elevated him, there seemed little point in fearing abstract threats beyond the reach of his reason.

His step lightened as he continued home, making his plans, relieved to be away from his screens. Had he been in front of them, there was little chance he would have detected the coming storm, the catastrophe he'd set in motion that would soon engulf him. The thing was too young, the signs too subtle to be seen from his vantage point. It fell to others, half a world away, to know fears that were far from abstract, and threats beyond anyone's reason.

Chapter 3: Waves of Consequence

Separated from Jack Kline's walk up Fifth Avenue by eight days and almost seven thousand miles, two other men were contemplating the Myanmarese debacle's implications. They had far greater insight into these than Jack, the kind of view one gets of a tidal wave just before it crashes down upon one's head.

The first was Heidiki Yamada, the chairman and CEO of the Takamura bank, the world's third largest. In all his eight decades he had never faced anything like the disaster now looming before him. He ran his hand through thinning gray hair as he sat at his desk, trying to compose himself. At the minimum he needed to appear in command when the young man who was coming to see him arrived at his office door. That man was the only other individual who understood the magnitude of the problem. Indeed, to the chairman's mind he was the author of Takamura's peril. Normally Yamada would have exploded, banished him from the firm, but this was not an option. Unfortunately, this person was also the main reason the bank had survived to see this day, and now its only chance at a future.

Heidiki's secretary buzzed in on the intercom to let the chairman know his visitor had arrived, and moments later Hiro Yamada, chief of the bank's capital markets operations, stepped into the room.

Thirty-seven years old, with fine features on a face that seemed perpetually bemused, Hiro gazed around the office. Its furnishings were Spartan, but on its walls hung two exquisite parchment paintings of mist-covered arboreal mountainsides. The windows offered a wrap-around view of the Tokyo skyline, glittering in the clear night air. Perfect serenity, except for the look on the old man's face, which reminded him of a pot of water at the boiling point.

Heidiki's secretary closed the door behind them and Hiro bowed, slightly too deeply. The hint of facetiousness in the gesture was not lost on

Yamada, who responded only by waving the trader into a chair. Unheard-of tolerance for outrageous behavior, but then the two men's relationship was far from the norm. They were both members of Takamura's founding family, members of a clan that still held controlling stakes in nearly a dozen of Japan's largest corporations, the Takamura *kieretsu*. This group of firms was linked to one another through interlocking directorships and cross-ownership of stock, creating a corporate armada led by its flagship, the Takamura bank.

The trader sat down across the desk from his chief. The two men locked eyes but remained silent. Heidiki Yamada was a master in matters of face, the subtle games of appearance that governed Japanese office politics. After a few icy moments, he was gratified to see the younger man first avert and then close his eyes. At last, some sign of contrition, of humility! Then he heard Hiro emit a low, soft snore.

"Hiro..."

The snoring grew louder.

"Hiro," the chairman sighed in exasperation, "I know you are not unconscious..."

The trader feigned waking with a start. "Huh? Oh, hello, Uncle. Have you been there long? Sorry, but I find a little nap at the end of a busy day so refreshing..."

"Must you engage in this kind of infantile behavior, even at a time like this?"

"I know I shouldn't, but there's something in your warm, comforting demeanor that brings out my inner child." Hiro knew he was the only man in Japan who could get away with a stunt like this, so at variance with traditional reverence for authority and elders. It ordinarily amused him to tweak his uncle this way, but now his antics served a higher purpose. They masked the fear he felt, and, oddly, reassured the chairman. The trader knew his uncle could not survive a loss of confidence in the one person who could save Takamura. Long ago the gulf between them had grown too wide to be bridged by expressions of respect or affection, but Hiro did not want to see the old man fail.

The chairman's tone was familiar in its impatience. "There is no time for what you consider levity. This has to be dealt with *now*. And the full extent of the matter must remain known only to us. I assume you realize what now rests on our shoulders."

"Uh... large, fleshy, vaguely round, in your case bearing a temple vein pulsing with anger ... I'm guessing you're referring to our heads."

The old man slammed his hand down on the desk.

"Oh seriously, Uncle, you cannot imagine the matter is obscure to me."

"You grasp the numbers, but there is far more at stake than that..."

Oh no, thought Hiro, *not the history lesson.* He'd heard this man make the speech countless times since he was a boy. How Takamura, like Mitsubishi, Mitsui, Sumitomo and the other *kieretsu*, traced its roots back to the seventeenth century, when the clan financed rice harvests and acted as bankers to samurai and shoguns. Traded with the Dutch at Nagasaki under the Tokugawa shogunate. In 1868 the Meiji Restoration brought to power an elite determined to modernize Japan, and Takamura was at the forefront of the new economy. They built factories, purchased lands and noble titles from the diminished samurai. Their wealth bloomed into the twentieth century, creating a colossus in steel, textiles, shipbuilding, mining and, of course, banking...

Yamada had gotten up to 1868 before Hiro interrupted.

"I believe, Uncle, that in the end this will indeed come down to the numbers..."

"If your late father and I had taken that attitude fifty years ago, we'd have given up hope."

"I find great hope in numbers."

Yamada glared at the younger man. "You know, your problem is you have never known true adversity."

Hiro rolled his eyes. This was the other leg of the speech: how Hiro's late father and Heidiki had saved Takmura from oblivion. Until the end of the Second World War, the various enterprises of the Takamuras were virtually divisions of the same company, a *zaibatsu*. The occupying MacArthur insisted on breaking up such intense concentrations of economic power, and the divisions were separated. As Japan reeled from defeat, Takmura nearly went under.

The brothers found a way to make the breakups largely a fiction. Through an intricate system of shared board members and equity holdings in each other the companies remained firmly linked. They supplied one another with products and distribution channels, and all received financing and guidance from the Takamura bank. The two men led Takamura out of the darkness and became key players in the rebuilding of an economy that, for a time, dazzled the globe. The bank was the still center of Takamura's turning worlds, owning interests in the other members of its *kieretsu*, which in turn held stakes in the bank.

Hiro smiled. "Well, I believe it was our last brush with adversity which caused you to drag me in here in the first place. Your *kieretsu* worked for four decades of the postwar "miracle," until Japan's bubble economy blew up in '89. Our bank took massive losses in the Tokyo market; lost billions more on overpriced American real estate. Perhaps you forget how our industrial companies suffocated under recession and foreign competition. By 1994 your empire sat on a precipice. Only obfuscatory accounting concealed the crisis from regulators and the public."

Heidiki gazed out at Tokyo's neon brilliance. "Had your father lived..." Four years earlier, Hiro's father succumbed to lung cancer. Missing him and his moderating influence was one sentiment the two men shared.

"I know. Had he lived you might not have had to bring me into the business. But as it was, you were left to face the abyss alone."

The old man sighed. "And it would appear you have delivered us, as your American friends say, from the frying pan to the fire."

"I think we both know we'd have been fried long ago were it not for me."

"I can be forgiven for believing you were the answer. Your gifts, obvious from childhood. You amazed your teachers, breezed through Tokyo University..."

"You might have just left me in academia..."

"Your father and I never could make you do anything against your will." Heidiki got out of his chair and turned away to gaze out at the sweeping view of the city, his hands clasped behind him. Hiro noted the whiteness of the knuckles. "Sadly, your intelligence came with a total lack of respect for authority. We'd hoped your years in America might help you get it out of your system, but that was foolishness on our part." The chairman glanced past his shoulder at the trader. "We may have pressured you to prepare yourself for a role in this concern. But can you sit there and honestly say you were uninterested in eventually leading Takamura?"

Hiro smiled again. He was right, of course. The idea of a life devoted to purely intellectual pursuits somehow paled when you had the chance to be one of the ten most powerful private citizens in Asia. He'd earned a Ph.D. in finance from Wharton, learning the techniques of financial engineering U.S. traders had employed for years. There he met and befriended some of the best and brightest of the next generation of American financiers. These included a certain physicist, sent by Stone & Co. to take advanced finance classes.

"In any case we did bring you in, and it is true your derivatives, these swaps, as you call them, were a great aid to us. Until now. I thought you were just helping our clients hedge risk. How could so simple an idea go so wrong?"

Hiro shook his head, musing that the name swap suggested simplicity; a swap of one thing for another, like children trading playthings. Yet swaps were perhaps the most complex financial instruments in existence. Creating them an enormously lucrative business dominated exclusively by American and European firms. Exclusively, that is, until Hiro arrived at Takamura. The revenue his swaps generated began to heal the wounds in the bank's balance sheet and allowed it to recapitalize the member corporations of the *kieretsu*. "You don't get a payoff like that we've had without risk, and I didn't hear any complaints while the money rolled in…"

A thin grimace came to the old man's lips. "Yes, we decided that you would be our salvation. We placed you on all our boards, even the bank's. This despite your age, your recklessness…"

"My inability to maintain the family trademark expression of barely contained fury for sixteen hours a day …In any case I've justified your faith, and not just with swaps. I restructured our real estate interests, salvaged underwater loans…. I've made us a power in bonds, underwriting paper backed by everything from mortgages to music royalties. Meanwhile, what have you done besides buy a piece of that U.S media group, Colmedia? How much have we lost on that? You can't expect me to solve everything."

"I was just hoping you wouldn't bring us to our knees, but you're divesting me of that silly notion by the minute. And I still don't understand what is it you've gotten us into."

Swaps were just that, a matter of exchange. A client might be receiving fixed interest payments in Swiss francs, but prefer to be paid in, say, euros, at a floating rate tied to the U.S treasury bill. Takamura would make that swap with the client, so long as that client paid a sufficient fee. Swaps could involve payments tied to any currency, interest rate, or commodity; yen, British gilts, jet fuel, even the Myanmarese kyat. Swaps might have sophisticated features, things with names like multiple legs and embedded options, and when Hiro thought of his Uncle trying to grasp such esoteric concepts he had to laugh inside. He knew these things were a mystery to the old man, and therein lay power. Swaps were tailor-made for the new breed of mathematically sophisticated trader of which Hiro was a prime example.

He shoved his hands in the pockets of his Saville Row bespoke suit and looked down at the polished tips of his Italian shoes. "Some reverses are inevitable in this business. It's why Takamura is so richly paid for its trouble."

"And today, trouble is very much the operative word, isn't it?" Heidiki shook his head in amazement. "Thanks to the kyat's collapse, your panacea now threatens to bring down everything we've built. I ask you again how this happened."

Hiro sighed. "When the bank does a swap with a client, or counterparty as we call them, we assume certain risks. One of these is the risk of the counterparty defaulting on its obligations to us under the swap agreement. We try to charge enough to compensate for taking on these risks, and we hedge our bets through a variety of methods. Above all, we try not to have too much exposure to any one counterparty, currency, or country. We try to diversify. When the kyat tanked, I knew there might be problems. BankBurma is Myanmar's second biggest bank and a longtime swap client. They took massive losses. Its management quickly informed me they would default on over two billion dollars' worth of kyat-dollar interest-rate swaps with us."

"A huge loss..."

Hiro leaned back in his chair and placed his interlaced fingers behind his head, but the slight flush that came to his face belied the cool he was trying to project. "I allowed my traders to be aggressive in dealing with the Myanmarese since BankBurma had a decent credit rating..."

"Until now."

Hiro ignored him. "I'd assumed, however, that this was the end of our Myanmarese exposure, since BankBurma was our only client in Myanmar." The trader paused, fighting to keep his voice steady. "I was wrong, of course. Two days after BankBurma's communication, the Australian mining firm Perth Holdings quietly notified Takamura that it could not make good on its end of a set of swaps tied to the price of aluminum. It seems the Aussies were counting on BankBurma to finance their offshore oil-drilling project. The Myanmarese bank can no longer make the loan. Perth now wants time to find new backing, and their financials are worse than is widely known. So we're facing another billion and a half in losses...Now I learn McKenzie-Kent had also made substantial Myanmarese investments, including a large stake in BankBurma." One of the earliest foreign trading houses, or *hongs*, in Hong Kong, the British-owned McKenzie was founded before the Opium War and had been trading with Takamura since the opening of Japan. "They've borrowed billions from us through a long-standing line of credit, and that money is now a fond memory."

The old man rubbed his temples, a pounding headache coming on. "So you allowed us to essentially bet our house on Myanmar without a second thought."

"I run trading, not lending. How was I supposed to know you'd let McKenzie's credit get so big? Now if you'd put in the firm-wide risk control software I recommended..."

"Or if *you'd* attended more board meetings, but of course you find these beneath you..."

"I wouldn't go that far. I just wish the pharmaceutical division would pay more attention to them."

"The pharmaceutical division? Why?"

"Think of it. A soporific which is the furthest thing from addictive. What a marvelous sedative..."

"Oh, this is pointless..."

Hiro got up and paced. He pictured Jack Kline's face and laughed, saying aloud in English, "Really got to hand it to you, Kline. You've screwed us big time here."

"What are you talking about?" Heidiki Yamada spoke only Japanese, and often suspected Hiro of saying something derisive about him in the other language.

"Nothing...just thinking of an old friend." He still talked to Jack on the phone from time to time, comparing notes on the market. Hiro couldn't believe Kline had been the author of his current predicament. Jack had always seemed a bright guy, but held back by ambivalence about the business. Liked the money, but couldn't shake the feeling the whole thing was a waste of gray matter. Hiro usually found Jack's analysis insightful but he never thought of him as a killer of currencies, or *kieretsu*, for that matter. Now it tuned out he was just another nerd who grew fangs. Anyway, he didn't hold it against him personally; even he couldn't have imagined the results of the kyat's fall, and he had a lot more information than Jack.

Heidiki spoke again. "Something must be done, and quickly. Between the swaps and the loan defaults, we will not have enough liquidity to make good on *our* obligations and still meet capital requirements. This leaves us..."

"Totally fucked," Hiro said in English.

"Will you speak Japanese?"

"In a somewhat delicate position."

"You mean we're fucked, I believe."

"Ah, you've learned some English."

"I've seen enough American cinema to be familiar with the expression. It's their every third word."

"There are options..."

"I'd be delighted to hear them..."

"We could attempt some sort of accounting legerdemain to get past the regulators of the Finance Ministry and the Bank for International Settlements."

Heidiki shook his head. "We're on thin ice with them already. We can't afford a scandal."

"We could hope for a foreign rescue of Myanmar and BankBurma, but the International Monetary Fund is tired of repeatedly bailing out over-indebted emerging nations, especially since the last Asian crisis. This time their aid will be slight and slow in coming. Unlike Mexico, Myanmar shares no border with the U.S, making any unilateral aid from that quarter unlikely. As for Japan, well, the Diet can't agree on bailing out banks in Tokyo, much less Yangon."

Hiro put his hands in his pockets again and closed his eyes. "This leaves one alternative: selling assets. The obvious choice is to liquidate our multibillion-dollar position in U.S. Treasury bonds. We've refrained from selling these at the urging of the Bank of Japan. A lot of large Japanese banks, the city banks, have huge Treasury positions, and the BOJ is worried that if we dump them it'll push up interest rates and crush the global markets, maybe even pull down the American economy. Japan's already in recession. Without the U.S. to export to, recession could become depression."

Heidiki folded his arms and listened. Despite his anger, he knew very well Hiro had saved them before. He believed in his nephew's intelligence if not his prudence.

Hiro continued. "This raises another question. Takamura isn't the only Japanese bank in trouble, and many of them want to raise capital. If we break ranks and sell, others might follow, causing a stampede. We could end up taking large losses on any bonds we keep. So to be safe, we'd have to execute our sale, quietly and completely, before the others move."

The chairman nodded slowly. "How would you proceed?"

"We can buy time by delaying some transactions. For example, Colmedia. You've planned an additional equity investment and a loan to them as well. We could stall them. Still, we must bail out of our bonds in a matter of weeks, maybe less."

Heidiki sighed. It was no mean thing to defy the Bank of Japan, but this crisis was turning lethal. Reaching across his desk, he lifted a ceramic paperweight off a pile of periodicals. It was in the shape of five chrysanthemums arranged in a pentagon, a stylized version of his firm's insignia. He ran his fingers over it. "The House of Takamura has stood for three centuries. We survived the swords of shoguns, Admiral Perry's cannons and the atomic bomb. We're not going to fall because some trader in New York shorted a third world currency."

"You understand what could happen if our bond sale starts a panic. This is a delicate time. America and Europe are on the edge of recession and Japan's economy is slumping again. If we crash the bond market and interest rates spike, there could be a spillover collapse in the world's stock markets, not to mention a global economic contraction, maybe worse..."

"Worse, yes..." The way those words were spoken told Hiro his uncle was seeing something he was not, a rare and disturbing thought. "But Hiro, Takamura survival is our paramount concern. As for other repercussions... regrettable, but these are risks we'll have to live with."

The younger man smiled slightly. "As always, your concern for the welfare of mankind moves me deeply. You should know we wouldn't be able to warn many others of this possibility. If word gets out before Takamura executes this sale, our bonds will collapse from under us. We might provide oblique warnings to a few valued and closed-mouthed clients..." But telling the Jack Klines of the world, Hiro thought to himself, was out of the question.

"Just finish it," the chairman said firmly. Heidiki's gaze fixed on his nephew, and he regarded him coolly. "Yours is the confidence of a man who knows his high place in the world is assured, even as he mocks those who created it for him. You'd do well to remember that this happy circumstance persists only so long as this house prospers. I indulge you because of your mind. Justify this forbearance now, or we will both look like the fools we may very well prove to be. This is a matter of great consequence to your future here."

Hiro's smile turned to smirk, his cockiness returning. "If this doesn't work, 'here' probably won't have a future."

Hiro closed his uncle's door behind him and exhaled, congratulating himself on preserving his nonplused demeanor. Now, thought the trader, his uncle was merely furious – far better then terrified. Anger would sustain him. Sometimes he felt for the old man; he had no sons and his single nephew must seem to him like some kind of sarcastic Martian.

Back in his own office, Hiro looked through his mail and found a magazine in the pile. There on the cover of the *Economist* was a picture of Ted Harris and Jack Kline. They'd been photographed walking through the lobby of Stone's headquarters on the day of the kyat's collapse. The physicist grinned in embarrassment above the caption: "The Boys Who Broke Burma."

Hiro smiled at this particularly silly photo and considered the effect on its subject that his plans might have. If Takamura's sale collapsed the markets, many players would take large losses. Smaller firms like Stone & Co. might go under. The idea gave Hiro no pleasure. Indeed, his friend's ascent was the only thing he liked about this whole quagmire. "Well, Jack, here's hoping you're not long too many T-bonds..."

"Hey, my partner in crime!" cried Ted Harris as Jack belatedly entered the conference room, to the general amusement of the assembled traders. "What, out on a modeling shoot?"

Would they ever get off his case about that *Economist* cover? It had been six weeks since the collapse of the kyat and they still wouldn't lay off. The photo had been snapped while Ted accompanied him on his egress from the building that fateful day. Jack thought the insipid, "What, me worry?" grin on his youthful face made him look like the Alfred E. Newman of global finance.

"Gosh, Ted, that humor is fresh as the day you first used it... sometime in the Paleozoic period, wasn't it?"

"Don't get Ted nostalgic, Jack," said Caroline. "You know how he pines for the good old days... wall paintings, mastodon hunts, dragging women back to his cave by their hair."

"Now there's no need to insult my old fraternity," laughed Ted. "And anyway, whose side are you on?" Caroline herself had been raging on Jack since the article came out.

"I think Jack's confused, goofy visage could be the new face of Wall Street. Anyway, don't let me interrupt your little dialogue. I do so enjoy watching mindless conflict."

"Yeah? Well, I enjoy watching you people make me money," replied Ted, who was now effectively running the meeting. While officially still senior partner, Pete was now often absent from the morning conference. In the wake of his defeat on the question of Jack's trade, he was attending mostly to old clients, seemingly in preparation for a now widely anticipated retirement from the firm. "What's the story on your yield curve trade?"

Caroline looked over at Jack. The two of them had been working on a trade together, betting that a slowing economy would cause a drop in the yield of long-term bonds, and hence a rise in their price.

"Well, we've acquired a modest position. Fifty million so far in principal-only Treasury strips," began Caroline. "Jack and I still think the thirty-year is about to break below through the six-and-a-quarter yield level, but they seem to be running into some unanticipated resistance."

"Jack, any thoughts on what's going on?" asked Ted.

Jack's mind was still on the *Economist* article. Actually, the unfortunate photograph aside, parts of the piece had made him feel better. It made clear the role of other players in the incident, notably the hedge funds. These large, often offshore investment vehicles invested billions of their well-heeled clients' dollars in virtually anything. Simon Ashcroft, whose fund, along with the likes of Soros and Julian Robertson, had been tied to many past currency debacles, was singled out for having been an aggressive seller of the kyat. The Stone traders were quite familiar with Ashcroft; the firm had frequently acted as one of his brokers, with Peter Torelli personally handling his trades. Having been previously noted for his role in the collapse of the Mexican peso and British pound, Ashcroft quipped, "Well, at least this time that kid at Stone's taken some of the heat off me."

It could have been worse. There had been some talk of congressional hearings in the first couple of days after the kyat sell-off, much as there had been when the peso tanked. Jack had feared he might be asked to testify. Myanmar wasn't Mexico, however. The national interest didn't seem to be at stake, and the pressure died down.

"Hey, Doc, you still with us here? Should I tell Scotty to beam you up?"

Ted's joke snapped Jack out of his reverie, and he replied, "Sorry. Yeah, I still like the bond; it's hard not to in the face of housing and inflation numbers as weak as we've been getting. I don't know why we're running into this resistance. My models hadn't predicted it and I don't see it in the fundamentals. It could be idiosyncratic; one large institution selling off its position for its own reasons."

Caroline turned to Hubie, who she knew talked to a phenomenal number of traders during the day, and, in between speeches inveighing against the oppression of the MTA, often picked up useful rumors. "Hubie, heard anything like that?"

"There's some buzz about big selling out of Asia, maybe a Japanese bank. Haven't got anything more specific, but I'll keep my ears open."

"You do that, Hubie," Ted directed. "O.K., now before we break this thing up, I want to discuss a change in strategy regarding our merchant banking fund. As you know, I originally conceived of this fund to participate in the upside of various corporate mergers. We'd take pieces of bridge loans to finance leveraged buyouts, maybe buy some of the target company's stock as well. However, as a result of certain changes in management philosophy..." He paused to exchange knowing smiles with Caroline and several other younger partners, taking satisfaction in their victory over Pete and the old guard. "Well, we'll be taking a more active role in acquisitions, in some cases making the buyout ourselves. I want everyone to be on the lookout for opportunities and to know I'm open to your ideas."

For the first time, Nate Henkel spoke up. "Making capital commitments that large raises a fair number of risk-control issues." He knew Ted's Young Turks had a considerable appetite for speculation. "I assume risk is still something you guys wish to control around here."

Ted laughed. "Yeah, Ned, it is. We'll run anything we do by you and get your input before we make a move." With his new power, Ted was taking it easy on Nate; he didn't want his traders thinking all restraint had been thrown aside. Everyone knew, however, the stakes were about to be raised to levels Pete would never have allowed.

After the conference, Jack returned to his desk. He was still stuck on the Myanmarese collapse. And it was turning into a *Myanmarese* collapse, not just a fall in the currency. As a result of the "kyat shock," Myanmar's gross domestic product, which had been growing 8% a year, was now projected to shrink by 5%. Further, that nation's inflation rate had soared to 100%. This combination of stagnation and hyperinflation would put a lot of Myanmarese workers out of a job, while simultaneously destroying their savings. Many economists argued it was inevitable, that the kyat's decline was necessary to narrow Myanmar's sixteen-billion-dollar current account deficit. It struck Jack that this was a hell of a way to close a trade gap and he was less than thrilled to have played a role in it. It was one thing to give up the ideals of pure research. This kyat fiasco was something very different.

He knew, as all traders knew, that the market was a destroyer as well as a creator. Now, for the first time, he saw himself as an agent of destruction, and knew many others held that view of him. He did not share it with his colleagues, but he felt tainted.

Ted came up behind him and sat on his desk. "So how's the new place?"

In the last few weeks he'd tried to take his mind off his doubts and recapture the euphoria he'd felt on that walk home the day of his victory. In what was for him an unprecedented spasm of acquisitiveness, he'd used his bonus to buy a three-million-dollar, six-room co-op in a building on Central Park West whose other inhabitants included a couple of movie stars, a network news anchor and a United States senator. It hadn't been easy getting in – co-op boards are loath to admit single young men, fearing loud parties and so forth. But the board's chairman was also a venture capitalist who wanted Stone to help take one of his companies public. A five-minute call from Ted, and suddenly Jack was a desirable owner. Besides, after the board interviewed Jack, he understood one member had remarked that it was "hard to imagine this guy at a party, let alone throwing one."

At least he'd been approved. He had not, however, purchased any new furnishings, so that his much vaster new domain contained only the meager contents of his old apartment.

Ted continued. "Get any new furniture, or are you just planning to park a DC-10 in there?" He and Caroline had visited Jack's new place shortly after its purchase.

"It's only been a couple of weeks."

"Look, this monastic thing was borderline even in the old place, but an empty classic six is just plain creepy. At least put something on the walls. Don't you have any kind of art?"

"Well, I've got some stuff I bought in college, like my 'Great Men of Physics' poster..."

"Sounds like a babe magnet," said Ted, shaking his head. "Tell you what, though. Why don't you see my dealer? He does mostly twentieth-century stuff. I bought a couple of Peter Maxxes and a Warhol off him last year. Tell him I sent you and he won't rip you off."

"Funny, you never impressed me as an art aficionado."

"I'm not interested in impressing you. You only have one X-chromosome."

Caroline turned around in her chair. "Ted Harris' Fifth Avenue Palace of Love. Must you try to bring him down to your level? I mean, you already have the protozoa to keep you company down there."

"Look, the man needs to make his space more female-friendly. When's the last time Jack mentioned a woman? I'm just trying to help him find something to do on Saturday night besides sitting at home playing with his...er...laptop."

"Maybe he's just trying to develop his own personal style," Caroline suggested.

"Thank you," said Jack, surprised to be defended.

"You've got to admit," Caroline continued, "His interior design currently has the virtue of simplicity. I mean, empty space has very clean lines. Besides, I think 'early twenty-first-century troubled loner' might be very big on the West Side this year."

Jack sighed. "Thank you both for your concern, but I'm sure I'll get along just fine."

"All the same, go see this guy." Ted reached into his wallet and handed Jack his art dealer's card. "Sixty-seventh and Madison. Just check it out."

"I'll think about it."

They heard a sudden swell of sound from a few trading desks away and Ted yelled over for an explanation.

"Colmedia just dropped 10%," Carl Rich called back, taking a break from his usual post at the mortgage-backed bond desk to check out the stock traders' screens. "Seems that their Japanese minority partner Takamura isn't extending a revolving line of credit to them, and it looks like they won't be making some planned second equity investment either."

"Sounds like they don't want to 'Tak' any 'mura' of Colmedia just now," Ted quipped.

"Ted, we just ate breakfast. No puns," replied Caroline.

"Actually, Colmedia's kind of an interesting company," Ted punched up the firm's financials on a Bloomberg. "Basically, they've got two businesses. They've got a record division, which produces the albums of some of the top pop artists in the world."

"Aren't they the ones that signed 'Angst'?" asked Caroline.

"Exactly. And in addition to their own artists they distribute for other labels. Music's been wildly profitable for them the last few years, and they'd be golden except for the other business, which is *Manhattanite* magazine. Caroline, that's the place you used to work, before you got your M.B.A., right?"

"I was an assistant editor for two years. Just a glorified internship, really."

"Then you know it's a huge loser and only seems to get worse. Not much of an audience for long essays and short fiction these days. Jack, what's that tag line they use in their television ads?"

"For when you've got some time on your hands."

"Right. Well, no one does. Not for that stuff, anyway. People are too busy watching reality shows."

"You've got a point there, Ted," replied Caroline. "I mean, they once published some of the finest writers in the world. How can you expect a rag like that to sell?"

"*Once* published. Hell, wasn't it you who told me they'd gone way downhill, reduced to celebrity profiles and, what did you call it? Oh yeah, 'the semi-autobiographical whine of the young and self-indulgent.' Didn't the boss there tell you he couldn't publish your work because it didn't bring out the voyeur in him?"

"Fred Colson, Sr., the founder and publisher. And actually he said my work wouldn't appeal to the voyeurs he thought were his readers now. No ugly personal confessions to leer at. I don't think he was happy about it. He was just trying to find literature that could sell in the age of Jerry Springer."

"Yeah, well if he didn't do right by you, *fuck him*." Jack marveled at this sudden flash of vehemence, but it instantly faded into cool financial logic as Ted continued. "Look, Colmedia has been using the profits from the music division to cover its losses on the magazine. Now if you could just get rid of that dog, you'd have yourself a clean music asset which a larger media conglomerate would pay a huge premium for. And with today's drop in the shares, I'm pretty sure the buyout price they'd pay for the record division *alone* would be a good 20%, maybe 30% over Colmedia's entire current market value."

Jack could see the wheels turning. "Ted, you want us to buy Colmedia?"

Caroline rolled her eyes. "Of course he does. He's been jonesing for a media deal since he set up our merchant-banking fund. But what about the *Manhattanite*? After we sell off the music division we'd still own the magazine, and we'd no longer have the music business to fund it."

Ted shrugged. "Well, we'd try to sell that too. Whatever you'd get for the magazine would just be gravy on top of the profits from selling the music business. Given its track record, though, the *Manhattanite* might be hard to move. If all else fails, we just shut it down."

"Just kill it off? It was a cultural treasure." Caroline shook her head.

"Was. Hey, you can't argue with the marketplace. Anyway, what are we here, the National Endowment for the Arts?"

"Ted, you're a beautiful human being."

"If this is such a great idea," asked Jack, "how come Colmedia hasn't done it already?"

"Typical entrenched management." Ted smirked with contempt for the concept. "Colmedia's CEO is this Fred Colson. He founded the *Manhattanite* decades ago and somehow staved off bankruptcy for years until his son Fred Jr. got them into the record business. Junior's the real brains over there."

Jack saw Caroline wince at the son's name. "After all, what's Dad done besides discover a score of the last three decades' finest artists?"

"Anyway", Ted went on, "Pops just won't part with the magazine. But if we could get our hands on Takamura's shares and do a tender offer, we could get control. Now I know Junior – I've met him at a couple of media conferences. He's got enough shares to put us over the top, and he's our kind of guy."

Jack smiled. "He doesn't really call himself Junior, does he?"

"Actually, he prefers Zane."

"Zane? How do you get that from Fred Colson Jr.?"

"You don't. He started using it in college, when he was promoting bands. Thought it sounded more, you know, MTV."

Caroline folded her arms. "Oh yeah, Ted, he's my kind of guy exactly. Jack, you're O.K with this?"

"Well, the logic is there. Shame about the magazine, though."

"Look, guys, if it's that big a deal to you I'll see if I can come up with a way to save the thing. You've got to know, though, that if this deal is as sweet as I think it is and we don't do it, someone else will. Kind of like a trade I heard about. You know, in a certain Southeast Asian currency?"

That Saturday, Jack found himself walking through midtown, having spent the early afternoon at the firm, trying to figure out what was keeping the bond from continuing its rally. No dice. All he knew was that someone out there had a lot of Treasuries and was selling every time the bond hit its resistance level.

It was a bright, cold December day, and he decided to get out of the Stone building's hermetically sealed atmosphere, hoping to clear his head. It was a few days before Christmas, and New York was decked out in all its commercial incandescence. He wandered to Madison, making his way through window-shopping crowds. Eventually he came to a door with "Phipps Gallery" printed in modern lowercase across its glass; the dealer Ted Harris had recommended.

Jack entered and found himself in a room with walls so white it hurt to look at them. "Dave Riley: Form in Space" in large black letters on the wall gave a name to an exhibit of sculpture displayed. Giant, amorphous blobs of what appeared to be clay and painted fiberglass hung on the walls. Jack had no idea what the artist was trying to express, but he had the odd sense he had seen these shapes before. His mind groped until he realized the objects reminded him of the wads of multicolored, fossilized chewing gum he had on occasion been unfortunate enough to discover on the underside of high school desks.

As he walked through the exhibit, a woman in her early twenties approached him, dressed entirely in black with a small ring through the left side of her nose. "Can I help you with something?" she inquired.

"Actually, I'm here to see Anton Phipps," Jack replied, wondering how the nostril ring handled a sneeze. "Please tell him I'm Jack Kline and my partner, Ted Harris, sent me."

"I'll see if Anton is here," she replied in a way that let him know Phipps wasn't in for everyone and, for him, probably wasn't even alive.

A few minutes later a slight, fortyish man with slicked-back, thinning hair and large, rose-tinted glasses emerged, extending his hand in a deferential manner. "Dr. Kline, Anton Phipps. I gather I'm in your debt."

As he shook Phipps' hand, he thought the man's appearance and gesture made him look very much like a praying mantis.

"Ted mentioned that his recent interest in a very nice Lichtenstein was motivated by the results of a certain transaction you executed. Something about Myanmar, I believe? I gather it increased his, shall we say, discretionary income."

"Glad to do what I can for the arts," Jack replied.

Phipps gestured to the sculptures on the wall. "Do you have an interest in Mr. Riley's work?"

"I'm afraid it's a bit too ...Bubbleicious for my taste."

"Uh, yes, well..." Jack could see his gum analogy wasn't appreciated, but he hadn't really expected this guy to have a sense of humor. "Anyway, we deal in a vast array of modern and contemporary art. Is there any particular period that interests you?"

"To tell you the truth I just stopped in to browse, on Ted's suggestion. Can you show me anything?"

"Certainly. We keep our more important works in the back."

Jack followed the dealer to his private showrooms, as Phipps explained that the pieces he kept there were acquired at auction or sold on consignment from various estates. Recently he'd come into possession of several early twentieth-century pieces, mostly Cubist. Jack knew enough about the art market to know the prices of many of these items would be well into the millions. That was far beyond what he was willing to part with, even with his windfall. He said nothing, however, since his curiosity was piqued.

They entered a room containing several works by Braque and Gris. Before Jack could ask any questions, however, the nose-ringed woman entered and whispered something to Phipps, who turned and excused himself, explaining that he had to attend to another buyer. Moments after the dealer and his assistant exited, he could hear what sounded like a negotiation taking place across the hall. The conversation was mostly inaudible, but he gathered Phipps was having a rapid exchange with a female buyer who spoke in a soft yet authoritative voice. He distinctly thought he heard the woman say something about a four-million-dollar bid. Then the dialogue ended abruptly as Phipps entered the hall, calling back that he would have to use the telephone.

The mention of any figure with the word "million" in it arouses a certain inquisitiveness among Wall Street types, and Jack was no exception. He went across the hall to see who was willing to part with that sum and for what.

Jack saw a slender woman in a blue Chanel suit, standing in front of a large canvas. At first Jack thought she might be about his age. However, when she folded her arms he glimpsed her hands, and they spoke to several more years. She wore no makeup. Her straight hair fell down past her shoulders, tied back in the manner of a graduate student sacrificing style for efficiency. The distress of that mane, its frayed ends, the light, discolored flecks in its darkness, suggested too many experiments with dyes. This was the only deviation from practical simplicity, and she would have seemed plain were it not for her expression. Concentration, the look of appraising intelligence he saw every day on the trading floor, but more than that. Something behind the eyes, moved by what they saw.

She seemed oblivious to his presence as he circled behind her, staring not at the painting but at its buyer. Then, for an instant, he caught her glance as it swept over him. Her lips curved in what seemed part smile, part silenced laugh.

Though no expert, he'd visited the museums of New York since he was a kid and taken art history classes in college. He knew enough to recognize what he was looking at as a Léger, its Cubist cylinders and disks striped with color and impossibly juxtaposed. As a student, he'd written an essay on the artist and now capitalized on that experience.

"Are you fond of Léger?" he ventured.

"That would be something of an understatement." She did not turn around as she spoke.

"To me, the fascinating thing about him is the way he seems to anticipate changes in the way twentieth-century man would look at the world. I mean, relativity and quantum mechanics were just beginning to be developed when Léger and the Cubists painted. Yet the warped objects and simultaneous views from multiple angles suggest the curved space-time of Einstein, the uncertainty of Heisenberg. You've got to wonder if they were somehow attuned to the coming evolution of man's conception of reality."

He'd gotten an "A" on that essay.

"Gee, that really is something." she replied, her back still turned.

"Thank you."

"I mean, when I want to be pretentious, I usually just start quoting Clement Greenberg. You're the first guy I've ever met who felt the need to haul in all that Stephen Hawking crap. Don't you think dumping the entire weight of the universe on Fernand Léger is a little extreme? Christ, what did the poor bastard ever do to you? That's just so...so *aggressively* pretentious."

As she finished her sentence she turned around and looked dead at him. There was the slightest hint of a smile on her lips, but her eyes, green and bright, were laughing.

Jack stared at her for a moment, speechless, then found himself bursting into an involuntary, convulsive fit of laughter. She also began to laugh, a surprisingly innocent-sounding giggle from a woman who only seconds earlier was cutting him off at the knees.

Jack put out his hand. "Jack Kline. And I'll have you know my father spent a fortune educating me to be this pretentious."

"Well, he obviously got his money's worth," she said, as Jack noted her firm grip. "Helen Cantos."

"Are you in the art business?" Jack asked.

Before she could answer, Phipps re-entered the room. "You have a deal, Ms. Cantos," he said. As he saw his client was no longer alone, Jack noticed the dealer seemed to pale slightly." Oh, Dr. Kline, I..."

Jack figured he knew what the problem was. Phipps' business was a secretive one, and many clients didn't wish their identity known.

"It's O.K., Anton," said Helen. "Dr. Kline was just explaining to me the physics of Cubism."

Phipps seemed to feel he now had to make some kind of introduction, so he said, "Helen, this is Jack Kline, a partner at Stone & Co." Turning to Jack, he said, " And of course this is Helen Cantos. Helen is..."

As the dealer hesitated, Jack thought he saw Helen slightly raise the forefinger of her right hand.

"Well...Helen is a most astute collector."

Phipps and Cantos excused themselves to finish their business, and Jack wandered about for a few minutes looking at the canvases. When dealer and client reemerged, he saw the woman was preparing to depart, and Jack told the dealer he was leaving as well.

"You haven't seen even a portion of our catalogue," Phipps protested.

"I know, but I'm afraid I need to get home," Jack lied.

"Where do you live?" asked Helen.

Jack told her his new address.

"That's only about five blocks down from my building," she replied, which Jack realized placed her in one of only two buildings on CPW considered better than his own. "My car's waiting out front. Can I offer you a lift?"

At that particular moment her proposal seemed the most attractive he'd gotten since arriving in New York, and he accepted. It was pretty unusual for a woman to offer a man she just met a ride, especially in Manhattan. He soon saw, however, that this lady had little to fear. Her car turned out to be a Mercedes driven by a six-foot, three-inch gentleman in sunglasses whose general appearance reminded Jack of an M-1 tank. A large bulge under his jacket strongly suggested the presence of a gun. Jack and Helen slipped into the back of the vehicle, and as the driver closed the door behind them the trader noted the thickness of the door's metal – like armor, he thought. The driver rolled up tinted power windows, also oddly thick, and Jack wondered if they were bulletproof. This was the kind of security usually reserved for heads of state and drug traffickers.

Whatever trepidation these observations induced in Jack was swept away the conversation that followed. The woman's knowledge of art was breathtaking. By the time they'd fought through traffic to the West Side, she had told him more about Léger, Picasso, Braque, and Miró than he had learned in four semesters of art courses. And it wasn't just her knowledge of Cubism that captivated him. She had a pair of the most beautiful legs he'd ever seen. Dancer's legs, he thought, and as she crossed them he tried not to stare. His interest was further enhanced by the lack of a wedding band.

There was something else, though. It was her happiness in sharing her ideas with him. As she spoke her face seemed to light up. It was the kind of joy in being listened to one finds in minds too much alone with their thoughts. That was a kind of loneliness he could understand, and sensing it in her only made him want to know more.

"So, when we were interrupted I was asking you whether you were in the art business."

"Yes, you were," she paused and grinned.

"Well?"

"I'm in many businesses. Investing in art is certainly one of them."

"I see." This was less than illuminating, and he had the distinct impression she didn't want to discuss the matter. Jack decided not to press just then. A Stone partner had significant information-gathering resources at his disposal. He could look into her background on his own.

As they pulled up in front of his building, he scribbled his private number on the back of his business card and handed it to her.

"Listen, if you'd ever like to further enlighten a physicist on art history, I would love to see you sometime." It had been a while since he'd hit on a woman, and with relief he heard her reply:

"Will you be in town the day after Christmas?"

"That... that would be great," he said, thinking his enthusiasm a little too obvious.

"Fine. In the meantime perhaps you can come up with a connection between Abstract Expressionism and organic chemistry."

After he got out of the car he tapped on her window, and she lowered it.

"You know, I'm pretty sure that Metzinger suggested a link between twentieth-century physics and modern art," he said.

"Actually he did. So you're saying that wasn't even *original* bullshit you were spouting back there, but actually *derivative* bullshit, inspired by the comment of higher authority?"

"Exactly."

"Now I'm infinitely more impressed," she laughed, and rolled up the tinted glass as the Mercedes sped away.

Chapter 4: Ghosts in the Machine

The next Monday morning Hubie, Rich and Jack gathered around Caroline's trading desk to sip coffee and contemplate the Treasury bond's odd price behavior. Ted Harris approached them, exclaiming, "Ladies and Gentlemen, an unexpected event has occurred of such earth-shaking magnitude that I think we have to completely reconsider our financial positions. We're talking the unthinkable here, and when word gets out on this, there could be global panic in the markets."

"What the hell happened?" asked Hubie.

"Kline got a date."

"I knew it was a mistake to tell you," moaned Jack. He'd only mentioned it in the hope Ted might have heard of the woman, but his colleague drew a blank.

"So who's the... and I use the phrase with trepidation... lucky lady?" inquired Caroline.

"Helen Cantos. Anybody here know the name?"

Heads shook all around, except for Caroline. "You know, that does ring a bell from someplace. Can't quite place it, though. Maybe it'll come to me."

"Well, I'm getting together with her next Tuesday, right after Christmas, so if you think of anything before then let me know."

"Why? Something suspicious about her?" asked Carl.

"Like the fact that she's willing to go out with you?" added Caroline.

"Caroline, and I mean this from the bottom of my heart... bite me," replied Jack.

"Hey, save that for your new girlfriend." Ted smirked. " What's her deal, anyway?"

Jack shrugged. "Like I told you, all I know is she's got a bodyguard and a brain like a one-woman art history department. I tried doing a Web search on her, but it turns out there's some sort of 'pet spiritualist' who goes by the same name and the first hundred listings are for her."

Caroline snapped her fingers. "I've seen that woman's infomercial – she wrote that book *My Dog Has Better Karma Than You.* It's a best seller – you're sure it's not her?'"

Jack nodded. "Yeah, I saw that woman's picture on her promotional site and she's not the woman I met. Besides, I doubt helping Rover reach Nirvana brings in the kind of money this lady has. She seems to buy million-dollar paintings the way ten-year-olds collect baseball cards."

"That, and a fabulous set of wheels," noted Ted, recalling Jack's earlier comments to him regarding Helen's legs. "Well, seeing how this babe obviously spun *your* wheels, I'll ask around and see if I can come up with anything on her. And speaking of asking around, Hubie, did you happen to hear anything about our mysterious seller of bonds from the East?"

"Word is that some big Japanese bank might be looking to unload Treasuries, but no one's been able to give me a name."

"The Bank of Japan's been putting a lot of pressure on Japanese banks to buy Treasuries," Jack commented. "They've been trying to keep interest rates down while they buy dollars to prop up the greenback against the yen, and make their exports more competitive. If some large Tokyo bank were selling when the BOJ wants them buying, there could be hell to pay. The BOJ and the Finance Ministry aren't normally ignored over there."

"Maybe so, but that's what I hear," said Hubie. "Might just be a rumor, though. For all I know there are multiple sellers, and this Japanese bank thing is just a red herring."

"While we're on the subject of the land of the rising sun," Ted interjected, "I had a very interesting conversation over the weekend with an old friend of yours, Jack. Hiro Yamada at Takamura. He's head of trading at the Takamura bank, but basically he's the guy to see if you want to do anything with any of the Takamura companies these days. They say his family still controls the *kieretsu*."

"Yeah. I met him while I was taking courses down at Wharton. Bright guy. Had a sense of humor, too."

"I called him to see if Takamura might be interested in parting with their stake in Colmedia. He speaks highly of you, Doc. I think it might be useful to bring you in on the discussions."

"Oh, you know me, Ted. Delighted to help in any way I can. Especially when you want to gut a cultural icon."

"Attaboy!" Ted slapped Jack on the shoulder. "Anyway, I wasn't disappointed in my chat with Hiro. I have a feeling we can pick up 25% of the voting shares for under a hundred million. That plus Fred Jr.'s shares would very nearly give us control. All we'd need is to pick up a few of the public shares on the open market."

"And what about Fred Colson Sr.?" asked Caroline.

"Once we acquire Takamura's stake and Fred Jr. makes his intentions known, the old man will have no choice but to acquiesce."

Caroline grimaced. "Leaving you and Jr. free to get rid of the *Manhattanite*?"

"Look, sometimes you're better off without a long-held asset. Take Carl here. He had that rug for a hell of a long time and I think you'd agree we're all better off now that it's gone."

The following morning in Tokyo, Heidiki and Hiro Yamada stood on the trading floor of the Takamura bank. They surveyed the vast room, nearly four times the size of Stone & Co.'s, brightly lit and filled with row after row of trading desks. Thousands of computer screens glowed. Takamura's twenty-five hundred traders, salesmen and clerks, though perhaps individually more reserved than those at Jack's firm, together made a terrific noise. It usually didn't bother Hiro, but this day he felt his head filled with the thunder of a coming storm. The added cacophony of his traders was not helping his concentration.

Hiro spoke coolly. "The process of selling the bonds is proving more difficult than we anticipated."

"We? Who is this we? Some of us have learned not to expect everything to come easily."

Normally Hiro would have had a snide reply at the ready, but he was too focused on survival to muster sarcasm. "Each time Takamura sells, the thirty-year Treasury bond retreats from its resistance level at a 6¼% yield. The other Japanese banks seem to be getting wind of a large seller and are starting to liquidate as well. This could encourage hedge funds and foreign investment houses to dump their bonds and even go short."

His uncle shook his head. "Not good. We own billions in U.S. Treasury debt. If your efforts to raise capital by selling some of those bonds results in losses on the unsold portion, the whole purpose of the exercise will be defeated."

Hiro nodded. "It gets worse, I'm afraid. If we try to unload a large part of our holdings, we may cause the entire bond market to fall. Then the disastrous scenario we've discussed becomes far more likely."

"The noose around our neck is tightening," the old man whispered. "There is no way BankBurma will be making good on its swap obligations absent a rescue from the Bank of Myanmar, and they can't do that without international assistance. It is now quite clear that any action to bail out Myanmar on the part of the IMF is months off at best."

Hiro rubbed his right temple. "Late last week I received a call from Alistair McKenzie, managing director of McKenzie-Kent in Hong Kong. I believe such a man is traditionally known on that island as a *tai-pan*, or big boss, which under the present circumstances I find particularly ludicrous. McKenzie informed me the problems at his *hong*, BankBurma bailing out of its loan agreement, had created what he called a 'short-term cash crunch.' He wanted to know if, in addition to forgoing payment on current obligations, Takamura might be willing to extend a further loan of, say, half a billion, just for a few months." Hiro rolled his eyes. It had taken all of his will to keep himself from slamming the receiver down hard enough to break its cradle.

"As for the Australians, it's all too depressing to contemplate now. Ironically, the only good news I've gotten is from the firm that had started this fiasco, Stone & Co. A partner of Jack Kline's at Stone, one Ted Harris, called wishing to enter into discussions regarding the purchase of Takamura's stake in Colmedia. He apparently smells blood, having noticed our decision to cut our financial commitments to your favorite music and publishing house. Normally I'd have told him to take a walk, but a sale could raise a few tens of millions we need, and relieve us of this foolish venture you got us into."

"Thank you for once again illuminating me with the rays of your false dawn," his uncle rasped.

"Uncle, I do have an idea."

"Ah, words I have learned to fear."

"Look, I spent the entire weekend staring at Takamura's projected cash flows and capital positions, to the point where I know them by heart. The inescapable conclusion is we must raise several billion dollars by the end of January or face a crisis, perhaps even a government takeover, and this is simply not an acceptable alternative."

Hiro saw the old man look away, his thin shoulders bent as if beneath a crushing load. He realized the chairman sensed looming failure and disgrace, and suddenly Hiro feared the strain would become too great.

"Uncle, I will not let that happen."

Hiro spoke the last words with a steel in his voice the chairman had never heard before. He turned to his nephew without reply, but his eyes were wide, almost beseeching.

The younger man continued. "The survival strategy I've spent the last few weeks formulating is already reaching its endgame." As the last few moves he would make crystallized in his mind, he felt a peace come over him. He could not know it, but what he felt was not unlike the calm Jack had felt when he had accepted what had happened with the kyat and decided to take the consequences. Hiro recalled the Hindu theory of right action: The certainty of knowing what your next move will be, and the serenity of understanding that it is the best you can do, whatever the outcome. A certainty that gave him the strength to bolster an old warrior for whom this was one battle too many.

"I'll try to sell piecemeal a few more times, waiting for periods of market strength so our trades don't coincide with other players selling. Maybe I can avoid spooking the market that way. If I can't sell an adequate amount in the next week or so, I will execute a massive sale as fast as possible, hoping to get out ahead of the inevitable liquidation of other firms' holdings. I believe if I spread my trades across the world's markets – selling bonds in the spot markets as well as selling futures, call options and so forth – I can effectively liquidate a very large portion of our holdings before other traders catch on. The rest of our exposure I'll hedge with puts and swaps so we don't get hurt when the bottom falls out. I think I can dump enough to bail us out before Takamura's predicament becomes apparent. When the truth is known, there could be wholesale panic selling by other Japanese banks. And once it's clear to the world that Japan's banks are getting out of Treasuries, the Chinese and the rest of America's creditors may follow. If the crash scenario I've envisioned comes to pass, it will be a catastrophe, for the Americans and for us. The degree to which Japan and the U.S. are dependent on one another, and the rest of the world on them, will suddenly become painfully clear."

"I hope that's the worst of it... if the markets lose faith in us, in the other banks..."

Again Hiro felt a nameless fear in the old man. "Uncle, a global crash would be bad, but we would survive, and..."

"Creditanstalt," the old man whispered

Hiro did not know the world, but the way the old man spoke it gave him pause. "Sorry?"

"A large Austrian bank. It collapsed, before your time, almost before mine. In 1931, almost two years after the Great Crash. Some say this was the real cause of the Great Depression. Rescue efforts were frustrated. Shock waves broke banks around the world and knocked everyone off the gold standard. The whole global economy fell to its knees, then... well, you know what happened then. And we are a far greater power in this world then the Creditanstalt ever was. If your sales start a rumor we are on the verge of collapse, even deposit insurance might run out in the face of the bank runs. Governments would have to print money, hyperinflation would set in..."

Crisis can give the strong a terrible resolve, and in sharing it the two men found an unspoken compact, bridging chasms of age and temperament, affirming loyalty to something very old.

Heidiki raised a thin, ancient finger. "We no longer have any choice. If not the kyat and Takamura, it would have been something else. Some other incident would have brought down the economic house of cards we and the Americans have spent decades constructing. Depression or no, this family's legacy will not die on our watch. Make us one of the survivors, Hiro. Do what you must, and do it quickly."

Jack spent Christmas at home. His parents were on vacation in Curaçao, the markets were closed, so he took the opportunity to relax, trying to regain his equilibrium.

The next evening, at around 6:00, he arrived at a small, trendy Italian restaurant on the Upper East Side, a spot suggested by Helen. The maître d' informed him that Ms. Cantos had not yet arrived and showed him to a table in the back. About fifteen minutes later Helen walked in, said a few quick words to the owner and sat down.

"You know him?" Jack inquired, having noted her exchange with the proprietor.

"Actually, I own an interest in this place."

He also observed that her driver/bodyguard was not in evidence.

"So, I take it you decided to leave your Praetorian guard at home this evening?"

"Well, you don't seem like that much of a threat."

"There's some people in Myanmar who might take issue with that."

"Yes, Anton told me you crush small countries for a living. You must find that very rewarding."

"I think the best part of it is the positive publicity it generates. After the kyat collapsed, the *Economist* described me as 'a young man who really knows when to go for the jugular.' "

"Your parents must be terribly proud."

He decided not to bring up the "Boys who Broke Burma" caption. "I suppose you've never had to deal with embarrassing PR. You seem like a person who keeps a low profile."

"I've, uh... had a little experience with publicity." She seemed to suppress a laugh. "How does a nice Jewish boy get into a business like that anyway?"

He gave her the short version, from the physics job market to the kyat, collapse to collapse. The conversation turned to her and he discovered she was half Portuguese, by way of Brazil, and half Italian. An only child. She'd grown up in Westchester, studied dance at Julliard - explains the legs, thought Jack. As for her knowledge of art, it turned out she'd picked up a dual degree in the conservatory's exchange program with Columbia: "Saved me from spending all my time with ballet dancers."

"They got on your nerves?"

"Some were fine, but in the main you're talking about people whose primary extracurricular interest is chain-smoking so they can get their body weight down to that of a dachshund. Anyway I'm out of that now."

"So what do you do?"

"You could say I'm involved in the recording industry."

Red lights went off in Jack's mind. "You're not with Colmedia, are you?" The last thing he needed was to get involved with anyone at a company that was to be a target of a Stone takeover attempt. After all, Ted wanted him in on the discussions with Takamura. He had enough heat on him as it was without creating even the appearance of some kind of insider-trading.

"No. I mean, I might do business with them but I'm not "with" them or anyone else. Why do you ask?"

"Nothing important. I know a few people there." It wasn't much of a lie. Once Stone got through with them, Colmedia would certainly know *him*.

"Actually, I own an independent label. Anodyne Records."

He laughed. "Is that truth in advertising?"

"Let's just say I know what business I'm in. Which is mostly pop, some alternative. I'm guessing not your thing."

"Well, I used to have a neighbor who subjected me to that stuff from time to time. Blasted it so loud I thought the building would come down. Given your background I wouldn't have pegged you as a rock mogul."

"You know how you were saying physics is a tough way to make a living? Compared to ballet it's a gold mine. When I got out of Julliard I danced with the Met for a couple of years, then helped found an experimental dance group. Did most of the choreography. We were a big deal for a while, some of the edgier critics loved us..."

"So what happened?"

"The NEA's budget got cut, we lost our funding. I laid off a bunch of friends already too skinny to tighten their belts, and I found a new line of work."

"Still, this seems pretty far from your sensibilities..."

"Sometimes sensibility has to yield to sense..."

"These days all the stuff you hear on the radio seems kind of the same to me. How do you decide what to put out?"

"The truth is you just said it. Nothing too innovative or complex, musically, I mean. And keep the lyrics about as deep as a dime. You're selling very simple feelings: a slightly post-pubescent mix of angst, anger and, above all, sex. Not any subtle sensuality, mind you. This is eroticism for teenage mall rats." She leaned forward, dropping her voice to an amused whisper. "The real secret is, you're looking for something which is, at its core, *boring*. Derivative, dull, but wrapped in a spasm of immature emotionalism and puerile lust. A sort of... 'snoregasm,' if you will."

"Nice business."

"Pays the bills. Some very big bills, in fact."

"Yet you seem kind of pissed about it."

She shrugged. "Not really. A little sad, maybe...I mean, I wish I could have found a way to sell something more... anyway, what are you gonna do? Like you guys say, what the market will bear."

"Yeah, or what my neighbor made *me* bear." She smiled, but he had a feeling his line of inquiry was troubling her. "Look, I'm not trying to get on your case here. Any job's cool so long as *you* can bear it."

"I'm probably giving you the wrong impression. It can be fun, in its way. Just gets to me once in a while."

"So you want to tell me what masterpieces you've bestowed on the world? There's a good chance I've heard some of them, albeit against my will."

"Maybe later. I don't want to spoil either of our appetites." She looked down at her menu. "Did you decide what to order?"

"I was thinking about the parpadelle with duck ragu."

"I usually don't order duck."

"Why?"

"When I was seven I took a school trip to a farm upstate. My mom came as class mother, and I made her rescue this little brown duckling. After fifteen minutes of crying she let me take it home as a pet. It was so traumatized it took about a week before it came out of this cardboard box hutch we made for it. You know the conditions they raise ducks under? Penned up, and, if they haven't been bred so they're too heavy to fly, they may even have their wings clipped. Left to wander aimlessly around some barnyard with nothing to do but..."

"Quack at one another?"

"Oh sure, blame the victims for aping their oppressors. That's just a manifestation of the Stockholm syndrome."

"Er...right." Great, thought Jack. One of those vegi-fascist animal rights nuts.

"Hey, don't let me ruin your dinner. You get what you want."

A waiter came, and Jack ordered a Portobello appetizer and some fuscilli primavera. She, to his amazement, ordered an arugula salad and the parpadelle.

"O.K., that's, like, seriously twisted."

"What?"

"You ordered the duck!"

"It's very good here. Why didn't you?"

"I was about to, but someone put this image of a terrified, helpless little duckling in my mind and made me feel like a war criminal for even considering the idea. I thought you said you didn't eat duck."

She beamed. "I said I usually don't. I told you I'm a part-owner of this place, and I insist they buy only wild duck. The birds are free to fly around and lead normal lives right up to the point some hunter blows them away and they become entrées. Poultry have a very limited sense of foreboding."

"So do you always mess with your dining companions' heads, or am I special?"

"I didn't mean to. Although this has been very informative."

"How?"

She touched his hand and her lips formed the same playful smile he'd seem in the gallery. "Myanmar notwithstanding, any guy who in the space of thirty seconds can be made to feel that sorry for a duck can't be all bad."

The conversation turned to other subjects. Again her erudition impressed Jack. She seemed to have seen, read or listened to absolutely everything. The woman could jump from Mozart to Goethe to Joyce to Garcia Marquez to Nirvana in the space of twenty minutes. She never seemed uncomfortable with a subject.

Rarer still, she made him comfortable enough to talk. He talked about cosmology and the breaking of the kyat. He talked about the antics of his colleagues and Ted Harris' term for incognito intellects on the Street, the "stealth nerds." Over espresso he spoke to her of the conflicts he felt over his work, and his sense of loss since leaving science. Thoughts he almost always consigned to the privacy of his mind.

"What's so funny?"

"You're a fairly tall guy, but I'm guessing you weren't a big kid."

"Why?"

"You don't seem to care that much about money, or at least not in the things it can buy. But it pissed you off that less talented guys were running the world while you starved with your equations. That's the schoolyard defiance of a kid whose mind and mouth matured before his body got big enough to defend them."

He was about to reply to that when he was distracted by a couple of men two tables over. He thought could feel their eyes on him. They were young and their suits screamed Wall Street. Jack thought he might have been recognized from the *Economist* cover, though that was weeks ago and he hadn't had the problem before. When she suggested they take a walk, he picked up the check (a point on which he had to insist) and they headed out into the night.

She suggested they walk to Rockefeller Center, and after walking a few blocks they stood looking down at the skaters circling the white rink, the Christmas tree and its thousands of lights towering overhead.

"Do you skate?" asked Jack.

"Not much. I was always worried I'd sprain an ankle and it would screw up my dancing. It is beautiful to watch, though."

"I've always loved the way ice dancers spin faster as they pull in their arms. Like a living illustration of the conservation of angular momentum."

Helen looked up and the growing smile on her face warned him of impending sarcasm. He preempted her.

"Now don't start with the geek jokes. Science can enhance one's appreciation of the beauty of nature."

"Yeah, I'll never look at spinning people the same way," she laughed, then touched his cheek and kissed him.

He forgot about angular momentum, putting his arm around her and drawing her close. Then he noticed a teenage couple about ten feet away; he had the eerie sensation they were staring at Helen and him. They wore leather jackets and the girl had a white streak dyed in her hair. Jack didn't think they looked much like readers of the *Economist*.

"What the hell are they looking at?" Jack cocked his head back toward the pair.

Helen glanced over his shoulder. "Probably just surprised someone would want to kiss a currency trader..." Yet Jack sensed she was rattled, something he hadn't imagined was even possible. "Uh... look, why don't we walk over to my place and I'll show you some of my art collection."

"Now that sounds like a come-on."

"If it is, it beats your 'cubism in warped spacetime' line..." She was herself again.

"It was all I could think of."

"I just keep seeing the Phipps gallery getting sucked down a black hole..."

"Well, that fiberglass stuff wouldn't be such a loss."

"Anton couldn't sell you on Riley's stuff?"

"Let's just say I didn't want to bite off more than I could chew."

She let out a laugh. "Like old chewing gum! Under your seat, right?"

Surprised, he saw her eyes shine with mirth again. "Exactly."

They walked and laughed, his arm around her, and after a block and a half something made Jack turn around. For an instant he thought he saw the same young couple following them, but the crowd on the street swallowed whomever he'd seen, and he couldn't be sure.

As they proceeded to the West Side, Jack wondered if the events of the last few weeks had made him paranoid. That was an occupational hazard in his business, and apparently in Helen's as well. He wasn't the one riding around in a panzer tank with a human Doberman, after all. Odd for a record producer. For the moment, though, Jack chalked that up to the eccentricities the rich can afford to indulge. He'd seen far stranger on the Street.

They walked up CPW in silence for a while. When Helen finally spoke, it was clear she was still amused by thoughts on ice skaters.

"So is that why you loved physics so much? All those equations helped you appreciate nature's beauty?"

"Well, yeah, but it wasn't just that. I guess, for me, it was an extension of faith, even religion. I guess that sounds contradictory, doesn't it? You don't think of faith when you think of science, of equations. Yet there is no *a priori* reason to assume you can understand the universe, that mystery will yield to reason. Just trying to understand is an act of faith."

"Back in Philly I always aced math, but it didn't make me feel any closer to God. Then again it was a Catholic school, and they discouraged mixing calculus and catechism." She started to grin. "Now I can see you doing integrals during your Bar Mitzvah."

"Might have made it more interesting. And the Jews like a little math with their mysticism. Know anything about Gematria? Talmudic numerology?"

She snapped her fingers. "The Kabalah didn't come up that much at St. Mary's."

"A lot of it's about mathematical patterns in holy text, based on the Hebrew alphabet. The *zohar*, the 'book of lights,' talks about these ten planes of existence, the *sefeirot*, through which God projected his presence at the creation. Numbers describe them, and if you understood those numbers, how they relate to each other, then you had the key to the universe. You knew why the world is as it is, and by extension who we are. Now physics is just an effort to find logical order in nature. In that sense it's really not that different from what those old mystics were trying to do. Einstein said he wanted to know God's thoughts. We're still trying."

"So did get you any answers? Find yourself in all that math?"

He shook his head. "Just more questions." He smiled. "Although a few weeks ago a divine hand emerged from my computer and pointed out this really sweet sell signal in kyat."

"If you can't find the meaning of life, you might as well make a nice piece of change."

"Some people I know think it's the same thing. This just all sounds like crap to you, doesn't it?"

"I think I get your thing with science. You felt connected with something bigger then yourself. Sometimes art does that for me. And dance. That's what I love about it. For a moment you can actually be that connection, *become* the art..." As she spoke, she spread her arms and did a turn on her toes.

She moved like a leaf on the wind.

Jack was transfixed by her motion. She shrugged. "Like being transported, you know? If you want to call that getting closer to God or whatever, fine. I don't feel the need to put a name on it - the feeling is eloquent enough." Then her face lit up. "Hey, that's an idea – we could go dancing!"

"Uh...you don't want to see that."

"You don't dance?"

"I don't think you'd call what I do *dancing*, exactly..."

She looked him up and down, admiringly, he thought. "Well, I mean, you're an athletic guy. You like music..."

"It's like watching a man with a squirrel in his pants."

"Sounds like one of those 'or are you just happy to see me' jokes. Anyway, if we're going to get along I'll have to do something about that. The dancing, I mean." She laughed, wrapping her arm around his waist. They continued, walking and laughing. Again, Jack felt oddly comfortable with her. Kindred.

When they reached her building, the doorman greeted her and they proceeded though an ornate lobby to a keyed elevator. They glided up to her apartment, which occupied the entirety of one of the uppermost floors. Helen used a magnetic card to open the door; high-tech security incongruous amid the elegant old marble and moldings of the hallway. As they entered there was no one in sight, and as far as he could tell they were alone.

They passed through a foyer into a large, dark room with grand windows facing east. The lights of Fifth Avenue shone across the park. When Helen hit a wall switch the room was illuminated, and Jack had difficulty believing his eyes. It was if someone had taken a wing of the Louvre and suspended it over Central Park. Manet, Degas, and Matisse hung from the walls. He said nothing as she led him over a huge Isfahan rug into a second similar chamber, but this time they were surrounded by Picasso, Miró, Léger, Rothko. A Warhol, not yet hung, was propped up against the wall. The room seemed a kind of study; two bookcases held several hundred volumes of literature, poetry and history. A large walnut Nakashima table was covered with papers.

Since coming to Wall Street, Jack had been in the homes of many wealthy people, but he had never seen anything like this in private hands. The trader in him might have tried calculating the market value of what he was viewing, but something silenced the mercantile instinct.

"Wow...I mean, this is...this is just unbelievable."

"To me, it's almost everything else that's beyond belief. Especially... well, let's just say that surrounded by the real thing, it's a little easier to keep from believing your own bullshit. Anyway, it's really an attempt at escape. I like to create spaces where I can avoid contemplating the material." She grinned. "Of course, doing that isn't always cheap."

He wondered if it worked for her.

"I'll tell you the truth. I feel kinda funny about all this locked up in a private home."

"Actually, I'm doing a social good. I lend maybe half out each year; sometimes to the MOMA or the Met, but usually to other museums that can't afford this kind of work, which are most of them these days. Without me, a lot of people would never see this stuff."

He'd expected her to begin describing her collection to him, but she said nothing as he stepped from painting to painting. She just watched him, then asked, "Want something to drink?"

He nodded and as she vanished into another room. While he waited for her return he gazed down at her table and the papers strewn across it. Some appeared to be musical scores, others contracts. He consciously averted his eyes from the latter, then noticed among the scores what appeared to be lines of handwritten poetry. He couldn't resist scanning these. They struck him as light, even silly. Little odes to love and dancing. Every once in a while there was a line he liked, something about a love driving the thoughts of all others away *"like the sun chases stars from the sky."* Enough corn and cheese for a decent order of nachos, but he figured the words were hers and warmed to them. Then he noticed a small photograph on a bookshelf. It was Helen, perhaps from a decade before. She was dancing with a ballet company, balanced *en pointe*, arms above her, seemingly weightless. A frozen moment of grace.

As he stared at the picture, chewing on the earpiece of his glasses, he was startled by the sound of music emanating from unseen speakers. One of the romantics, he thought. Brahms, maybe. He turned as she returned with an uncorked bottle and two wine glasses, already filled.

"Sorry, had to let this breath a bit. Just got a case in and I wanted to try it. Château Pétrus Pomerol, '62. I hope you like Bordeaux."

They swirled wine in their glasses and he raised his to hers in a crystal clink.

"To us?"

"You see anyone else here?"

Jack knew little about wine but what he tasted was spectacular.

"That really is very good. Where did you get this?"

"I have a very good dealer in Paris, but it was hell to obtain."

"Must be expensive."

"You don't want to know."

"Are we celebrating something?"

"Us meeting, and the ability to afford very expensive forms of fermentation."

He held up the photo. "From your Julliard days?"

"Uh-huh. Back when dinosaurs ruled the earth."

She motioned for him to sit down and as they settled on a large sofa in front of the table he asked, "So that's where you found your truth? In dance?"

She sipped her drink, reflecting for a moment. "Being transported is about a feeling, and feelings aren't always truth. Speaking of which, what was a scientist doing fooling around with Hebrew mysticism?"

"It was a phase. Lots of analogies have been made between cosmology and religious creation myths. You know, 'Let there be light,' the dance of Shiva, that sort of thing. Grad students tend to get sucked into it for a while. I just went for the most familiar flavor. And it resonated with some things I was studying, like compactification."

"You were studying compactors? Hey, something useful! This building's trash compactor makes this really weird, loud noise..."

"It's actually a feature of certain theories, where spacetime starts out having ten dimensions instead of just time and the three spatial dimensions we experience in our daily lives. The extra dimensions get curled up so they're not noticed."

"*That's* in the zohar?"

"No, but there's this thing called the *tzimtzum...* "

"Exactly the noise our compactor makes – wakes the whole place up in the morning, and you know these walls are prewar."

"Supposedly when God created the world, when he projected his being through those ten planes, he drew himself inward to make room for the universe. It reminds some people of the way dimensions are supposed to curl up on themselves."

"I haven't seen a stretch like that outside of my yoga class. You really think there's a connection between that stuff and theoretical physics?"

"I think when people are displaced and oppressed and almost helpless, they create myth to explain the world to themselves, and to make themselves feel powerful. Centuries later, a few coincidental resemblances of that myth to modern theory are inevitable. But, sometimes, coincidence can be beautiful. Anyway, like I said, it was a phase. You don't subscribe to any particular philosophy?"

"Well, I describe myself as a tautologist."

"I've never heard of such a thing."

A grin began to play across her face. "It's my own belief system, based on an acceptance of the tediously self-evident, the manifestly obvious. It's a realization of the inevitable triumph of the trivial."

He laughed. "You ought to meet my partner Ted. You're both really into coining these little phrases..."

"I like to consign some things to an annex of the language. Helps me avoid thinking about them too seriously..."

Jack had noted her word games possessed a slightly bitter edge. "Given the state of the culture, your own comments about your business, it sounds like you're simply a realist. You wouldn't get an argument from me, anyway."

"Realism somehow misses the deeper banality of what I'm striving to embrace." Helen turned to look past him, out beyond her windows into a darkness that for a moment seemed mirrored in her expression. "Mine is a very particular kind of cynicism." Then she glanced down at the poetry on the table and brightened. He realized with embarrassment that he'd left the pages visibly disturbed.

"Now you haven't been reading these."

He smiled apologetically. "Only the poems. I'm sorry. I was just curious."

"See what I mean by embracing banality?"

The music playing on her stereo swelled in a crescendo. Not Brahms, thought Jack, but he still couldn't place it. "What is this, anyway - Debussy?"

"Elgar - the 'Enigma Variations.'"

"Figures. Could be your theme music."

She stifled a laugh. "If I have a theme it certainly isn't by Elgar."

"Look, you're obviously not a trivial person, and this certainly doesn't strike me as the home of a woman who embraces the banal. I really don't get it."

Helen put her hand on his chin. "I know." She looked at him with what he thought was a mixture of amusement and something else, almost like sadness. "I think that's what I like best about you." She brushed her fingers through his hair and slowly shook her head. "You will, though. Get it, I mean. Soon. It's...well, inevitable, I'm afraid."

"That sounds kind of ominous." He sat back and unconsciously removed his glasses, placing an earpiece in his mouth in the manner Ted mocked.

She laughed a little and made a dismissive motion with her hand. "I don't mean anything by that. Just what happens when two people get to know each other better. Look, I'm sorry. I can get a little morose at times. Anyway, I didn't mean to get you so upset you'd start smoking..."

"What?"

"Let me put it to you another way. How do you feel about Magritte?"

"I'm afraid I don't follow..."

She smiled and gently pulled the glasses he'd been chewing on from his mouth. "This is not a pipe."

"Ah...yeah. Ted gives me crap about that too, although his humor contains fewer references to surrealism."

"Your trading floor sounds surreal enough." She gestured toward the papers on the table. "Not exactly Yeats, is it?"

"Its not bad. I like the part about the sun and stars. Is it yours?"

"Afraid so. Actually, they sound a little better when they're sung."

"These are lyrics?"

She nodded.

"I thought you just produced records."

"I do, but..." she smiled, "well, lets just say sometimes I dabble."

"Let's hear what the musical version sounds like."

"I'm not really in a singing mode tonight. Besides which, I don't really see you as a guy who thinks of women in terms of suns and stars."

Jack looked at her. There was something about her so utterly out of place. It was a condition with which he was very familiar, and seeing it in her moved him. Words he'd read once came to him, and as he took her in his arms he found himself speaking them.

"She was like the sun making red in her rising the clouds of dawn with the flame of her light."

She blinked, surprised. "Who wrote that?"

"A guy named Judah Halevi. Twelfth-century Sephardic poet."

Helen smiled "Now that's a line." As they kissed she pressed against him with an urgency he hadn't expected. He opened his mouth to say something; he still had many questions about her, but she brought her fingers to his lips. "Whatever you're about to ask is part of a world I want to go away right now, O.K.?"

The logical part of his brain, the part molded by science and hardened by Wall Street, told him it was definitely not O.K. But as he looked into her eyes, smart and sad and lost, that part of his mind was not in control, and he just kissed her.

Later, lying with her in the darkness, there'd been something else, more than cool skin warmed under a caress, or her sudden beauty as he brushed her long hair across her breast. Their paths had left them sharing an emptiness, a void which drew them into each other as vacuum draws in air, annihilating itself. And so, for a time, they made the world go away.

On the last day of the year, Stone & Co.'s trading floor was at less than half-staff. It was a Thursday, and trading volume was next to nonexistent ahead of the holiday weekend. Normally, Jack would have blown the day off. However, Ted was meeting with Fred Colson Jr. of Colmedia and wanted Caroline and him to sit in. Led by Ted, the three young partners had formed a triumvirate, which, in Pete Torelli's absence, had become the defacto ruling committee of the firm. Stone's traders and bankers had begun referring to the three as the troika. In truth, Jack was very much the junior member of this trio; the other two had decided to include him, given his visibility after Stone's kyat victory. After all, great buzz.

As the three partners sat in Ted's spacious office waiting for Colson to arrive, Ted and Caroline chatted about the Colmedia deal, the mysterious Japanese seller of Treasuries, and Carl Rich's disturbing new toupee, which seemed to have highlights. Jack's mind was a million miles away from their dialogue. He stared out the window, looking west and uptown over the park in the general direction of CPW and Helen's apartment.

"Shit, Jack, is this how it's gonna be now?" Ted snapped him out of his reverie.

"Is what how it's gonna be?"

"You staring out the window like an idiot with that insipid little smile on your face. 'Cause if it is, I want the old Jack back. The guy who analyzed markets to death and never got laid."

"I'm listening to you guys. Really. And I never said anything about getting laid."

"Oh, *please!* " Caroline laughed. "I haven't seen anyone this happy since that time an LIRR conductor forgot to collect Hubie's fare."

Jack *was* happy, and until now he hadn't realized how unfamiliar the emotion had become. He felt he had found an island of sanity, shelter from a world of gyrating markets, collapsing currencies and corporate takeovers. Helen had fashioned a separate peace, and she had shared it with him.

Here, however, he had to deal with reality. The discussion of the partners turned back to the behavior of the bond market.

"I really hate to change the subject, but I'm inclined to believe the rumor Hubie heard about there being a single big seller of U.S. bonds." Jack began. "The fact that the selling seems to hit at around the same market level every time suggests there's one big player out there with a particular liquidation price in mind."

"It might not be a liquidation *per se*," interrupted Caroline. "It could be someone going short Treasuries."

"A hedge fund, maybe," added Ted.

Jack nodded. "That's all true, but these sales are big. Big enough to repeatedly back the market up. Now a bunch of hedge funds could do that, but as I said earlier the selling pattern suggests a single player. Even the biggest single hedge fund would have difficulty mustering the capital for that much short selling. They'd have to use huge leverage. I find it unlikely that someone out there would make that big a speculative bet against the bond in the face of a slowing American economy."

"Then who's the seller?" asked Ted.

"I'm thinking a bank," replied Jack. "A big bank. A lot of the selling seems to hit when Tokyo is open so like Hubie said, Asian, probably Japanese. Trying to liquidate a large portion of their bond inventory."

"That's the whole problem with the theory," countered Caroline. "We know the Bank of Japan has been pushing the big Tokyo banks to buy Treasuries. And right now, with all their other problems, like the real estate loan bailout, the last thing those banks would want to do is piss in the Bank of Japan's sake."

"That's quite right," replied Jack. "The only way I can see one of the Tokyo banks thumbing their nose at the BOJ right now is if they're in desperate need of funds."

Ted frowned. "Wouldn't we have heard if one of the biggest banks on earth had its balls to the wall?"

"That's where I'm stuck," said Jack.

Just then the door opened and Judy, Ted's assistant, poked her blond head in.

"Ted, Fred Colson is here to see you."

"Great. Send him on in." Ted turned to his partners. "O.K., kids, playtime is over. I'm dying to know whether Colonel Mustard killed the bond market in the kitchen with a candlestick, but we'll have to return to that mystery later. Right now I want you both to meet the man whose going to make the Colmedia acquisition work for us. Oh, and by the way, guys, he's got a plan to rescue that magazine both of you seem to think is so crucial to the survival of Western civilization. He's visionary in a very, uh, information-age, online sort of way. You'll see what I mean."

"Hey, Zane!" Ted called as Judy re-entered the room followed by Fred Colson Jr. He looked about thirty-five and was dressed in an Armani suit and a Hermès tie. His hair was slicked back with enough gel to make Jack wonder how the guy could stand touching his own head. He also noticed that Zane's eyes never left Judy's posterior.

Ted made the introductions. Colson emphasized that his friends call him "Zane," which made Jack wonder what his enemies called him. They sat down around a coffee table and Ted spoke. "Why don't I begin by reviewing the plan as we've discussed it?"

"It's your party," Zane replied.

"The thing's quite simple, really. Zane and his father each control 30% of the voting stock of Colmedia. Now Takamura's stake is 20% and the remaining 20% is held by the public. Or rather it was. Our merchant banking fund has already purchased just under a fourth of the public float, which is to say just under 5% of the voting shares. Any more and we'd have to file a 13-D with the S.E.C., revealing our holdings. We don't want to have to tip our hand as to our intentions until our takeover is a *fait acompli.*"

"Don't fire 'till you see the whites of their eyes," said Zane with a smirk. "Did I say fire? I meant file." Jack marveled at the executive's enthusiasm; after all, the eyes he was talking about belonged to his father.

"Precisely," said Ted, and continued. "Now we're in substantive discussions with Takamura to purchase their stake, and when that deal is about to close, we'll simultaneously make purchases of the public shares sufficient to bring Stone's holdings to 30%. Between Stone's fund and Zane here we'll then control 60% of the voting shares and hence Colmedia. We'll appoint a new board, put Zane in as CEO, and restructure the company."

"And that restructuring would entail exactly what?" asked Caroline.

"Zane, why don't you lay it out for us?" said Ted.

"No problem," Zane leaned back in his chair. "Essentially, what we want to do is separate the magazine from our music division. Ted figures our record business alone is worth 30% more than current market price of Colmedia today, and I'd say that's conservative. If we spin off the

Manhattanite, we can unlock that value. The stock market will see we're no longer using our music profits to keep that publication alive, and they'll assign Colmedia its proper share price."

"And what happens to the magazine?" asked Jack. "The shareholders will now own both Colmedia, which is to say the music business, and the *Manhattanite* as two separate companies. This means Stone also holds 30% of the magazine."

Zane shrugged. "As would I. Now on one level the answer to that question is: who gives a damn? We'll have already made a truckload of money through the spin-off."

Ted nodded. "So even if the stock in the new *Manhattanite* turns out to be worthless, we'll have made out."

"Right," Zane's smirk became a broad, toothy grin. "Hey, but why leave money on the table? The fact is the *Manhattanite* could be a winner for us if we can just change its skew."

"Skew?" asked Caroline.

"What's needed over there is a total paradigm shift. We've got to appeal to the young reader with disposable income. That means Gen X and Gen Y. Consumers who are cyber-hip and media savvy. Looking to cruise the Infobahn and jack into the continuous digital rave that the global village has become."

"Right...right." Jack had no idea what the guy was talking about, though he sounded like every gee-whiz article on the Internet he'd ever read.

"Look, print media is dead. The future is online, and that's where we have to go. Were gonna shut down the presses and put whatever's worth keeping on the Web. Sell links to advertisers. Update continuously. That's not the really exciting part, though. The real cherry here is the interactivity."

"How so?" asked Jack.

"At Colmedia, *we're working a whole new attitude*. We'll go way beyond the crap other Web-zines are offering. First, there's music. Colmedia's recording division already has an in-house group putting up websites to promote our albums and concert tours, and we're moving into selling music downloads like all the other record houses. We can do a joint venture with the *Manhattanite*... album reviews, videos, interviews with artists, ticket sales. Right now Pops won't let me do any of that stuff. Not 'literate' enough, he says, but that'll change once we're in the driver's seat. The thing is, though, interactivity's gone pretty far with music. We've got online fan chats with stars, people mixing favorite tracks; hell, if it wasn't for all the illegal swapping I'd be thrilled. On the other hand, no one's brought true interactivity to literature. I mean, imagine what I could do for fiction..."

"Imagine..." said Caroline. Jack thought he saw her shudder.

"You know what the problem with fiction is? Too linear. Just one possible ending. No chance for the reader to log in and have his say. Today's consumers were brought up on video games. They expect to participate in their entertainment. To be players, not observers. Now, with the new online *Manhattanite,* the reader is in the driver's seat. Playing the characters, becoming them in a virtual world, and not just accepting some writer's crap. And I'm not just talking new fiction here. You could make the classics interactive. Think of it: all the bummer endings of every novel you've read or play you've seen wiped out with a mouse click. All the buzz-kills morphed away. And what happens when we get this technology into the schools, when every book a kid picks up is a virtual reality interactive experience. Maybe this time Romeo and Juliet elope and get a condo outside of Verona. Willy Loman makes a killing in soybeans. Ahab offs the whale."

"Sort of like *virtual* culture," said Ted, and Jack caught him flashing Caroline his "I put the frog in your lunchbox" smile.

Zane waxed expansive. "I'm telling you this could bring back reading. It could even be a group activity. If a few players - I mean readers, think Tennessee Williams is a little heavy, then their characters do an intervention and Stanley checks into rehab."

"Democracy in cyberspace," Ted volunteered.

"Pure and simple," replied Zane. "And of course we can do it for movies as well. Take *Casablanca*. Great flick, but Bogie not hopping on that plane with the babe? Please. Now, through the magic of computer-altered video downloads, we can make that happen."

Caroline gave Zane a look of cold disbelief. "Why stop there? You could let the user, as *himself*, 'interact' directly with the characters. You know, go fishing with the Old Man and the Sea."

"Or lay Madam Bovary", Ted chimed in.

Zane snapped his fingers. "You might just have something with that last one. Literary cyberporn. We could keep it classy. Steal a march on Playboy. Man, I'm gonna love working with you guys! You think way outside of the box – right on the bleeding edge!"

"And who wouldn't want to be there…" said Caroline.

"The shame of it is we could have done this a year ago, but my old man is a paper-and-print kind of guy. Strictly Gutenberg. Hey, I love him, and back in the day he found a couple of pretty decent wordsmiths, but the fact is he's a speed bump on the information superhighway. And I'm all about the Web. E-publishing, e-commerce…"

"E-go," Caroline whispered to Jack, who could see she was about to explode. He decided to move things along. "About this change in control, if we put you in as CEO, what happens to your father?"

"With your stock and mine, we'll control the board, so we can put in who we want. We'll offer him a seat and some title like 'honorary chairman,' but in terms of management decisions or editorial control of the *Manhattanite*, he's out. He could never understand our vision. Bottom line: he's tired, not wired." Zane looked at his watch. "Look guys, I've got a meeting, then I'm checking out a new band we're thinking of signing. *The Cud Munchers*. They're at the forefront of the new Albany sound."

"Albany?" asked Caroline.

"Yeah. I tell you, upstate New York could be the next Portland."

"Did the Seattle scene move up to Oregon?"

"Portland, *Maine*. The Northwest thing died years ago. Even Portland's finished. I've found a whole new reservoir of pent-up teenage rage in dairy country. Kind of a hard rock, bovine motif. Just goes to show you, with all the people I've got out there looking for talent, I'm still the one with the ear, my own best A & R man. After all, I did discover 'Angst.'"

"And here I thought he just induced it," Jack whispered to Caroline.

"Sorry?"

"Jack was just saying he thought you'd produced it - 'Angst's' first record, I mean." Caroline smiled at Jack.

"Yeah," said Jack, recalling his neighbor's thunderous stereo, "A sterling achievement. I'd hate to think of all that genius wasted."

"Actually I'm still developing them. I just had them start spelling their name with a backwards 'z' instead of the 's'... pop music 101: everything's cooler when it's misspelled."

"America's educators, take note," said Caroline.

"Anyway, can I expect to hear your answer in short order? My old man's in London and won't be getting back for a few days. This would be a good time to strike."

Ted stuck out his hand and shook Zane's as they got up. "I think we should have something for you within a week."

"Excellent. Hey, you guys give great meeting. Looking forward to doing the business with you." Zane shook Jack and Caroline's hands. Ted opened the door and Judy appeared. As she led Zane away, Ted called out "Hope you'll be able to stop by my place tonight. Best New Years party on the East Side.."

"I don't know that that's saying much. I'm a TriBeCa kind of guy myself, but I'll try to drop in. Might be a little late, though. Æther's doing a concert at Madison Square Garden, and we do her distribution so I'm going. Actually that's who I'm meeting next. You see her new shtick with the chrome body paint?" He laughed. "Got to hand it to her makeup guys. She gets a mirror finish so you could do a line off her ass and not miss a speck."

Jack turned to Caroline. "See how wonderful it can be when art embraces technology?"

Ted ignored him. "Well, stop by if you can."

"I'll try. And thanks for drinking the Kool-Aid."

When the Colmedia record chief had left, the three Stone partners stood in silence for a moment. Then Caroline held out the hand Junior had just shaken and said with mock panic, "It...it *touched* me."

Jack nodded. "You do feel the need to bathe after talking to that guy. And what the hell does 'drinking the Kool-Aid' mean?"

"It's from before the dot-com bubble burst. Investment banking speak for taking a leap of faith. You know, like those Jim Jones freaks in Guyana with the poisoned punch." Ted laughed. "O.K., so he's a reptile. So what else is new? If we refused to do business with every Gila monster on the Street we wouldn't even be trading with ourselves. Look, just relax and take in all the interactive, new media goodness. The fact is the numbers work on this deal, and that means we gotta do it."

The partners worked through lunch analyzing the transaction. The markets would be closing by 1:00 pm on account of the holiday. As that time approached, the Stone troika made their way down to the trading floor. In the elevator Caroline asked, "Why doesn't Takamura do this deal with Zane? Why sell to us, and at a discount?"

"Takamura is a very Japanese firm," said Ted. "They aren't into hostile takeovers of American companies, especially family-run ones. They like to cooperate with management. If they don't like the way a company's run, they sell. The alternative is just too unseemly for them. Gives 'em a stomach ache."

"We, of course, aren't subject to that kind of dyspepsia," said Caroline.

"Let's just say I'll still be able to finish my porterhouse at the closing dinner," replied Ted.

As they got off the elevator and walked onto the trading floor, Jack was stuck by the uncharacteristic peacefulness of the place. With only a skeleton crew of traders present, the room was quiet enough that he could hear the click of fingers on computer keyboards. With so small a complement of personnel, the handful of conversations going on echoed in the cavernous chamber. Even the vibration of the floor beneath his feet, normally an angry rumble this time of day, was reduced to a gentle tremor. He looked out through the trading room's wrap-around windows. Manhattan was laid out under a crystal clear blue sky. This wasn't such a bad place after all, Jack thought. All you had to do was get rid of the traders.

The three partners walked to their trading desks, which they had rearranged in a cluster in the center of the floor so they could communicate with each other without shouting. When they sat down, Jack noticed the image of a spinning envelope in the upper left-hand corner of his laptop screen, the icon for incoming e-mail. He checked it and found it had been sent from something called "webshop" at a Colmedia address. A few mouse clicks and the document appeared on his screen, the text was a single line:

Present fears are less than horrible imaginings.

Jack printed the message. "Hey, kids," Jack said, waving the document for his partners to see. "Looks like Ted's friends at Colmedia have decided they'd rather talk to me."

Ted looked at the sheet. "That's fucked up. The only guy at Colmedia who's supposed to know about this deal is Zane, and I didn't tell him I'd be bringing you into the discussions until this morning."

"Maybe Junior decided to jump at the chance to deal with someone else," Caroline suggested with a smile.

Ted was clearly annoyed. "Seriously, that really is a breach of protocol. That "webshop" sounds like Colmedia's website development group, and I don't see why anyone there would know shit about our deal. And what the fuck is it supposed to mean?"

Jack shrugged. "Like I have a clue?"

"It's Shakespeare, from *Macbeth*." said Caroline. "Given the choice of line I'd have to say the sender intended to induce a sense of foreboding in the recipient."

"Thanks, Professor. And to think I was sure that was a love note. See Jack? That's why it's crucial to have a Yalie with a comp lit degree around here." "It does sound like the work of a man of letters. You think Fred Colson Sr. got wind of Junior's activities and decided to send us a warning?" Jack suggested.

"Possible," said Ted, "but unlikely. First of all Zane and I have been very careful about security. He never even calls from Colmedia's offices. Second, as he said, Dad's been out of town. The time stamp on this thing indicates it was sent from Colmedia today. Third, if Dad wanted to send a message, why send it to you? Everybody knows I'm in charge of merchant banking here."

Jack looked again at the note. "What's with sending it from this 'webshop' address?"

"Maybe it's more anonymous that way," Caroline offered. "It's a departmental e-mail account, probably used for feedback on their websites. It doesn't belong to a single individual. My guess is someone else in the Colmedia organization found out about our plan and didn't like it. By now they've probably told Fred Sr., so we should assume we may have some kind of fight on our hands."

Ted shook his head. "Even if that's true, it won't matter that much. Fred Sr. doesn't have the cash to buy out Takamura or even purchase enough of the public float to stop us. He's tapped out."

The three sat silently for a few moments. It was one o'clock, and they glanced at their screens as the markets quietly closed.

"Look, we've already got this 'Who sold the bonds?' mystery," said Ted "Let's not obsess on who our new Elizabethan friend is. The fact is if Takamura sells us their shares, then that stake plus our current holdings and Zane's stock gives us control, period. There's nothing Fred Sr. or anyone else can do about it." Ted folded his arms. "On another subject, I presume the two of you are up for New Year's tonight?"

Caroline rolled her eyes. "And *I* presume this'll be your usual gathering of the young, overpaid and intoxicated, hitting on models searching for husbands whose net worth makes them attractive even when they hurl?"

"But it's so much more. You're just not grasping a little something that, well, *I* like to call, the 'Ted Harris Experience'..."

"Uh, yeah," Jack sighed. Ted was dropping serious coin to throw a party in his duplex on Fifth, and most of the firm's senior personnel, along with a fair slice of the cream of thirtyish and fortyish Wall Street, would be there. The bonuses at Stone had been announced a few days earlier. They were the largest the firm had ever paid out, thanks in no small measure to Jack's assault on the kyat. Jack knew Ted was counting on that windfall to lend some buoyancy to what would otherwise be a lame gathering of people old enough to be out of place at the clubs, and unlucky enough not to have escaped to warmer climes. Hell, Caroline and Ted would probably be on some island themselves but for their coup d'état;

they felt they needed to keep an eye on the place while things cooled down, and had persuaded Jack to do the same.

Still, cash has a way of improving moods, and so morale was at an all-time high at Stone. Even the older partners, who had seen their power erode, were mollified by the windfall. All except Pete, who despite a massive payout had informed the firm's new leadership of his impending resignation.

"Well, I might as well have the experience of watching you pay to have strangers wreck your apartment," said Caroline.

That surprised Jack. Knowing Ted, this thing would have the atmosphere of a kegger thrown by some geriatric frat with a seven-figure social budget, and that didn't sound like Caroline's scene. She was attractive and unattached, and, though he knew nothing of her personal life, he'd have thought she'd have somewhere else to go.

"See, Jack? Caroline's coming, and that alone makes it an A-list affair. Why don't you bring your new friend? "

With all the upheaval at the firm it really wouldn't do for any member of the troika to blow off a party thrown by another. "I'm not proud of this, but I'll be there," said Jack. "Helen won't, though. She said she had to take care of some business over the holiday." He had hoped to spend New Year's with Helen, and her statement might have raised suspicions of another guy, but there was a resignation in the way she said it that made him believe her.

With the markets shut down, the few traders still on the floor began to melt away. Ted and Caroline were themselves leaving. They asked Jack to walk out with them, but he wanted to look at a few charts before he left. He told them he'd see them at Ted's.

When he got to his new office on the fifty-third floor he placed his laptop on his desk and flopped into a high-backed leather chair. The room was empty except for the standard-issue oak office furniture and a Bloomberg terminal. Across from his desk hung a poster of Monet's water lilies from the Museum of Modern Art; otherwise the walls were bare. He used the place as a refuge from the noise of the trading floor, a quiet place to think. And he needed to think now. He felt he was missing something. Takamura and Colmedia, the inexplicable sell-offs in the bond market, cryptic and threatening notes, the creepy feeling he'd been followed on a date. It was all getting so damn *weird*, and it was ruining what should have been the best time of his life. He was rich, a partner in a Wall Street investment house, and he'd found the most fascinating woman he'd ever met. Yet he sensed there was something out there, dark and pernicious, just beyond his vision. Ghosts in the machine. A pattern he should be seeing, but couldn't. Too tired to hunt for it now, he leaned back in his chair and closed his eyes.

Chapter 5: Horrible Imaginings

Jack woke to the warble of his desk phone. Through his office window he saw the lights of the skyline against the darkness of night. He glanced at his watch:

9:15 p.m.

Shit. He'd stayed up half the previous night looking at the currency markets, and he hadn't realized the sleep deficit he'd built up.

He picked up the receiver. "Kline," he rasped.

"Happy New Year to you too," said Helen. 'Did I wake you?"

"Guess I dozed off."

"I tried you at your place, but I should have known you'd want to spend the evening alone with your computers. I'm guessing you're sitting in a room right now with nothing but bare walls and glowing screens."

"You're right about the screens, but I do have a poster on the wall. Monet. 'Water Lilies.'"

"A small sign of sanity."

"Actually I've always liked his lilies. About three years ago on Valentine's Day I'd arranged to meet an old girlfriend at noon at the Museum of Modern Art, in that room with the huge water lily triptych wrapped around the walls. It was sort of in lieu of giving her flowers."

"Jeez, you're cheap."

"It had nothing to do with money. Haven't you ever wondered about what you're really saying by giving flowers? It's like 'I love you, so I had these beautiful living things ripped from the earth so you can watch them slowly wither and die.'"

"Now who's seriously twisted?"

"It's still not as weird as your duck thing."

"So what happened with the girl?"

"I got stood up."

"Go figure."

"She ran off with some accountant who bought her a Lexus. Anyway, looking at that canvas, it didn't even bother me. I still go back there every February 14. Sort of guarantees I always get flowers on Valentine's."

"I don't think I've ever met anyone who celebrates the anniversary of getting dumped before."

"I think you're missing the poetry of the thing. I'm trying to show you my sensitive side."

She laughed, "Nice to know it's as strange as the rest of you."

He heard voices and she covered the phone for a moment. Then she returned. "Hon, I've got to split. I'm involved with a New Year's production."

"Some kind of record promotion?"

"Yeah, you could say that. You're still going to your friend's party?"

"Afraid so."

"Well this thing I'm doing may run really late. l could try to give you a buzz on your cell after midnight. I'll probably sleep through brunch tomorrow but how about we grab something in the afternoon?"

"Come over to my place. I'll show you my space."

"Sounds good. Later, hon."

He'd been dying to tell her about Zane; after all, she and Colson were in the same business, and he could just imagine what she thought of him. But Jack dared not bring up the subject in the middle of takeover talks.

He grabbed his coat and headed out, figuring he'd stop by his place, change clothes and head over to Ted's before midnight. Before he left, however, he took the elevator at the fiftieth floor and headed into the trading room.

The florescent ceiling lights were off. The room was lit only by millions of glowing colored characters on trading screens, and by the lights of the city beyond the window. In the darkness it was difficult to tell where the screens ended and the skyline began. As Jack walked across the empty floor to his desk, he had the sensation of floating in a vast, shimmering sea of information.

He just needed to check a few things out before going to Ted's party. He sighed. As if he didn't have enough problems, at Ted's he faced the prospect of seeing Zane again. Happy New Year indeed.

As he sat down, Jack looked across the floor through the ocean of luminous data. He noticed two small, brilliant red lights on the floor a few feet away. At first he thought they might be the fuse indicators of a power strip, but then he saw them move, and he jumped. A rat. The traders usually ate breakfast and lunch at their desks. Crumbs often fell through the holes in the false floor through which cables were strung. This provided a food supply for rodents who lived below. They occasionally made their presence felt when they supplemented their diet by gnawing through the insulation of the wires.

Jack watched the creature slip though a floor hole and thought back to his friend with the postdoctoral fellowship and the bats in his tower office. On Wall Street the vermin stayed closer to the ground.

Something Ted said was eating at him. He didn't buy his explanation of why Takamura didn't do Ted's deal with Zane on its own. Maybe most Japanese institutions would shy away from so hostile a move, but not one led by Hiro Yamada. Jack remembered Hiro from his days taking classes at Wharton. The only thing about the guy sharper than his wit was his financial mind, and he took no prisoners. Jack thought he'd be very much at home in the world of American mergers and acquisitions, and would have little patience for incompetent management.

And why the low-ball price Takamura was asking? Given that a buyer could make such a killing from spinning the Colmedia's publishing business off, why not take a few months and shop Takamura's stake around? Surely a bidder might emerge willing to pay more than Stone. Hiro was no fool; he wasn't one to sell at a fire-sale price. Unless, of course, there was a fire.

Jack flicked on his Bloomberg and pulled up all the news stories on Takamura over the past sixty days. There were hundreds related to Takamura's various lines of business, and as he scrolled through them he saw nothing unusual. Then an item caught his eye. The Hong Kong trading house McKenzie-Kent was considering filing for protection from creditors while it reorganized. This following the cancellation of a cash infusion from BankBurma of Myanmar. It was well known in the markets that BankBurma was struggling to survive in the wake of the kyat's collapse. The only reason the story appeared under his search was that Takamura was named as a creditor of McKenzie's, with exposure in the billions.

Then he noticed that Perth Holdings, the Australian mining giant, was also seeking to renegotiate its arrangements with lenders. The firm cited adverse market conditions and the default by BankBurma on certain swaps. Again, Takamura was named as a creditor.

Finally, there was a series of stories on BankBurma itself, noting the Myanmarese bank owed money to dozens of financial institutions around the world, including Takamura.

None of this in and of itself would have signaled to the markets that Takamura had a serious problem. The Takamura bank was a colossus at the center of one of Japan's oldest and most powerful *kieretsu*. It had dealings with thousands of firms around the world, and some were always in default. Jack punched up a graph of Takamura's stock. The bank's share price on the Tokyo exchange had been stable.

There was something else, though. The set of problems he was looking at were all linked to BankBurma and the kyat, and hence clustered close together in time. And no one really knew how big Takamura's *total* exposure was, except for Takamura. Jack knew Hiro had vastly expanded Takamura's swap business; indeed, he'd discussed it with him periodically. Swaps were off-balance-sheet transactions, so exposures could become enormous without anyone knowing. Further, these problems were taking place against the backdrop of difficulties Takamura and the other Tokyo banks were having with their real estate loans and collapsed Japanese stock holdings.

Yet the market had no reason to think Takamura was destabilized. They had not seen any aberrant behavior on the part of the bank. Like, for example, attempting to unload valuable assets at deep discounts in a desperate effort to raise cash.

Jack shook his head. It was ridiculous to think that was why Hiro was dumping his stake in Colmedia. As Ted said, that sale would raise less then a hundred million. If Takamura really were in the hole for billions, a few sales like that would at best buy a little time. Were Takamura really in a jam, they'd have to raise serious money, and that would mean massive selling of some large, liquid component of their portfolio. Like their Treasury bond holdings.

Jack felt the blood drain from his face.

A single Japanese bank trying to unload billions in Treasuries. That had been Jack's theory, based on the rumors Hubie had heard and the price action he'd observed. As he'd told Ted, there was one only reason that he could see for a big Tokyo bank defying the Bank of Japan and engaging in massive Treasury selling: absolute desperation. The market had seen no signs of crisis. Only Stone was aware of the Colmedia deal, and when he put that transaction together with the rest of the data...

If he were right, the consequences could be devastating. Once Takamura's selling became public, the other Japanese banks could follow suit. The BOJ itself might be forced to go along. The panic would drive interest rates through the roof. Stock markets around the world would hit the deck, and there was a pretty good chance of a global recession. As for Stone, they'd take big losses on their stock and bond holdings, but, having been forewarned they could minimize the impact, perhaps even profit. There was a more serious problem however, and for Jack, a personal one. In the aftermath of a financial catastrophe of such a magnitude, the post-mortem would surely trace the chain of events back to the collapse of the kyat, and hence, of course, to him. It was bad enough to be one of "The Boys Who Broke Burma." What would he be now? "The Kid Who Crushed Capitalism?" "The Rat Who Wrecked the World?"

His mind turned to the e-mail he had received that afternoon. "Horrible Imaginings." He wondered if the sender might have been communicating not a threat but a warning. Sounded ridiculous. How would someone at Colmedia know anything about an impending global crisis?

Actually, the whole thing sounded crazy. These were, after all, the imaginings of a guy who thought people were following him and his date around.

Anyway, he knew how to test his theory. He'd call Hiro tonight at his office in Tokyo, where it was already New Year's day. The Hiro Yamada he'd known at Wharton wasn't exactly the life of the party, but there was no way he'd be hanging around Takamura's headquarters on New Year's Day unless all hell had broken loose.

Ninety minutes remained before midnight in New York, which made it 12:30 in the Tokyo afternoon. He reached for his phone but thought better of it. The trading lines were recorded, and this might not be a conversation he'd want preserved for posterity. He'd stop by his place, make his call, then head for Ted's.

Jack stood on his terrace in the cold night air, cordless phone in hand. He looked across the park as he punched in the number for Hiro's office at Takamura. He braced himself and counted the rings: one, two... he's not in, thought Jack. Maybe this Sword of Damocles hanging over the markets really was nothing more than a figment of his paranoid imagination.

The third ring was interrupted by a voice: "Hi" - yes in Japanese. It was the voice of Hiro Yamada.

Damn, thought Jack. He took in a deep breath and steadied himself. "Hiro, Jack Kline. Happy New Year, man. How've you been?"

Hiro replied in flawless English. "Better than you, Jack, if all you've got to do on New Year's Eve is call me. How the hell are you?"

"Can't complain. Actually, I'm headed over to Ted Harris' later. I believe you spoke to him recently."

"Indeed. Looks like we'll be doing business. And I have of course followed your recent exploits. Nice photo in the *Economist*, by the way."

"Yeah, I'm very proud of it. So, Hiro, I understand Ted Harris is talking to you about buying your stake in Colmedia."

"That's what I've discussed with your colleague, or should I say partner. Congratulations, by the way."

"Thanks, although from where you sit we must all look like ants."

"Only because I'm nearsighted. Anyway, is there a problem with the transaction?"

"Well, I know the price under discussion is under a hundred million. Seems kinda light."

"Now I see why Stone made you a partner. Clever strategy, trying to negotiate your purchase price up." Hiro began to laugh. "Sure, you lose money on every deal, but you can try to make it up in volume."

"Very funny. The thing is, Hiro, I can't help but wonder why you'd be willing to sell at that price, unless of course Takamura needed to raise liquidity in a hurry."

"With all due respect, Jack, a hundred million may be a lot of liquidity to Stone, but not to Takamura."

"That's my point, actually. This should be chump change to you. So why sell for less than it's worth? And I've noticed some other things. The problems you've had with McKenzie-Kent, with Perth Holdings, and of course with BankBurma, which seems to be the root of the other defaults. And there's the Diet's decision to delay the property loan bailout..."

"Are you actually suggesting that Takamura is selling its Colmedia stake to deal with those difficulties?"

"No, Hiro, I know the Colmedia sale is just pocket change. To deal with those 'difficulties,' as you put it, you'd have to raise serious cash. Perhaps, for example, by selling off those billions in Treasuries the Ministry of Finance and the Bank of Japan have been shoving down your throat."

There was silence on the other end of the line. Jack closed his eyes. *Say it ain't so, Hiro.* He continued.

"I've been watching the bond market, Hiro, and I'm pretty sure there's a single, large seller of Treasuries in Asia. In Japan, to be exact. Too big to be a hedge fund, and with a particular liquidation price in mind. The way I see it, that means the seller is a large Tokyo bank. The only way one of those would sell its bonds in defiance of the BOJ is if it had no other choice. Before a bank would do that it would raise whatever it could to buy time, by selling off assets like its Colmedia stock."

More silence from Tokyo.

Jack lowered his voice, as if someone might hear. "Look, man, the theory has a lot of explanatory power. Even explains why the guy who runs the whole show over there is sitting in his office on New Year's Day." He paused, uncomfortable with his inquisitory tone. "Hiro, if I know what the deal is, soon the whole damn market will figure it out. I promise you I wont be the one who spills this. Just tell me, how bad is it?"

A few seconds ticked by before he heard Hiro say softly, "Bad."

Jack leaned against the railing and shook his head. "I thought you had most of the brush fires put out over there."

"I did until you came along, my friend."

"So it's the kyat thing."

"Yeah, that little thing. It was really just a matter of timing. We were almost out of the woods, and if nothing else had gone wrong we would have been O.K, even with the real estate bailout delayed. Then, of course, you decide to blow the shit out of Myanmar, which tanked BankBurma. We were prudent, you know. BankBurma was sound. They could have handled a drop in the kyat, even a twenty percent decline. No one anticipated the thing would fall almost fifty percent. We had exposure there, and we could have absorbed the blow, but we didn't realize BankBurma would take down McKenzie-Kent and Perth. Those losses are simply more than we could handle just now."

"And now you've got a cash flow problem."

"You could put it like that. By the end of January I've got to plug a multi-billion dollar hole in our balance sheet, or we'll default on our own obligations. The regulators will look at our numbers and go berserk."

"Hiro, if you start dumping those bonds wholesale, do you realize what that will do to the markets? What happens if the rest of the Tokyo banks follow suit? Jeez, you could end up forcing the BOJ to dump its bonds just to avoid getting burned themselves."

"I don't know if the other banks will follow. They may be cowed by the BOJ. They may not. If it happens, so be it. It can't be helped."

"It won't just be the U.S. that gets screwed. When interest rates spike, America won't be able to finance its trade deficit with Japan. We'll have to cut imports, which will pummel your export sector. And you're already in recession. With both the U.S. and Japanese economic engines unavailable to pull global growth along, I'm guessing were looking at a worldwide dive. And if people even think Takamura might go under...ever hear of Creditanstalt?"

The man in Tokyo rolled his eyes. "Yeah, Jack, everyone seems to want to give me history lessons. Look, my responsibility is to protect the interests of my house. I suggest you do the same for yours. And I trust I have your word of honor that this information does not travel outside of Stone & Co."

"Of course."

"And I also want your assurance you're not going to tell Ted Harris to use what you know to stick it to us on the Colmedia sale. He called me from home two hours ago. We're talking about a price of around ninety-five million."

Ted worked fast, thought Jack. Zane's sparkling personality must have inspired him. "I'm not looking to help Ted screw you out of your lunch money. Listen, no one else knows about this except for the two of us?"

"Just my uncle."

"Oh." Hiro had told Jack a little of his strained relations with Takamura's chairman.

"Don't ask. Anyway, besides our high and mystical ruler, know one else has the whole story. A couple of my bond traders know some of it, but they can be trusted. I've also warned a few longtime clients who understand discretion. I wanted to give them a chance to protect themselves. And now there's you. Everyone else is on their own as far as I'm concerned."

At least for the moment the information was contained, thought Jack, although God knew how long that would last. "Look, we've still got some time here. Maybe we can think of some other way out of this."

"Well if you think of something, give me a call. I'm still trying to make piecemeal sales of our bonds without moving the market. I'll give that strategy a few more days before I just blow out our position."

"Hey, Hiro, I'm sorry. Obviously I'd no idea any of this was going to happen."

"You couldn't have. No one could. It's chaos theory, like we used to talk about. You sit there like a bug on a leaf, and you never know when your next burp is going to scare up a typhoon."

"An analogy much on my mind lately."

"I'll talk to you. Meanwhile, do yourself a favor and build a storm shelter." Hiro hung up.

For a moment Jack just stood there looking out into the night. The view of the park and city lights was much the same as that from Helen's apartment. Yet none of the magic he'd felt that night came to him. The city's vastness now seemed threatening, and he noticed the lights less than the dark.

It was just incredible, he thought. Some guy is too busy complaining about his commute to get a trade order straight, and the next thing you know the world is on the edge of an economic precipice. And the beautiful part of it was the only two guys who knew the truth were a couple of math dweebs staring into little screens.

He looked down at the pedestrians on the street, people just looking to have a good time and celebrate the holiday. If they had any idea what was really going on in the world...

Speaking of celebrations, it was 11:15 and he had to get over to Fifth Avenue. He suddenly felt a real need to help Ted and Caroline ring in the New Year.

By the time Jack was able to hail a cab and get over to Ted's it was a quarter to midnight. The place was packed. He waded through the crowd, searching for his host and Caroline. Various Stone people slapped him on the back, thanking him for increasing their bonuses. He heard one inebriated trader from another house tell a blonde in a skin-tight dress that "that's the fucker who got all these S.O.B.'s rich this year."

Jack finally heard a familiar voice, and turned to see its owner, drink in hand, lecturing a conversation pit full of people.

"So the point is," said a triumphant Hubie, "I've found cases where it's cheaper to book a flight from New York to Vegas via Chicago than to fly from New York to Chicago without a connection. If you're headed for Chicago you can just throw away the Vegas ticket and you're still ahead."

"Hubie, I hate to interrupt...?" Jack interjected.

"They've set up a system so complicated they're screwing themselves. I say fuck 'em. I'm wondering if there's a business in this. If I had the time I'd do it just to make fools of the bloodsuckers."

"Hubie," Jack almost shouted, putting his hand on the trader's shoulder. When this guy started talking transit it was next to impossible to stop him.

"Hey Jack, Happy New Year."

"Yeah, same to you. Where's Ted?"

"I think I saw him and Caroline head upstairs."

Jack immediately made his way up the stairs and started searching from room to room. God, the place was big. Finally, from behind a half-open door he thought he heard a woman's voice cry out "Animal!" He knocked against the doorframe, and, getting no reply, entered.

The lights were off and Jack tripped on something. He hit a wall switch and saw one of Ted's monogrammed Turnbull & Asser shirts wrapped around his shoe. He looked up and glimpsed a naked Caroline astride Ted on the bed.

"Oh, for God's sake," sighed Jack, covering his eyes and withdrawing.

He headed downstairs and ran into Carl Rich just as the crowd was counting down the last few seconds of the year. Carl tried to say something to him but was drowned out in shouts of "Happy New Year!" Suddenly the celebrants were enveloped in a blizzard of silver confetti that seemed to come from nowhere.

Jack's head swam and he found himself sitting in a Le Corbusier chair pretending to listen to Hubie and Carl talk about some ski trip they were planning. About ten minutes later he looked up to see Ted and Caroline, both looking slightly disheveled.

Ted grinned. "Mind if we talk to you for a sec, Jack?"

Jack followed the pair into a gleaming metal kitchen suitable for servicing an ocean liner. Caterers toiled around the three as Jack addressed his partners.

"So I guess that's what you meant by the 'full Ted Harris Experience'..."

Caroline was blushing, which Jack had assumed was impossible.

"Beats the hell out of watching that ball drop..." said a smiling Ted, and Caroline punched him in the arm.

"Jeez, don't you people ever lock the door?"

"Sort of an oversight," said Caroline "Look, Jack, you have to understand...".

"But I do. I mean, I've always considered Ted to be at least half animal."

"Jack..."

"Part man, part beast. A man-beast, really..."

"Oh, fuck off..." Ted sighed. "Just don't mention this to anyone, O.K.? We're not ready to have this thing come out yet."

"Guys, it's your business. I'm happy for you, that you're... getting along so well. No one else at the firm knows?"

Caroline shook her head. "Pete found out, but he wasn't interested in making it public. Thought our taking over the firm had put the value of his stake in enough jeopardy without any added gossip." Jack sensed she shared that concern.

Ted, on the other hand, seemed amused. "We figure you're old enough to deal with it, but some of the younger kids may not be ready to find out what Mommy and Daddy do when the lights go out." Caroline punched Ted's arm again.

"My lips are sealed, I swear. Now I've really got to talk to you two about something..."

Jack could see his partners had had a few, and the incident upstairs hadn't made anyone steadier. He slowly laid out the substance of his conversation with Hiro.

When he was done, Ted whistled slowly. "Man, I could get him down on the price of that stock..."

"That's all you can say? I mean, do you understand the magnitude of this? And besides, Ted, I gave him my word."

"I know, I know. Just thinking out loud. It doesn't matter anyway. If we're on the right side of this bond blow-off we'll make more money than we know what to do with." Ted turned to Caroline. "That's not a problem, right?"

"Actually it should be pretty simple. We dump our bonds and sell the bond short. Buy put options, too. We can do the same thing on equities, since the stock markets will probably take a dive on something like this. Some of our hedges may not be perfect, but as long as we're on the right side of this thing we should do fine."

Jack knew all this already, but couldn't believe how nonplused his partners were. "I'm not sure you guys are thinking through the repercussions of something like this." He explained his fear of blowback from their connection to the kyat collapse.

Ted was unmoved. "Hey, Chicken Little, we don't even know if the sky's gonna fall. The other Japanese banks and the BOJ may sit tight. If there is this giant sell-off then, hey, we can handle the heat. We haven't done anything wrong. So maybe we have to sit in front of a Senate committee for an afternoon and explain that markets go up and down, and we're better than most at guessing the next move. Fuck, it's free publicity. We'll pick up some clients."

"It doesn't bother you that this thing could set off a global economic shock, driving markets through the floor and putting millions of people out of work?"

Ted shrugged. "Am I blown away by the world being turned on its head? Sure. Do I have any moral responsibility for it? Absolutely not. If it's going to happen, it'll happen, whether we make money on it or not."

"I don't believe this. You don't care that we had a role in this? That we could be blamed?"

"Jack, I gotta tell 'ya. In the vast, gray ocean of things I care nothing about, the opprobrium of the masses stands out only for its singular insignificance. Besides which, we won't be condemned. Not really. Fact is, this country loves winners and forgives them a lot more than this."

Caroline laughed. "See why I fell for him? I never could resist a starry-eyed idealist. Anyway, first thing tomorrow morning we'll set up a trading strategy to deal with the situation."

"So you're fine with this too."

"Jack, it's the market. What can you do?" She put her hand on his shoulder. "Come on, there's a party out there..."

"Thanks, but I think I had enough excitement for the day. What I really need right now is a little quiet."

It was nearly 1:00 when Ted and Caroline walked Jack to the door. As they did they ran into the arriving Fred Colson Jr., with a woman on each arm, neither of whom seem old enough to have voted more than once.

"The weasel has landed," Jack whispered to his colleagues.

"Hey, partners," Colson called to them, "Just managed to claw my way uptown. You should have seen the traffic snarl around the Garden. We were at Æther's concert there. I do her distribution. Anyway, when that thing let out, bang! Instant gridlock. Becky, Shauna and I were stuck in the limo for a half hour. We just had to ring in the New Year on our own." This elicited a chorus of giggles from the girls.

"Bully for you," said Jack, excusing himself. Caroline walked Jack out as Colson chatted with Ted.

"Sure you won't stay and help us deal with that?" Caroline pointed a thumb toward Colson.

"That thrill's all yours. Go back there and talk to Zane. You know, he's working a whole new attitude."

Jack awoke late on Saturday morning, New Year's Day. He'd only slept a couple of hours, and he was still feeling wired from his conversation with Hiro. Deciding a jog might give him perspective, he planned to head down CPW and continue to a record store he knew on Fifty-seventh Street. The way things were going, he wanted all the information he could lay his hands on. He felt some of it was waiting for him there.

The morning was clear and cold. As he hit the sidewalk he turned on a portable CD player. His ears filled with Bach's double violin concerto as his lungs took in the winter air. It was a struggle to fend off grogginess. Helen had called again at two in the morning, then he'd stayed up half the night trying to think of a way to avoid the Takamura bond sale.

He wasn't even sure he should bother. Ted was right - maybe it would cause a panic, maybe it wouldn't. And they were forewarned; the Stone traders could profit from the event if they played their cards right. As for public condemnation, it was true his kyat trade might be linked with the crisis, if there was a crisis. At worst, however, the Myanmar collapse would be called the straw that broke the camel's back, not the root cause of the debacle. Maybe he'd take flack from some on Capitol Hill looking for a scapegoat, but there really was nothing anyone could do to him.

The problem was that the idea of having helped create this mess made him sick. And that was just it. Jack didn't even feel he'd chosen this. It was as if a riptide were dragging him along. He wanted to exert some form of control, to guide the process, change its course.

When he attempted to formulate a plan, however, the only strategies he'd come up with seemed foolish. Rectifying the situation meant some kind of bailout; of Takamura and the firms that owed it money, of Myanmar itself. Stone was far too small to attempt anything like that alone. Besides, the risk involved would be next to impossible to justify, especially given the ease with which they could now deal with the sell-off he'd be trying to prevent.

Even if he did come up with a scheme, if he wanted the Stone partners to go along with it, he'd have to use at least one of the two principal motivators of Wall Street: fear and greed. Their prior knowledge of Takamura's plans had eliminated most of the fear factor. Greed, on the other hand, sprung eternal. That particular instinct was having an effect on Jack as well. It wasn't so much the concept of making money as the idea of profiting from conscious decisions that appealed to him. Just getting lucky didn't quite feel like winning.

On the other hand, as Ted Harris would have been the first to point out, this was about the Benjamins, not warm fuzzies. They were not international relief workers. If just letting the Takamura sale happen was the easy, safe, and profitable thing to do, then it should be done. The world did no favors for traders, so what the hell did he owe the world?

By the time he got to Fifty-eighth Street, Jack was feeling better. At least now he knew the parameters of his situation. He knew the players and the game. Maybe there were a few loose ends, he still didn't know what the deal was with that bizarre e-mail, but basically all the cats were out of the bag. Whatever his decision was, it would be just that. *His* decision. No more surprises. He was in control.

He did feel the need for a bit more data regarding another aspect of his life. He'd meant to do a Web search on Anodyne records and try to figure out what Helen's cryptic remarks were all about. In all the tumult over Takamura it had slipped his mind, but before he returned to his computer he decided to check out her products directly. The music and video megastore on Fifty-seventh was part of a chain of noisome pop culture fortresses that had invaded Manhattan. Four brightly lit floors of CD's, DVD's and cassettes. Jack entered, passing under large screens suspended from the ceiling. Music videos blazed across them, the accompanying music tracks pumped into the room from hidden speakers. The pulsing bass tones suddenly reminded him of the midnight concerts his neighbor had treated him to in his old apartment.

A sullen-looking teen-aged clerk stood behind a counter, staring into a computer. Jack approached him.

"Pardon me. I'm interested in getting a list of artists recording on a particular record label. Can you pull up that information?"

"This thing could get you a list of artists by substance abuse problem," said the kid, clearly too cool to look up from his screen at a patron. "Label?"

"Anodyne."

The clerk laughed, and as he did Jack noticed some sort of tribal tatoo on his right temple. "That's an easy one. You're listening to some of their stuff right now. Well, her stuff. That's Æther's label. Ever hear of her?"

"Rings a bell," said Jack. It was too early for sarcasm from a twerp with an illustrated head.

"She's got a couple of other artists on it as well, but basically it's her. That's a clip of her New Year's Eve concert at the Garden," said the clerk, gesturing toward the screens hanging in the air. "She's doing some new song she just wrote; it's on her new release..."

Jack turned around and looked at one of the video displays. A woman, clad in reflective latex body paint, sang into a microphone. Her hair, dyed several colors not existing in nature, seemed to defy gravity. Yet she moved with a grace both oddly familiar and totally incongruous with her appearance. And there was something else beneath the synthesized rhythm and camp eroticism. A lyric, something about the sun chasing the stars from the sky...

"I have the list of albums here if you want it," said the clerk.

Jack didn't hear him. He didn't notice his CD player slip from his hand, or how its case cracked against the tiled floor. He didn't see the silver-legged chips that flew from the machine's insides and scattered like startled insects.

For as he stared at the figure on the screen, any certainty this world held for him vanished, and he could not bring himself to hope to understand. Not even when she came to him later that afternoon.

Chapter 6: The Medusa

The disciples of Einstein taught that you couldn't actually watch someone fall into a black hole, at least not without sharing his fate. As the unfortunate individual approached the event horizon, the point of no return, time would seem to slow for him so that to an outside observer he would appear to have stopped, frozen at the edge of oblivion. Of course, for the victim time would move on, and he'd descend into the consuming darkness.

Sitting alone in his apartment, these ideas came to Jack, but he felt himself more observer than observed. It was his sense of himself, dragged and held by forces unseen, suspended over an abyss. Even with the Takamura thing he'd thought he had a handle on it all, right up until the moment he'd looked up and seen the image of Helen Cantos dancing on that screen. Now he was just watching himself floating, falling. The strange thing was he found the sensation comforting. He felt remote from himself, from what he observed, as if he were viewing television. The feelings he would have expected: anger at deception, embarrassment at having been deceived... these were nearly absent. There was instead only a distant curiosity; like that he'd known as a scientist wondering about some astrophysical phenomenon in a far-off galaxy.

How could they be the same person?   A classical dancer, an educated, brilliant woman. Julliard, Columbia... He could comprehend how someone like that could run a record company, just as a cosmologist could end up trading currencies. But this?

Contrary to the clerk's snide remark, he knew who Æther was, and would have known even without his erstwhile neighbor's blaring stereo. He'd have had to live on the moon for the last decade to have avoided the knowledge. Her music and stage antics had made her one of the more famous people in the world. It was sad testimony to just how out of touch with the *zeitgeist* Jack was that he hadn't recognized her on the spot, even out of costume. *Now* he knew what the men in the restaurant and those kids in Rockefeller Center were looking at, and it wasn't some trader who'd made the cover of the *Economist*. He felt moronic for having thought so.

Solving that mystery seemed paltry compensation for the questions that now filled his thoughts. Why hadn't she told him or become involved with him at all? And her act. He'd even heard something about Æther doing something lewd onstage with... what was it, some kind of potato?

It was insane, but there he sat on his futon, staring at his laptop computer's display, watching her dance. It was a video on a website promoting her new album and tour. The image, even with the costume and makeup, was unmistakable. It was Helen. Through his machine's speakers her voice sang the lyrics he'd read a few nights before.

He sat there waiting for her arrival, to see her again with his own eyes and make real what seemed absurd. He'd told his doorman to send her right up, telling him to expect a Helen Cantos. He couldn't use her stage name with a straight face and anyway the guy would never believe him, unless of course he got a good look at her.

Just after 3:00 came the knock on his door.

"It's open," he called out, turning down his laptop's screen brightness and sound. Helen entered and walked into the large, nearly empty room Jack was sitting in. She looked around and grinned.

"Nice place. Someone really ought to move in here."

He didn't get up, and when she bent down to kiss him she could tell by his expression that something was wrong.

"What's the matter?" She pointed at the computer. "Somebody run the batteries down on your toy?"

Jack stared at her for a moment. The stage makeup was gone, her hair dark now, hastily dyed back from the colors of the prior night's performance. Only a few strands of alien pigment testified to the transformation.

"Let me ask you something, Helen. You said the other night you were an only child, right?"

"Uh-huh."

"Well, there goes my evil twin theory. So how about genetic engineering? Ever been involved in any cloning experiments, for example?"

"What the hell are you... oh." She paused and the smile left her face. She walked to the window and stood there, her hands clasped behind her back. "So what happened? You tried to turn on CNBC and accidentally got MTV?"

"Something like that." He touched a button on his laptop and turned the machine toward Helen. Æther's dancing, mirrored figure re-materialized on the screen, a looking glass spinning in silence.

She glanced down at her image. "Look, I just thought we'd get to know each other without her getting in the way. I was going to tell you."

"Before or after a picture of us turned up on page six of the *New York Post*?"

"Touching that your principal concern is the public relations fallout."

"Well, there's also the little matter of me having no idea who the hell you are!" The abstraction was gone. Everything seemed very real to him now.

"You're one of the few people who do. You think those fifty thousand fools at the Garden last night have any idea?"

"That's what I just don't get." He gestured toward the screen. "I mean, *Æther*?"

"At least my stage name keeps me from being confused with that pet mystic. Have you seen her infomercial? She probes a poodle's aura."

"But how can you possibly *be*... since when do you sing, anyway?"

She shrugged. "Well, there was the choir in high school, and I sang with a couple of bands while I was studying here. Not my greatest gift, but with a voice coach and enough electronic shit to make a bullfrog sound like Maria Callas, I get by. And, of course, I *can* dance. It just kind of snowballed from there."

"But how do you go from ballet to this?"

"I told you what happened to my dance company. After it cratered I had a few revelations. I started to have a problem with a field whose aesthetic revolves around anorexia. And the foot thing. Ever see the feet of a forty-year-old ballet dancer? You should if you have a strong interest in stress fractures and acute tendonitis. Assuming of course that she gets enough work to acquire the injuries. That's the main thing. I swore I'd never again try selling what the world won't buy. The whole audience for that stuff wouldn't fill a tenth of the seats for one of my concert tours. Most of the major companies run in the red. It may interest you to know there's one in this city whose lights are on only because I wrote them an anonymous check."

"What about art? Your studies at Columbia..."

"Art history? Well, let's see. Basically, you've got two options with an art history degree. There's academia, and I think you're familiar with the security and generous compensation that route affords. Then of course there are the galleries and auction houses." She laughed. "And I've got to tell you, between trying to sell to that Ted you told me about and being a buyer myself, I'll take the latter."

"So instead you decide to do this...this..."

"What do mean 'this...this...'? You make it sound so evil. It's not like I've brought back disco or something. I've performed in front of more people in one night than would have seen me in a lifetime of my old career. I'm a star. And I make people happy."

"Yeah, that's what I gather. For example, I'm sure that costume you wore last night made thousands of teenage boys very happy."

"Oh, so that's it. You weren't such a prude the other night. So I've never been a particularly inhibited person..."

"No kidding."

"Hey, I've got news for you. When you're dancing at Lincoln Center, half the guys in the audience are just staring at your ass."

"What was that about you at the Hollywood bowl doing something un-natural with a vegetable..."

She rolled her eyes. "Yam."

"What?"

"It was a yam." She turned toward him. "I was kidding around. It was a Thanksgiving Day concert. Some roadies wheeled this enormous turkey dinner on-stage, and there was this suggestively-shaped yam..."

"God."

"I just know the humor that works with my audience, and it happens to make Benny Hill look like Voltaire." Her eyes narrowed and she folded her arms. "Anyway, why I'm defending myself here. I'm not one of the 'Boys who Broke Burma.'"

"*You* read the *Economist?*" Even while discussing his discomfort with the publicity he'd received, he'd never mentioned the caption on the magazine's cover.

"Sweetheart, my label sells in fifty countries. I had foreign exchange exposure coming out of my ears while you were still sitting in graduate school playing with your protons. In fact, my firm's a financial innovator. Anodyne was one of the first issuers of bonds backed by music royalties. Got the Japanese to underwrite them for me before most of Wall Street had even heard of the things. I'm sure I know a hell of a lot more about your business than you do about mine. So yeah, I saw your cover."

He sighed. "Someone told me if you wreck a foreign country you generate great buzz."

"Now just think if you could cause another Great Depression..." Her voice oozed scorn. "Why, you'd be bigger than Elvis, or the Beatles, or..."

"You?"

"Fuck off."

He sat down on the futon and shook his head. "Look, I'm just trying to grasp how someone with your mind does this stuff."

"How does a guy who studied the birth of the universe spend his days trading little bits of paper back and forth?" She sat down next to him. "We don't choose the world we're born into, and this one doesn't value a lot of the things you and I might think are important. You can't sell people what they don't want to buy." She laughed. "Look who I'm explaining the free market to."

Helen leaned toward him and dropped her voice as if seducing him into conspiracy. "So you've got two choices. You can choose martyrdom to art, science, the whole 'higher mind' thing, but there's a fine line between a martyr and a *schmuck*. The alternative is compromise, reconciling your talents with the realities of the marketplace. Subordinating creativity to ambition. That's what we've both done."

"I think there's a little difference between you and me on that score."

She nodded. "You're right. There is. I'm better at it than you. I could buy and sell you twenty times over, and I didn't have to destroy any small countries to get where I am."

"What about your effect on the culture?"

She laughed. "Yeah, if it wasn't for me they'd all be listening to Elgar, right? We live in a country that spends more on the NFL than the NEA. You know how many years I spent trying to survive as an artist? To change that 'culture'? The one that spends billions on movies about aliens but won't shell out a few bucks to find out what's actually out there, remember?" Her smile hardened. "You don't think I know most of the stuff I put out's junk? Believe me, I know...I know and sometimes I hate it, but it's what I can sell. I told you I wished there was a way I could have sold something better, but... screw 'em. I give the morons what they want and keep my art for myself." She pointed at his laptop's screen "She's exactly what they deserve. Just don't blame me for the 'culture's' bankruptcy, 'cause it was broke when I got here."

"In your position you could try to do something about it..."

"Oh, yeah, like you finance guys. At least my music doesn't hurt anyone. And it's possible to say something in rock. Look at Morrison, Lennon, Hendrix..."

"No offense, but you're not seriously comparing your stuff to theirs..."

"They wouldn't make it today. Once in a blue moon I slip in a glimpse of what I like, when I can get away with it. A lyric, an image in a video...at worst it's silly. And I do try to be a good influence. One time, when I was accepting a Grammy, I even quoted Tennyson. Probably the only exposure a couple of million kids will ever have to him."

"Splendid. Maybe if Tennyson had danced around with his butt covered in chrome he'd have gotten more attention."

"Hey, don't knock the outfits. Fewer people recognize me when I'm not in costume, which makes it a lot easier to walk down the street..."

"And that's why you have yourself made up as a human mirror?"

"A human metaphor. Up there, reflected in me, they see what they really want to see - themselves. If that looks ridiculous, well some things are easier to deal with when reflected into abstraction. Remember the Medusa?" She shrugged, laughing. "Hey, it's art, if you think about it a certain way. A lot of art is really just someone's private joke."

"Gee, you love your public, don't you."

"I give them what they want."

"Which isn't really you."

"Just a few aspects with commercial viability. It's a matter of projecting an image with mass appeal."

Jack considered this for a moment. "More hologram than mirror, " he said quietly.

"What do you mean?"

"Holograms are a kind of three-dimensional image..."

"I know what a hologram is."

"The thing is, if you make one on glass and shatter it, each piece contains an image of the whole, but viewed only from certain angles."

She nodded. "So I show them the angles that sell." She smiled slightly. "A ghost in a shard of reality, but one people will pay to see."

"And it doesn't embarrass you?"

"I laid off twenty people who followed my dream. That made me ashamed. This is just silly, and the world makes people do a lot of silly things. As I understand it, you use a fair bit of twenty-five hundred years of mankind's mathematical learning to figure out when to sell something called a kyat. You don't find that just a tad ludicrous?"

"The thought has crossed my mind."

They sat silently for a moment, and when Helen spoke her voice was softer than before. "Once, when I was sitting on the library steps at Columbia, I watched a bunch of pigeons flocking in the courtyard. There was this one bird. Small, brown, with a hooked-down beak and funny-shaped eyes. Some kind of freak, I thought. The others stayed away from it, like they were shunning it. It looked pathetic. Then this thing takes off and soars into the sky, and it was so..." She paused, her eyes closed. "You know how Brancusi tried to sculpt the arc of a rising bird's flight? He said he was trying to give the world pure joy. When I saw this thing take off I knew what he meant. And I realized it wasn't a pigeon at all. It was a young hawk, probably one of those red-tails you see once in a while around Central Park. Maybe separated from its nest..."

"So the pigeons shunned your little buddy because they were afraid of becoming lunch. You know, between this and the duck thing...what is it with you and birds, anyway? Don't you have stories about anything without feathers?"

She sighed. "My point is when this bird was alone in the sky, it was beautiful. It was only when it was on the ground with the pigeons that it looked absurd. Sometimes, though, you have to come down to survive."

"I think I see what you're getting at, and it's about the most elitist fucking thing I've ever heard in my life."

"Well, if you'd just been escorted by the NYPD through a crowd of screaming maniacs trying to tear your clothing off, you'd be a little elitist yourself."

"Anyway, like I said, hawks are birds of prey. They eat pigeons."

"Well, the one I saw was too small; sparrows would have been more its speed. Besides, that just makes the analogy work better for you than me."

"If you're referring to the kyat thing, that doesn't make me a predator. The markets do what they want...The kayt was a bubble, a big balloon, and if I hadn't burst it someone else would have."

"And clerks in counting rooms observe, 'twas only a balloon...'"

"What?"

"Dickinson. She liked things with feathers, too. I know you don't control the 'Invisible Hand' and all that. You just slipped a set of brass knuckles on it, didn't you?"

"That's really not fair. If something is inevitable, why shouldn't I profit from it?"

"In other words, a far-off part of the world was going to hell and since nothing was stopping you from exploiting the situation, well, you know that thing you told me about God withdrawing his presence to make room for the universe... the yum yum?"

"*Tzimtzum.*"

"Yeah... did it ever occur to you that we find out who we really are not in the presence of God, but in his absence? Now you and your friends, high up in that tower of yours, you saw dreams dying in a far-away place, and you cashed in. You're right, actually. You're not so much a predator as a scavenger, like some kind of carrion bird. You've done for Capitalism what the Donner party did for dining *al fresco.*"

"If you think I'm such a vulture, why did you go out with me in the first place?"

She smiled a little. "Well, I guess I liked the way you circled. I didn't consider what you'd be like when you landed."

"Like you said, sometimes you've got to come down to survive." He looked at her, and her face seemed older than the night before, and very tired. "Helen, why you didn't say who you were in the first place?"

She looked away from him, out the window to the horizon. "I don't know. Maybe I just wanted a break. To spend time with someone who cares about ideas. You know that joke your friend has about 'stealth nerds'? You're looking at the arts version. You want to talk about having to conceal your true nature? Try my business. If you knew the crude, shallow, lowlife jerks I have to deal with..."

A picture of Zane's smirking face formed in Jack's mind, and he felt sympathy for Helen rising in him.

"I can imagine."

Eyes closed, she almost hissed under her breath. "It just gets so fucking *boring.*"

She opened her eyes and stared at him for a moment. "Didn't you ever want to forget who you are, what you've become? Just for a little while?"

"At this point, I could see it becoming kind of a hobby."

She stood, straightening her dress. "Look, Jack, last night went very long and I just don't have the energy for this right now. I'm going home."

He watched her walk away, and she seemed as he first saw her. Alone.

"Helen... can I call you later?"

"Whatever."

As she reached the door he called after her. "Hey, I didn't mean to hurt your feelings. I was just kind of shocked..."

She turned to face him. "Nothing personal, Jack, but I really don't give a shit what you think of me. I learned a long time ago that if you see yourself as a reflection in the eyes of others, all they have to do is blink and you cease to exist." She opened the door and looked back at him. "Two days ago the fact that I read the *Economist* wouldn't have surprised you. You and your friends should be on your knees thanking me – its people's obsession with me and what I do that keeps them too numb to notice you've got your fingers in the guts of their lives. You think I gave myself that name to seem otherworldly? I am your anesthesia, Doctor."

And she was gone.

Chapter 7: Scylla and Charybdis

Jack spent the evening alone. No longer removed from himself, conscious of falling, he wanted to put the scene with Helen out of his mind. His pressing problem was Takamura's impending bond sale, and he wanted to formulate his strategy before the markets opened on Monday. Yet her words kept leaking into his thoughts.

In the end, the decision came down to either letting the scenario unfold and trying to make a buck, or attempting to alter the future to something more benign. The former was easy money. Stone had the advantage of superior market intelligence. Place their bets correctly and they could sit back and make a killing. Like Ted said, that was why they were in business. When Jack had made partner, Ted had gotten him a gold pen desk set with a motto of Horace engraved in its base:

Make money! If you can, make money honestly; if not, by whatever means you can, make money.

On presenting the gift, Ted turned to Caroline and said, "You know you're right. You can learn so much from the classics." Jack had decided against displaying the item on his desk.

Given that attitude, it was unlikely Ted or any of the other partners would be particularly interested in having the firm exposed to additional risk just to avoid a crisis that they could profit from anyway. Unless, of course, Jack could arrange it so the payoff from their intervention would be far greater than the money they could make on a collapse. He had a few ideas about how to make that happen. Stone would need allies and would have to act very fast. And take a hell of a chance.

Jack shook his head. Why the fuck bother? If anyone on the Street knew one of "The Boys Who Broke Burma" was sitting in the dark worrying about moral imperatives, they'd laugh themselves sick.

Especially when such an easy trade had been laid out in front of him. As a partner, he had a fiduciary responsibility to the firm; he was supposed to represent Stone's interests alone. The Stone partners didn't give a damn about what kind of financial whirlpool Takamura's bond liquidation unleashed so long as they weren't dragged down by it. The thing was, following this afternoon, Jack couldn't bring himself to feel the same way.

A thought came to him and he started to grin. Caught between Stone and a whirlpool. Like an ancient mariner trying to navigate between Scylla and Charybdis. He might have enjoyed giving his situation mythic proportions were it not so... what was Helen's phrase? "Aggressively pretentious."

Anyway, it wasn't his problem. He hadn't created the conditions that allowed the kyat to collapse, or the confluence of events that now placed the bond market on the edge of disaster. He'd just placed a trade, and by accident for that matter. A trade, which, if not placed by him, surely would have been executed by someone else. The markets were bigger than any one man. Only a fool would attempt to impose his will on them. All he could do was look out for himself. And that was a morally defensible position.

The phone rang with Hubie on the line.

"Jack, if you're not watching the business channel, switch it on and check out the "Year in Review" show. They're about to do a segment on the Burma blowout."

Jack had almost forgotten the flat-panel set he'd had mounted on the wall. He picked up a remote and flicked on the screen. It was the sole source of illumination, and he sat bathed in its light. The Myanmar piece began. Mercifully, they didn't begin with his name; they only referred to "large-scale speculation by investment banks and hedge funds."

"Aw damn, no shots of you and Ted. I was hoping they'd show that *Economist* cover."

"Uh, yeah Hubie, that would've been neat."

"Following the kyat implosion, Thai purchases of Myanmar's natural gas from the Andaman Sea have not been sufficient to bail out the economy. The opium trade is flourishing again as a police crackdown evaporates, and some say the government is actually using drug traffic to

generate currency. Here, in the northern Kachin territory, the regime is attempting to exploit the green jadeite mines of Hpakant, in an effort to raise cash to pay the nation's debt. As under the former junta, conditions are brutal. The jade mines are worked round the clock with no thought to safety. Teenage prostitutes and heroin, tolerated or facilitated by the government-controlled mine operators, provide solace to desperate workers. As unsafe sex and hypodermics pass between them so does HIV, and what they call the 'jade disease' long ago become rampant in this region. Poverty drives many to Yangon. With the economy devastated in the wake of the Kyat's collapse, for most the search for jobs proves fruitless. Now drugs and prostitution are on the rise in the capital as well...."

Hubie's voice dropped a little. "Man, must be getting pretty harsh over there."

Jack wasn't sure if it was this program, the scene with Helen or what he'd learned from Hiro, but a wave of nausea came over him. "Makes you feel good about your job."

"As a result of this activity the World Health Organization projects the AIDS epidemic may explode across the country..."

"Hey, it was a beauty trade, Jack, even if it did make Pete Torelli take his balls and go home. Anyway, the kyat would have tanked with or without us. Your model predicted it, right?"

As the report concluded a clip of some girls, apparently prostitutes, in a Yangon dance club was shown. They looked about fourteen.

"Jack, it *was* just the market at work." Hubie sounded slightly plaintive, beseeching. "We knew would've happened no matter what we did, didn't we?"

Jack wasn't sure what he knew, save that Hubie would never intentionally hurt anyone, and that sharing doubts with him would only cause him pain. At that moment, more than any other in his life, Jack did not want to increase the sum total of pain in the world.

"Yeah, Hubie. No matter what we did."

Jack snapped off the screen and sat alone in the darkness. Twenty stories above the street yet he could still hear the faint sound of traffic, the distant wail of sirens. And her words. He forgot the phone in his hand.

"...but in his absence..."

"Whose absence? Pete's?"

"What? Oh... no, Hubie, not Pete."

"Then who? You're not starting to talk to yourself, are you? You know, New York's got enough of those guys."

Jack closed his eyes, listening, the streets sounds barely audible.

"Jack... Hey, you alright?"

"Yeah... yeah, Hubie, I'm O.K.... but listen, about Pete... you wouldn't happen to have his home number, would you?"

The next morning Jack was driving through the Sunday quiet of a snow-covered Greenwich, Connecticut, in the ten-year-old Ford Escort he'd had since graduate school. He'd driven it only a handful of times since arriving in New York, where he now kept it garaged a block from his building. He'd almost forgotten he had it, and now he prayed it didn't break down.

The homes along the road he was driving on weren't visible from the street; only the numbers on the private gates indicated which residences lay behind them. Jack pulled up to the one he was looking for, spoke into an intercom and watched as the electronic doors opened. He drove through them along a private road a quarter-mile long until he came to the circular driveway of a white-columned Georgian mansion. He stepped out of the car and listened to the crunch of icy gravel beneath his feet. The estate fronted the Long Island Sound, and his ears were stung by the freezing wind blowing off the water.

He rang the bell and moments later the door was opened by a tall, slender woman in her fifties, her hair pulled into a bun, a few streaks of its former strawberry still visible in the gray, Pete's wife Susan looked at him as if he were a dead bird her cat had just deposited on her doorstep. Jack could only imagine what Pete had told her.

"Hi, Susan. It's good to see you again." It was obvious to him that the feeling wasn't mutual.

"Peter is waiting for you in his study, Doctor Kline."

It was even colder in here than outside, thought Jack. Still, he respected her loyalty to her husband. In the mood he was in, any stand on principle was appealing.

He followed her down a long hallway to the open door of Peter Torelli's inner sanctum. The room had the feel of a captain's stateroom, teak wainscoting with brass fixtures. Bookcases filled with volumes on finance and naval history lined the walls, and several models of racing sailboats were encased in glass. A single bay window over the desk looked out across the water.

Pete sat in a high-backed leather chair behind an antique roll-top desk. He swiveled to face Jack and gestured him to take a seat. Susan closed the door behind her, and Jack thought he heard her say something under her breath, which sounded suspiciously like "rat-bastard."

The older man regarded him with what Jack thought was more indifference than anger. "So what's so important you'd drive through the tundra to see me?"

"Pete, a crisis of potentially devastating proportions is threatening to arise in the bond market. As Senior Partner, I feel you need to be made aware of the situation, and I've come here to seek your counsel and leadership."

Pete looked at him for a moment and then broke into laughter. "Kid, who are you trying to bullshit here? Ever since your little adventure in Myanmar, Stone's been run by you and your two buddies. I'm out. I'll be tendering my resignation in a few weeks. So why should you give a fuck what I think about your 'crisis'?"

"Because you're the only person I know who could help me do something about it."

It took Jack twenty minutes to explain the scenario to Pete. When he was finished, Pete reached into his desk and pulled a cigar from a small humidor. "You want one? Think of it as the gift of a slow poison."

"No thanks."

The senior trader lit the robusto, inhaled deeply and blew a plume of smoke into the air. "Look, Doc, that's a fascinating story you've got there, but you don't need me to tell you what to do about it. If all this is true and you know about it ahead of time, then you've got the market by the short hairs. Just go short, clean up. Hell, I'll cheer you on. It'll increase my payment when I cash out of the partnership."

"Pete, I don't want to go short. I will if I have to, but I think there's another way for us to make money and simultaneously keep the bottom from falling out."

"Yeah, what's that?"

"The kyat has lost half its value in this collapse. Now I knew Myanmar's economic mess justified devaluation of its currency; 10% or maybe 20% would have been appropriate. But 50% is just too extreme. Myanmar still has great potential. The kyat is undervalued at these levels, but the market's been traumatized. Buyers won't step up to the plate. Now BankBurma would have been able to make good on its swap obligations and investment promises had a normal correction occurred. It's this crazy plunge that's killing them."

"So?" Pete seemed unimpressed.

"What if we could get the kyat back up to the point where it's only 20% off its pre-crash value? Then BankBurma could pay off at least part of its obligations, which would allow McKenzie-Kent and Perth to do the same. Takamura would get its cash before the end of the month. Between that and a few asset sales like the Colmedia deal they should have enough to avoid having to do the bond liquidation."

Pete shook his head. "You know, I've seen a lot of guys make it on Wall Street, and it's amazing how a little money can lead to delusions of influence. But you're the first I've seen who thinks he can raise the dead. And just how do you propose to perform this act of necromancy?"

"Normally, the central banks might have done it for us. The Fed, the European Central Bank, the Bank of Japan; they all might have bought kyat to prop up the currency. They'd have done it just to increase the stability of the financial system. Given the ferocity of the sell-off, however, they'd run the risk it wouldn't work. The truth is, central banks only have so much power. If they stand against a runaway market, and lose, they blow their credibility, and they can't afford that. Besides, they usually act under the leadership of the U.S. Treasury, and Myanmar isn't Mexico. Treasury doesn't feel the national interest is at stake. Now, the Secretary of the Treasury was quoted last week as saying he'd like to see a higher kyat. He could direct the Fed to buy kyat on Treasury's behalf, but given the pressure on the kyat right now, Treasury won't move. They'd be afraid the intervention wouldn't work. That could change if they sensed that market sentiment had shifted. If they saw major players purchasing kyat, they might start buying to encourage the kyat's recovery."

Pete shrugged. "Well, like you say. The market's screwed up right now. Eventually they'll calm down and recognize the underlying value in Myanmar. It'll just take time. Until then you can't expect O'Connor and the other finance ministers to stick their necks out." James O'Connor, one-time star Wall Street trader and Hubie's former boss, was the current Secretary of the Treasury.

"There isn't any time," snapped Jack. "Takamura needs the money by the end of the month. We don't even have that long, because Hiro Yamada has already started selling. He's going to dump the whole load well before the end of January."

"So I ask you again, Doc. What the fuck do you want to do about it?"

Jack leaned forward. "J. Pierpont Morgan once organized a private bailout of the American banking system, back during the Panic of 1907."

"So what, you want to bail out BankBurma? Takamura? Stone doesn't have anything like the capital for something like that. Anyway, neither your partners nor any other firms on the Street are gonna risk a nickel on those dogs. Not while Myanmar's flat on its ass."

"I know that, Pete. That's why I want to try to organize a private bailout of Myanmar. Get the hedge funds and investment banks to start buying kyat. The same ones who made a bundle on its decline. Once the central bankers see the kyat start to rise, they'll step in to support it."

Pete exploded with laughter. "I was wrong, you don't have delusions of influence, but of omnipotence! Doc, I gotta hand it to you. When you showed up on the Street, you were just some geek with a couple of fancy degrees. Then you make a few bucks and all of a sudden you think you're J.P. Morgan!"

Jack didn't smile. "No, Pete," he said quietly, "But maybe you are."

Pete was still struggling to contain his amusement. "What are you talking about?"

"You're the one guy at Stone with enough connections and reputation to talk to the big hedge fund managers. You've been acting as Simon Ashcroft's favorite broker for what, twenty years? You could explain it to him. Make him believe in the plan. Suppose he were to start buying kyat publicly, and we did the same. Everyone knows we're the one's who made the call on the kyat in the first place. If Stone and Ashcroft start buying kyat, it could scare the bears into covering their shorts. Especially if the central banks follow our lead. And I'm telling you, Pete, this can work. I've run it through my models, and the kyat is ready to rise if given a chance."

Pete's smile had faded. "Those would be the same models that told you to piss on my trading limits and risk the whole firm?"

Jack looked at the man's face and knew that behind the grin were humiliation and the pain of betrayal. It was now or never. "Pete, there's something I need to tell you. I told Hubie to short forty million in kyat. I said something about shorting four hundred as a joke, but he was on the phone and misheard me."

Pete stared at Jack in silence for a moment; then said evenly, "You know, I can accept being outmaneuvered, the young usurping the old. It's in the nature of things…"

"We didn't usurp you, Pete. The partners just didn't go along with you firing me. Nobody's forcing you out…"

Pete ignored him. "I think, though, that I've earned enough respect not to have my intelligence insulted with a cock-and-bull story like the one you just spewed. If I hadn't paid two hundred thousand to have this paneling ripped out of a Burgundy chateau and shipped here, I'd put your overeducated head through the wall."

"Pete, it's the truth."

"Then why didn't you tell me at the time?"

"It wasn't to advance myself – like you said, I'd have made partner anyway. I was in a no-win situation. If you'd believed me, you would have fired Hubie, and I didn't want that. It was an honest mistake on his part. You know how he is. Hell, *I* know how he is, and, knowing him, maybe it was my fault for kidding around at a time like that. And, then again, if I'd told you the truth, it was more likely you'd just think I was trying to lay the blame on someone else and consider me an even bigger dick than you do now."

"Well, kid, I'm going with option two."

Jack could see his request wasn't even under consideration, and all the confusion and frustration of the last few weeks welled up in him and exploded.

"You know what, Pete? I don't give a fuck what you believe." He rose from his chair, his voice rising in a crescendo of fury. "In the last few weeks I've watched a guy's bitching over his morning commute trigger a nation's collapse. I'm doing business with a man who wants to turn the supreme achievements of Western literature into some kind of arcade game. And now, it seems this amazing woman I'm seeing is on the rebound from a very public affair with a sweet potato. *You* don't believe it? Well, I'm here to tell you a lot of things are un-fucking-believable, but that doesn't make them any less true, and it doesn't mean they won't sneak up and bite you on the ass!"

Pete stood just as his wife opened the door, obviously alarmed at Jack's outburst.

Her husband waved her away. "It's O.K., Susan. We're fine."

Susan gave Jack a look that could've curdled milk as she closed the door.

Pete took a long draw on his cigar and exhaled, peering at the flushed young man in front of him through wisps of smoke. "I don't know what all that was about, son, but I think you'd better take it easy, before you have a stroke. Tell me something, Jack. What do you care if the bond market crashes? If you know what's going to happen, why not just go for the easy money? If you're worried about heat from Washington or the press, you shouldn't be. Look at Ashcroft. He's been in the middle of a score of these things over the years and he's still an admired figure."

Jack was still flustered. "Look, in the long run it can't be good for our business to have a global collapse. Think what it will do to Stone's underwriting business or Ted's merchant banking fund. We have all these plans for expansion and in a negative growth environment they'll be blown to hell."

Pete smiled. "What was it Keynes said? 'In the long run, we're all dead.'" He tapped some ash into a tray. "Look, I'll have cashed out long before most of the profits from that stuff are realized. Anyway, I find it hard to believe that's what's got you hyperventilating here, trying to find a reason not to make an obvious trade."

Jack took a moment to regain his composure. He'd always felt in Pete a humanity rare in his business. He saw it in the tolerance he had for the quirks of the people who worked for him, the Hubies and Carl Richs of the world. In the patience he'd shown teaching the ways of the Street to a refugee from particle physics. He was a mensch, and that trait was worth betting on. It was Jack's last card.

"Believe me, Pete, normally I would just cash in. Usually we don't guide markets or shape history; we just try to stay ahead of the game and make a profit on whatever happens. Usually. Every once in a while you get a chance to be more than flotsam on the ocean. You get to have a say in what the world will look like. It may not be a big say, and what you do may not have a lasting impact at all." He paused, gazing out the window at freezing sea. "The thing is, when you get that chance, it's the only time you get to find out who you are. I'd like to be more than just..."

Jack stared at Pete, not fully sure what he was trying to express, let alone how he could reach his audience. "Someone told me you don't get to choose the world you live in, only what you do in that world. We have a choice here. We could do something that will still make us money. We'll still be traders. And we'll have done something... decent."

Pete rubbed his chin. "Have you told your partners about this plan of yours yet?"

"No. I want you to endorse it with me at the next trading meeting. Then maybe they'll go along with trying it. If it doesn't work, we can always dump the kyat and go short."

"Assuming we have time and the kyat doesn't fall out from under us."

"Obviously this is not without risk."

The senior partner nodded. "Tell you what I'll do. I'll come back and tell Ted and Caroline that if they want to give this a shot, I'll help. Ashcroft's based in the Caymans, and I wouldn't mind flying down there for a day anyway. We'll see if we can convince him to go along with it. You gotta know, though, it's going to be a tough sell. These people aren't exactly obsessed with the commonweal."

"There's a lot of money to be made doing it my way, too."

"And a lot of risk. You'll have to convince them you can handle it."

"That's why I came to see you."

"You realize if Stone takes a big enough hit on this you could find yourself kicked out of the partnership."

"I hope to avoid that outcome." That was an understatement; given what he'd just put down on his new apartment, he prayed to avoid that outcome. Finding another position after screwing this thing up wouldn't be easy, and bankruptcy did not appeal to him.

Pete showed him out, and as they came to the front door Jack asked, "My appeal to conscience actually swayed you?"

"Kid, if you want to survive on the Street you can't get all squishy about the human condition. You'll have to come up with something better than that if you want to persuade your colleagues to go along with you on this thing. I've been in this game for decades. You throw moral arguments at them and all you'll see is ice in their eyes."

Jack looked back at the older man. "It couldn't have been easy, seeing that all these years."

"Only in the morning."

"When you're in the trading meeting?"

"When I'm shaving."

Chapter 8: Tilting at Windmills

Jack had warned Ted and Caroline that he was bringing Peter Torelli to the regular trading conference on Monday. He didn't want them to think this was some kind of power play. Pete's renewed presence raised eyebrows among the traders, but Ted still did most of the talking, however, and it was clear the troika was still in control.

After the meeting ended Ted, Caroline, Jack and Pete remained behind. Jack repeated the plan he'd explained to Pete the previous morning, and Pete indicated his willingness to help. Ted sat back in his chair and turned to Caroline. "Whaddya think?"

She stared at the physicist. "Let me ask you something, Jack. Have you suddenly developed an overwhelming attraction to me?"

"What? No, I mean..."

"How about me?" asked Ted. "Have I somehow become irresistibly beautiful in your eyes?"

"What the hell are you guys talking about?"

Ted shrugged. "We're just wondering why you seem so determined to fuck us."

Pete grimaced. "Funny. You two should take that act on the road."

Caroline smiled. "It's a hobby. Some people go camping, we do snide. Look, Jack, we just don't see the point here. Why take a risk? Going short's a sure thing."

Jack had carefully considered Pete's warning about discourses on morality. He decided to stress the effect on Stone's bottom line. "First of all, it's true we'd be taking a greater chance by using my approach, but my models show the upside is considerably larger as well. And there are other factors to consider. There's of course scrutiny from Washington; they'll have the Street under a magnifying glass if the markets collapse. More important, imagine the effect a global slump would have on our business, on our future plans for Stone."

Ted laughed. "You're sure it's about us and not you? We remember your New Year's attack of conscience. On top of which Hubie told us about your reaction to the 'Year in Review' coverage of your little triumph, so we know you've got issues with the human fallout from the Burma thing. And I gotta tell ya, this whole scheme sounds like some bad Kung Fu movie sequel: *Kyat II,* starring Jack Kline - *'This time it's personal'* ".

"Give me some credit for callousness, Ted; everybody else does. Look, you're just now turning our merchant-banking fund into a buy-out vehicle. You've expanded our M&A advisory. Caroline's almost tripled our trading, and we're breaking into client derivative services. All this has huge profit potential, but we had to spend a lot of money up front. It's going to be very difficult to get a decent return on that investment in a lousy economic environment." A slight nod from Ted; the argument was having its effect. "Thing is, folks, in a depression, Wall Street isn't nearly as much fun."

"And you're so sure you can stop that from happening?" asked Caroline.

"I'm pretty far from sure, but it's worth a try. Everyone on the Street knows the whole idea of perfectly efficient, rational markets is just so much social science fiction. The market got a little carried away here, that's all. All we have to do is give it a shove in the right direction. We'll agree on a pre-set limit for our losses, say a fall in the kyat of ten percent. If it's clear it's not working, we could should still have time to reverse our position and go short."

Caroline looked doubtful. "Perhaps."

"Hey, you're the queen of quick trades, and we've got Hubie working for us. We'd pull it off." Jack had no idea if his last statement were true.

Ted looked out of the glass walls at the trading floor below. "What will you tell Ashcroft about the Takamura situation?"

"Absolutely nothing. We want him interested in buying kyat, not short-selling Treasury bonds."

"Which is probably what we ought to be doing," muttered Caroline. She looked at Jack and smiled. "Oh, what the hell. You made us a pile on the kyat collapse. I'm willing to give you a free-at-bat here."

Ted turned to Jack. "O.K., talk to Ashcroft and see if he and some other players will go along with this. We'll see what happens."

"If we're all agreed," said Pete, "I'm going to go and call Ashcroft. If he'll see us tomorrow, Jack and I'll fly to Grand Cayman in the morning. It's a shame to rush back up to this icebox but since time's short we'll make it a day trip."

"Take the company car," suggested Ted, referring to the Gulfstream jet in which Stone maintained a fractional ownership share.

As Pete left, the other three partners headed out on the floor. They sat down at their trading desks and Ted said, "Jack, Caroline and I would like to talk to you about certain personal matters."

"If you're pissed I brought Pete in on this..."

"No, we can live with that, although I've got to warn you, this thing's a little out there, and if it goes really south I wouldn't count on that 'free at bat.' The partners may get pissed off, and just might hold a tribal council and vote you both off the island. Nothing personal, dude."

"Ah, strategic management inspired by a televised game in which contestants are forced to eat small animals."

"Don't worry, we already buried Carl's rug. Anyway, we want to talk about something else."

"Look, Ted, if it's about you and Caroline, it's really none of my business. Like I told you before, I'm happy for you guys and I promise I won't say anything to anyone."

Caroline looked like she was trying to stifle a laugh. "We're not really too concerned about that prospect anymore." She slowly pulled her pen out from her ponytail's beret as if drawing a blade. "I believe the operative dynamic here is the old Cold War concept of mutual assured destruction."

"I'm sorry?"

Ted grinned. "Let me ask you something, Doc. How's it going with the new girlfriend?"

As the markets opened, the morning roar began echoing through the trading room and Jack had to raise his voice to be heard clearly.

"Things could be better."

"What do you mean?"

"There are certain philosophical problems." Jack's voice dropped to a mumble. "Like on our last little get together she called me a carrion bird."

Ted strained to hear Jack's lowered voice above the din. "A carry-on bag? She thinks you're luggage?"

"A carrion bird," Caroline clarified. "You know, like a vulture. A scavenger that feasts on the flesh of the dead."

"Thank you, Caroline," said Jack.

"Well, at least she's getting to know the real you." Ted was smiling broadly now. "Which is a coincidence, since Caroline and I have been getting to know a little more about her as well."

Jack began to feel queasy.

"You see," Ted continued, "After you left my party we hung out with Fred Colson Jr. for a while. Zane had just come back form Æther's concert at the Garden. Turns out she's got her own label but Colmedia handles her distribution and promotion. Anyway, Caroline here remembers that your new friend is in the music business, too. So she asks him if he's ever heard of Helen Cantos."

By now Caroline was slumped back in her chair laughing uncontrollably.

"And hey, guess what?" Ted was breaking into hysterics as well. "He actually knows her pretty damn well."

Jack put the fingers of right hand to his temple, knowing he should have seen this coming.

"So I take it you're aware of Ms. Cantos' musical endeavors?" asked Caroline, barely in control of herself.

"She happens to be a very brilliant woman..."

Ted nodded. "Modest too. I think she demonstrated that when she did that thing with the carrot..."

Jack shook his head. "Yam."

"Come again?" said Ted.

"It was a fucking yam, O.K.? She was doing some kind of a Thanksgiving thing and... look, I'm not going to get into this with you."

Caroline chuckled. "Anyway, I hope you won't let this interfere with your relationship. It seems like a natural match. I mean, you like to probe the outer reaches of the universe, and she likes to probe the inner reaches of her..."

"Yeah, Caroline. Great. Thanks again." Jack cut her off. "Haven't you people ever heard of freedom of artistic expression?"

Caroline raised her hands. "But what about the yam's needs? I'm sure it felt cheap. Used."

"Anyway I don't know where this is going, and until I do I'd appreciate if you could both keep your mouths shut."

"We won't tell on you if you don't tell on us." said Caroline.

"You didn't say anything to that slime mold, did you?"

Ted rolled his eyes. "Zane? In the middle of a deal? Of course not. You didn't talk to her about the Colmedia takeover?"

"I'm not an idiot either." Jack got up from his chair. "I'm going to assume you two will zip it. I'd just as soon keep my private life off Wall Street."

As Jack walked away Ted called out, "Hey, Doc, my niece is a big fan. Can you get her an autograph?"

Before Jack could muster enough sarcasm for a reply, the phone rang on Ted's trading desk. He turned to leave again but heard his partner calling him back.

Ted hung up the receiver. "Guess who just showed up without an appointment, asking for Caroline and me?"

"The producers of 'America's Scariest Couples'?"

"No, they'd be more interested in you and your new friend. Actually its Fred Colson Sr. "

"Shit." Caroline tossed her pen against her screens.

Jack looked from Ted to Caroline. "You think the jig is up?"

"Naw. He probably just wants to thank us for being such a help with his son's career goals," Caroline ventured, "especially this new corporate patricide phase."

Ted picked up his receiver again. "Maybe that Elizabethan e-mail was from him after all. Caroline, I have to do this, but you can blow it off if this is uncomfortable for you."

"Well, we are about to obliterate his life's work. I suppose I might give him a few minutes."

Ted turned to Jack. "You ought to join us; he asked for you too."

"What for? All I did was sit in on the meeting with his kid."

"Yeah, well, maybe he saw that troika stuff in the *Journal*. Face it, man; you've thrown in with the pirates now. Anyway, it's a chance for you to meet a legend of publishing."

Caroline nodded. "And completely destroy him. Nice."

Jack steeled himself for confrontation as they rode the elevator up to the sixtieth floor. He'd never seen a photo of Colson, but pictured the editor as a gray-haired, bow-tied, Ivy League professor type. When he saw the man in Ted's office, he found that gray hair pulled back in a short ponytail. With his jeans and tweed jacket he looked like one of those aging refugees from the Sixties he'd seen haunting bookstores in Harvard Square.

"Fred Colson," he said softly, smiling, "the elder. But of course one of you already knows me." He nodded at Caroline.

They sat down, Colson tossing an arm over the back of a sofa, a picture of ease.

"I hope my dropping in hasn't put you people out, though I gather that's exactly what you intend to do to me. Anyway, seeing as your firm is about to become a major shareholder in Colmedia, I thought you might want to meet the chairman before you fire him."

Ted propped an elbow on his desk. "Mr. Colson, Stone & Co. routinely engages in conversations with executives of corporations - I can assure you of the propriety of any discussions we may have conducted with representatives of Colmedia..."

"Please, Mr. Harris, let's spare each other. Junior's a braggart, and thus a very poor custodian of confidences. And there's still quite a few people loyal to the old man." He spoke so offhandedly he might have been talking about the weather.

Catherine broke the silence that followed. "Well, frankly we surmised as much when we received your e-mail."

"Come again?"

"Your e-mail. The line from Macbeth."

Colson grinned. "You must have me confused with someone else. I don't do e-mail. Or e-commerce, or e-publishing, or any other e-nonsense. I'm sure Junior shared with you his displeasure with my views."

"I think your son feels you may be missing opportunities he'd like a chance to capitalize on..." Ted spoke in the practiced bland language of an investment banker. "I like to think of him as more than an entrepreneur. He has a real vision of the Web, a sort of social philosophy. Perhaps one day he'll be to the Internet what Marshall McLuhan was to television."

"Ted, we both know the kid's to philosophy what McLuhan was to judo. Now I'm no Luddite, but I'll admit I'm not a machine kind of guy. You're talking to someone who spent a year on an ashram. Nevertheless, I've given Junior a free hand. Look at our music division, if you call what he sells music. You'll laugh, but when he started it, I had dreams of him finding the next Dylan. Obviously that wasn't to be, but with my backing he's become one of the world's leading purveyors of mindless noise. The problem is he doesn't want to be burdened by the publication that put me in a position to support him in the first place." He shook his head. "My own personal argument for birth control."

"Please understand this is just business," Catherine interjected, "we're not interlopers in, ah, family matters..."

"Buy into a family business and you buy into the family. Anyway it's really not his fault. I set the example. When I started the thing in '68 it was on the cutting edge, but these days I don't even think there is an edge out there to be on. Recycled crap's still crap, even if you throw it up on a Web page."

"Actually I still think a lot of the *Manhattanite*. I learned a great deal working for you."

"Like the fact that you didn't want to write the kind of stuff I've published lately. Not that I entirely blame you, Ms. Stewart. When I saw the articles in the *Journal* and the *Economist*, I took great interest in your rise and that of your Dr. Kline here. A writer dealing in debts, a physicist trading money." He smiled, shaking his head. "What hath we wrought? Tell me, Caroline, are you no longer quite so enamored of the literati? Well I am, you see. That's my curse. I love writers even though I know we're talking about people who secretly thank God for all the misery in the world, theirs and everyone else's, because it gives them something to write about. I love the young ones, even as they try to top each other in laying bare the most shocking personal history." He sighed "I'm waiting for the day one of them sends me a manuscript detailing his dysfunctional relationship with a parrot. And I love the old ones, ones I discovered, even though half of them have become fatuous poseurs competing in a triathlon of pretense, cynicism and the stealing of each other's mates. Of course, some of them found they had personal miseries to share as well. Old wrongs, vintage whines, like 'when we were young we were so poor we couldn't afford air, so I had to hold my breath until I was thirty.' I love these people because sometimes; once in a great while, but sometimes, one of them sings in the storm of refuse that is what is marketable, and I lift that voice above the noise, and people hear the music."

Colson shrugged. "That's why I can't lose this gig, my friends. I give wings to angels. The only similar position has been filled for some time."

"Shame you couldn't find a way to bestow any of that flying equipment on Caroline." The edge in Ted's voice was no longer a mystery to Jack.

"Well, there was a time I might have, but things changed. I had to change too, to survive. And, I thought, at least people might read this stuff; better than having a nation of talk-show viewers. Besides, you run a company, you become a suit, even if you never put one on. Next thing you know you're 'rethinking the organization,' 'managing for excellence,' all the rest of that crap. Creativity has to support the bottom line, instead of the other way 'round, and sooner or later that's too much weight to bear. I tried to find a middle ground between good writing and good business, and I ended up with neither. Idealism gave way to profit. The kid's just taking that logic to its inevitable conclusion. That's sort of the story with a lot of people your age, isn't it?"

"Now, Mr. Colson..." Ted interjected.

"It's perfect. My generation taught yours how to sell out, and man, you were attentive pupils. Perhaps, Caroline, you and your colleagues have acquired a different sort of wing from the type I would have wished for you. There's an old Spanish saying: 'raise crows and one day they'll fly home and peck out your eyes.' And it's not just Junior or you Wall Street people. My son's got the distribution rights for that woman, the singer with the shiny finish. You know who I mean..."

"Æther." said Ted. "Jack, didn't you recently become familiar with her, uh, stuff?" Ted turned toward the trader, smiling innocently.

Colson shrugged. "Well, there's no accounting for taste. Thing is, you know who she used to be? Years ago, before she was this Æther, she went by her real name - Helen Cantos. Not that dog psychic, mind you...Junior will never forgive me for not giving her a column. No, she was a dancer and choreographer. Something of a prodigy in that latter endeavor. Brilliance and real guts. I saw her perform with a company she used to have. She had the nerve to do programs with all new music, the most innovative composers. I think she saw herself as doing for them what Diaghilev did for Stravinsky. New *Firebirds*, so to speak...but these days the world has no use for firebirds. She went belly up." The publisher shook his head. "Strange to think that was an artist once..."

"I tend to think people change what they do for a living, not who they are," Jack said quietly.

"I imagine you'd have to, seeing as how you've gone from atom smashers to smashing countries..."

Ted cut him off. "Look, Mr. Colson, we'd love to sit here and debate inter-generational politics, but we really have to get back down to the trading floor, so if we've no further business to discuss..."

"I'm sorry, Mr. Harris. Here I've been talking to you about history, and of course the only subject that carries any weight in a place like this is cash, specifically the amount it would take to get you people to leave my company alone. You see, I'm still fool enough to pay for a chance to fix what I've broken."

"We're not looking for a bribe, Mr. Colson. We won't be paid to go away." Ted's voice hardened. "We're not in this for greenmail."

"Really? How's ten million sound? Between my personal assets and some help from friends..."

"Quite frankly, sir, you'd need to add at least a zero to that figure just to get in the game."

Colson opened his mouth, then closed it again, like a poker player who'd thought the better of calling a hand.

Ted smiled. "You don't even know the value of your own assets, do you? I'm afraid that's something neither your shareholders nor the markets can tolerate. Not anymore. It isn't Stone. Hell, for Caroline, this deal's like acid in her mouth, but it doesn't matter because if it weren't us, someone else'd pull the trigger. It's just that, right now, we're the fastest guns in town."

Colson stared wide-eyed at Ted, and Jack thought he looked less angry than amazed, in an almost innocent way. Then the publisher nodded once, slowly. Wordless, he rose and started toward the door. At the last moment he turned toward the partners, his eyes meeting Caroline's.

"So you've finally flown home."

When the door closed, Ted turned to his partners, smirking. "Well, obviously we're dealing with a father and son committed to old-fashioned family values..."

Jack nodded. "So long as the old-fashioned family we're talking about are the Borgias..."

Ted laughed but when he looked at Caroline she turned away. As Ted's smile faded, Jack knew he needed to be somewhere else, As he left, neither of his partners said anything.

Stone's plane prepared for takeoff, and Jack felt his lids get heavy. He hadn't slept much in the past few days. Something about the sensation of being lifted into the air calmed him, as if he were rising above the chaos of the last few weeks. A few minutes after ascent from JFK, he drifted off.

When the Gulfstream touched down outside of George Town, at Grand Cayman's airport, Jack awoke with a start. He rubbed his eyes and focused on the face of Peter Torelli, who held the orange-pink pages of the

Financial Times in his hands. Pete looked up at Jack over the frames of wire-rimmed reading glasses.

"Have a nice snooze, kid?"

Jack had slept like the dead. He stayed up the night before talking to Hiro Yamada. He'd described to him the plan he'd formulated and managed to extract from him a promise not to dump Takamura's bonds for three more days. That was the maximum Hiro would wait; he didn't want to cut it any closer to the end of the month lest he have to sell too fast. Further delay increased the odds of tanking the market in the middle of the sale, costing Takamura billions. Jack had also gotten Hiro to agree to buy several hundred million dollars worth of kyat at the appropriate time. This was particularly dangerous for the Japanese bank in its present condition, but they figured if the bailout fell through the bond sale would cover a kyat loss as well. Besides, thought Jack, if Stone were going to gamble, Takamura sure as hell would too.

The Stone partners stepped off the plane with Jack carrying a laptop computer and Pete nothing at all. They'd get back on the aircraft in a few hours and thus required no luggage. A driver sent by Ashcroft picked them up at the airport. The two traders sat in the back of a Range Rover during the twenty-minute drive to Ashcoroft's home. Jack got his first look at the island. He caught glimpses of white beach and azure blue sea, palms swaying in the tropical breeze. Oh yeah, thought Jack, good thing we'll be racing right back up to New York. Wouldn't want to miss a minute of winter in Manhattan for this.

Simon Ashcroft was said to be a billionaire twice over. His home turned out to be a compound on Seven Mile Beach, the Gold Coast of the Caymans. It consisted of three guesthouses surrounding an enormous main complex; a Spanish fantasy rendered in stucco and tiled roof. Landscaped floral gardens embraced a set of connected pools, artificial ponds like a string of sapphires shining in the sun. At the edge of this manicured oasis, a pristine private beach was caressed by foamy waves.

If a cover of *Vogue* could come to life, then that was what greeted the Stone partners. An impossibly perfect vision wrapped in a sari that seemed to match both her eyes and the color of the sea. Pete introduced her as Kerry Ashcroft, and they followed her to a verandah that looked across one of the enormous pools to the ocean beyond. Jack figured the woman for about twenty-four, and as she turned to address them she tossed her auburn hair in a way that made him suspect she knew exactly how breathtaking she was. She informed them that Simon would be arriving presently, then stepped away to arrange for some drinks. Jack whispered to Peter.

"His daughter?"

"His wife. Number three, I think. Or maybe four – I'm not sure that Russian girl ever got a ring out of him. He trades them like bonds. This one's a model. Very famous, I understand. She's got that five story poster of herself in her underwear in Times Square."

Jack heard the beating sound of rotors and turned to see a helicopter approaching the compound. As it approached, the trader shouted into Pete's ear. "Terrific. We're trying to save the financial world and we're asking for help from a guy who, judging by his lifestyle, thinks he's a James Bond villain."

"He makes even Ted's consumption level look modest, doesn't he?" The chopper touched down on a pad fifty yards away.

Jack shook his head. "Who lives like this?"

"Zeus. He lived better."

"He was a mythological deity."

"So's Ash – just ask him. And don't underestimate the man. He's one of the few guys I know who's as smart as present company."

Jack nodded, surprised at the compliment.

Ashcroft approached. He was a silver-haired Englishman, around sixty yet with a tanned, athletic appearance. He was dressed in a polo shirt, cotton pants, and loafers without socks; wiser attire than the Stone traders' suits, given the tropical heat. Jack had seen the man's picture many times in business magazines. Pete's joke notwithstanding, Ashcroft's success and secrecy had indeed made him a figure of awe in the business.

Ashcroft shook Pete's hand and spoke with an accent that was pure Oxbridge. "Peter, how's life treating you?"

"Can't complain, Ash. I'd ask you the same question, but I think the answer is pretty obvious."

Ashcroft turned to Jack. "And you, sir, must be the estimable Dr. Kline. I should thank you; we did rather well on that kyat thing."

Jack shook the man's hand. Before he could say anything Kerry returned, followed by a maid with a pitcher of iced tea and glasses. She set these on a circular table under a yellow umbrella, and Jack, Pete and the Ashcrofts sat down in wicker chairs around it. The four of them spoke for a few minutes about how the weather here contrasted with that of New York. Ashcroft also spoke about the rising value of real estate in Miami, which he'd just flown in from. Jack gathered the guy owned about a quarter of South Beach. Kerry said something about a having to pack for a modeling assignment in Paris and excused herself. The conversation turned to business.

"So my old friend here tells me you have a proposal you'd like to present."

"I appreciate your taking the time to listen to it."

"Given your role in Southeast Asian current events, I can assure you my undivided attention."

For the third time in as many days Jack explained his scheme, this time *sans* the part about Takamura and the impending crisis. He pitched it as a simple trading opportunity - a chance to buy an undervalued currency. When he finished, Ashcroft put his elbows on the table and formed a steeple with his fingers. He smiled at Jack for a few seconds.

"Tell me, Jack," said the hedge fund manager. "Have you lined up the cooperation of any other major institutions yet?"

"I am assured that a major Asian bank is already on board."

"That wouldn't happen to be Hiro Yamada's bank, perchance? The Takamura bank?"

Jack was dumbstruck.

Ashcroft's blue eyes seemed to shine. Jack suspected it was the gleam mice see in a cat's eye before being consumed. "I ask this," continued Ashcroft, "because one of my traders was at Wharton when Hiro and you were there, and he mentioned to me what good friends you were. Very smart fellow, Yamada. Met him once in Singapore. He's run into a spot of trouble lately, though. All those bad loans he inherited. And then there's this kyat thing." Ashcroft leaned back and smiled. "My people in Singapore tell me Takamura took quite a bath on swaps with BankBurma. Worse, I understand Takamura has significant exposure to McKenzie-Kent of Hong Kong and Perth Holdings of Australia, both of which are having a rather nasty time dealing with BankBurma's collapse. Or, so I'm told."

The Stone partners were silent as they watched Ashcroft sip his tea. He put his glass down and continued. "You know, gentlemen, I can't help but wonder if Takamura's difficulties have something to do with the rather odd behavior I've seen in the bond market recently. Patterns of selling consistent with a large Japanese bank trying to liquidate its Treasury holdings. Patterns I'm quite sure you're astute enough to have detected, Dr. Kline. It would take quite a crisis to compel a Tokyo money center bank to sell its bonds right now. The Bank of Japan would not be pleased. Before resorting to something like that, I would think Hiro Yamada would try everything else. Like selling off various assets. I hear he's been shopping their stake in Colmedia, for example. He might also turn to old friends for help in bailing out the kyat. Try to put the genie back in the bottle, as it were." Ashcroft smiled broadly, revealing a set of perfectly white teeth. "So, gentlemen, what do you think of my analysis?"

Jack opened his mouth to say something, though he hadn't the faintest idea what. Fortunately, Pete put his hand on Jack's wrist and began to speak. "O.K., Ash," he said calmly. "So you know what we know. The question right now is what we're going to do about it."

"I should think that would be rather obvious. Go short. Bonds, stocks, just about everything. Except perhaps gold; might buy some while I'm at it. As for the kyat, it may be undervalued, but there's hardly any point in buying any until after the markets collapse. You certainly don't need me to tell you that, Pete, and neither does your young friend here. What's beyond me is why you two would contemplate doing anything else?"

Jack was rattled, but knew he had to make his case. "Have you considered the broader macroeconomic consequences of a massive decline in the markets? I think it's quite likely we're talking about a worldwide crash here, perhaps even a depression."

"Which I imagine might impair some of Stone's business activities. I'm running a hedge fund, you understand. I don't really care which way the economies of the world go so long as I'm on the right side of the movement. That's my concern in its entirety." Ashcroft took another sip of his tea. "I wouldn't worry too much, though. Position your trades correctly and you should be able to make enough to see your firm through whatever heavy weather blows in. I still don't see why you chaps are here, unless you just came down for the sun."

Pete saw Jack's knuckles whiten as he gripped the arm of his chair. The younger man was beside himself with frustration. He couldn't believe he'd been so completely found out, and with the Takamura situation revealed he saw no way to turn Ashcroft to his purpose. In desperation he ignored Pete's warning. "Have you considered the human cost of such a crisis?" he asked.

"My clients don't pay me to take that into consideration." Ashcroft's tone conveyed amusement. "I suppose, though, that the human factor was paramount in your mind when you shorted all that kyat? I think you should look to your priorities here, my friend." Ashcroft grinned. "You know, Jack, I'm somewhat familiar with your erstwhile profession. I've read some of the popular books on physics and cosmology. All those fine minds looking for God in the atom. I don't know if you found him there, but I hope you don't imagine you'll discover him in the markets." The financier fixed his gaze on Jack and his face lost all expression. "Economics is the practice of a darker calculus. You can't trap the market's chaos in a crystal of logic, or bend the global economy to your particular moral view. If you persist in trying, you will succeed only in impoverishing yourself, and you will grow old in your enterprise."

Jack stared at the Englishman for a moment. "Let me ask you something, Mr. Ashcroft. Are you actually *trying* to sound like the heavy in some B-movie?"

"Uh... Jack?" Pete interrupted.

"I'm sorry, Pete, but I've had enough of this guy's oracular condescension. Look, Goldfinger, let me tell you exactly where you can stick *your* enterprise..."

"Jack," Pete cut in again, firmly now, "you were telling me you've never been to the islands before. Why don't you take a walk on the beach for a few minutes? Give me and my old friend here a chance to get reacquainted." As he spoke, Pete's gaze never left Ashcroft.

Jack looked from one face to the other, then pushed himself up out of his seat. "What the fuck. Mr. Ashcroft, please continue to blather on in my absence." The other men watched Jack walk past the pools and down a set of slate steps to Ashcroft's private beach.

"You know, your boy has Burma so far up his backside he must sneeze kyat."

"Makes him and his friends rather vulnerable, doesn't it?"

"Oh? The thought hadn't crossed my mind."

Pete smiled at Ashcroft. "You know, it really is good to see you again, Ash."

"Likewise. How's Susan?"

"Very well, thank you. You're happy with Kerry?"

"Well, it's only been a few months, although for me that's not bad. You got it right the first time, I suppose. Always admired that about you."

"Listen Ash, about this kyat thing..."

"You're about to tell me I have to buy kyat for the sake of my fellow man?"

Pete laughed. "Yeah, Ash, I've gone so soft in the head as to think you capable of humanitarian action..."

"You know, Peter, I do realize what this is really about..."

"Really?"

"You coming down here promoting that fool's errand." He pointed his thumb at Jack's receding form. "You know full well his scheme has almost no chance of working. Myanmar's sunk even if you could get the currency back up, and if the Japanese blow up and there's a global meltdown, it's going to happen whatever we do. Yet you help this twit convince those two pit vipers he runs your firm with to go along with this rubbish."

"Say I agree with your assessment of the odds; why would I burn my own firm like that?"

"Because you know when your partners lose a packet on Kline's idiocy, they'll be screaming for blood. The good doctor and the other two, the three individuals who've been pushing you aside, will be out on their respective arses. Then the only leadership that will reassure the partnership or the Street will be the strong, sure hand of experience. Which of course resides at the end of your arm."

Pete looked out toward the sea. "Well, suppose I told you I wasn't going to walk because of Kline and his friends. That when I first came to the Street it wasn't like Shangri-la, but somehow the whole thing got warped into a big, mean game of Monopoly and that I wanted out until this kid... " He paused, raising his eyebrows as he began to smirk. "Buying this crap?"

"That's a right lovely tale, Pete. A mid-life crisis. I fear I may cry," he chuckled. "Please don't insult my intelligence. This plan's doomed, and when it falls apart you'll be back in charge. You know it, I know it, and further you knew I'd realize it the minute you told me about it..."

Pete nodded. "I'm afraid we really are two of a kind." He began to laugh. "Hey, you should have seen that stuff work on that punk..."

"So are you going to tell me why you thought I'd get involved with all this?"

"Because I'll deal you in. When the kyat hits the fan, so to speak, Stone's going to take some serious losses. The kind that make a firm start looking for outside investors to shore up its capital base. The market will be shot, so an IPO will be out of the question. The partners might accept a cash infusion from sources they might not normally look favorably upon. Certain oft-vilified hedge fund managers, for example."

"Ah... Just because Americans can't invest in offshore funds like mine..."

"I know... you're forced to take capital from other sources. Colombian ones, for example, and we're not talking Juan Valdez here. Anyway, Ash, don't deny you haven't wanted a piece of a major American investment bank. We'll turn the place around in a year, and when the market recovers we'll go public and both make a fortune."

Ashcroft clapped his hands. "Now that's the Peter Torelli I know and love! O.K., I'll tell you what I'll do. If you and Takamura come in and buy a few hundred million dollars worth of kyat, I'll do the same. I'll drop hints to a few other money managers as to the possibility of a kyat rally, just to make things look real. When that rally falls apart I'll accept, say, a 10% downside on my kyat position, then sell and short everything in sight."

"This'll be a thing of beauty."

"And after all hell breaks loose?"

"I think two hundred million dollars should plug the hole this'll blow in our balance sheet, in exchange for 10% of the equity. You can use the profits from your short sales to pay for it."

"I think 30% would be more like it."

"You're not the only disreputable hedge fund manager I know, Ash.... twenty's as high as I'll go."

"Ah yes, the old Peter." Ashcroft thin smile slowly reappeared. "Very well, then. Twenty."

"Of course, you understand that on the off chance Kline's plan somehow works, this arrangement is off and you'll have to console yourself with your profits on his trade. Naturally, however, I'll do everything I can to make sure that scenario never transpires."

"I've no doubt." They sat quietly for a few moments, sipping their drinks. As the first rays of sunset reflected pink-orange in the waves offshore, Ashcroft said, "Why don't we call Sir Jacob of Rangoon back here and tell him he'll get his chance to tilt at windmills?"

Sixty hours later, sitting cross-legged on the floor of his apartment, Jack Kline stared into the screen of his laptop computer and wondered if his was indeed a futile quest. Stone and its allies had begun executing their plan, and their efforts were being thwarted.

When he'd flown home with Pete, he'd felt elated. Somehow the senior partner had brought Ashcroft around, and that night, staring east over the blue-black expanse of the Atlantic, he really thought it could work. When he'd arrived home, he'd immediately called Hiro Yamada in Tokyo and they finalized their strategy:

"So your discussion with Ashcroft was a success?"

"If your idea of a successful discussion is an exchange of veiled insults leading to an equilibrium of mutual contempt, then yeah, it was a home run."

"Sounds like a chat with my uncle. Anyway, your new pal's in, right?"

"If his word can be trusted. What's happening on your end?"

"I've talked with the heads of the BankBurma and the Bank of Myanmar," said Hiro. "I informed them that Takamura was in a position to arrange what amounted to a private bailout of the kyat."

"Did you extract the concessions we discussed?"

"They were only too happy to oblige. Once the kyat hits an acceptable level, BankBurma will immediately make good on its obligations to Takamura, as well as to Perth and McKenzie-Kent. Neither of those last two has entered bankruptcy yet, and I've told them they can avoid it now; the price of that escape being of course that they honor their prior commitments to us."

"What level do we have to get the kyat back up to if BankBurma and the others are to make their payments?"

"I've gone over the books and they'll be O.K. at 33 to the dollar. That represents a little more than a 20% decline from the kyat's pre-crash level."

"And a 58% appreciation from its current price. Its a very tall order, Hiro."

"As you said, Jack, a 20% decline would have represented a justifiable devaluation of the kyat. All we have to do is inject a little rationality into the market."

"In the space of forty-eight hours."

"Think of it like basketball, Jack. Without the element of time, where would the excitement be?"

Jack was getting the feeling that Hiro was actually enjoying this.

"It may interest you to know," Hiro continued, "that BankBurma's capital position is actually a bit worse than I'd realized. We actually would have had to get the kyat up to around thirty to the dollar were it not for a little twist I came up with."

"*Twist?* Like what my insides are doing right now?"

"Relax. The Bank of Myanmar was going to do a long-term bond sale just prior to the kyat crash. Takamura was going to be the lead underwriter. Of course after the kyat went through the floor no one would touch the bonds, so we suspended the sale. If we can get the kyat up to thirty-three, I'm confident we can sell a portion of the bonds. The Bank of Myanmar has agreed to use the proceeds to bail out BankBurma before they do anything else."

"What's a portion, exactly?"

"One billion dollars' worth."

"One *billion?*"

"Exactly. I spoke to your partners Ted Harris and Caroline Stewart. When they heard the good news from the Caymans, they agreed to have Stone join the underwriting group and sell about two hundred million dollars' worth of kyat. Of course should the kyat fail to rise, we could get stuck with some seriously underwater paper. If this thing works, though, we'll make a decent fee here, especially if we increase the size of the bond sale. The original issue was going to be two billion, but I figure we don't want to bite off more then we can chew."

"Oh no," said Jack, rolling his eyes. "We wouldn't want to do that. I'm amazed Caroline and Ted went for this."

"Well, there was a price..."

"Let me guess. Colmedia?"

"Four hours ago the deal closed. Stone bought us out for seventy-five million. I know I got you to agree not to change the price, but that was before I realized I'd need your help with the Myanmarese bonds. Had to give you something for that. Ted seemed very happy; he really does want into Colmedia, doesn't he?"

"He just wants to do something for world culture."

"Well, you helped make it happen for him."

Jack sighed. "Yeah, something else I can be proud of."

A lot more than pride was at stake. The transaction was ballooning, bordering on recklessness. If it blew up, he'd get the blame and probably find himself drummed out of the partnership. Again, the thought of the price he'd paid for his apartment made him nauseous. Now he could only press on.

"O.K., Hiro, let's talk execution. Takamura, the Ashcroft fund, and Stone will start buying kyat in rounds of a hundred million dollars' worth each. The purchases will start at 8:00 p.m. New York time, 8:00 a.m. in Yangon. We want the first couple of purchases to be made when the Myanmarese markets are open, to maximize liquidity. We'll try not to move the markets too much at first. Then we'll keep buying through the New York open the next morning, now in as noisy a way as possible. By then both Ashcroft and I will have put statements out on the wires saying we think the kyat is significantly undervalued. Given that we dumped the kyat before its crash, we should have a lot of credibility with the markets; they'll figure our buying is a signal that the kyat's about to rally. Hopefully, if the kyat starts to rise, the central banks will see this as an opportunity to support the currency and start buying. Then, we'll get a short squeeze; the players still shorting the kyat will panic and buy in a rapidly rising market. If everything goes perfectly, we just might be able to get the kyat up to where we need it to be."

"Sounds reasonable. How do we coordinate?"

"Through Caroline and Mike Hubert, our best market operations man."

"We'll be ready on this end. Anything else?"

"Yeah. Talk to your contacts at the Bank of Japan and get them to watch the kyat over the next twenty-four hours. If they see the kyat recovering in Asia, maybe they'll step in and intervene, even if Treasury and the Fed hesitate."

"I'll do what I can, but I know they'd prefer if Treasury moved first. The kyat is part of the dollar block, you know." Hiro was referring to the set of currencies seen as linked to the dollar and thus in the U.S. Treasury's bailiwick.

"I'd prefer if the U.S. moved as well, but the actions of finance ministers and central bankers are less than sure things. Stay in touch, Hiro."

"You know it. And Jack...thanks, man."

"Likewise."

There hadn't been much more to it. Jack spent the following day with Caroline and Hubie, ironing out details. That night, Stone began buying kyat through its Hong Kong office, with Hubie overseeing the action from his house on Long Island. He in turn reported to Caroline and Jack, the three trading phone calls all night, watching the kyat on their screens.

By now it was 5:00 a.m. The sky was still dark, but computer and television screens lit Jack's apartment. He was watching CNBC, which had just begun its Asian markets summary with a report of heavy kyat buying. Jack and Ashcroft's remarks about the currency had already been released, and the rumor was that Stone and the Ashcroft hedge fund were taking down huge amounts of the Myanmarese currency. A Japanese bank was rumored to be a major purchaser as well. In reality, Stone's buying group had already committed almost six hundred million dollars to their strategy.

Jack stared at his laptop screen. A green line traced the price of the kyat through the night. As the buying began, the currency had rallied. The price had risen slowly at first, to fifty to the dollar, then forty-eight, then with greater speed to forty-five. And there it had stopped dead. For two hours it had remained stuck at that resistance level.

For what seemed the hundredth time that morning, Jack's phone rang.

"Yeah?"

"It's Hubie. The way I hear it, there's a lot of hedge funds out there that aren't buying this rally. They think it's a selling opportunity, and they're dumping more kyat."

"Shit. You haven't seen any central banks come in? The Bank of Japan?"

"Nothing."

"O.K. Look, I'm about to go the office. Might as well make the last stand on the trading floor."

"I'll see you there."

Before leaving he placed one last call.

"Yamada."

"Hiro, it's Jack."

"Big zero so far, huh."

"Whole lot of nothing. What are your friends at the Bank of Japan telling you?"

"They simply aren't willing to move on this without the U.S. Treasury, especially given all this short selling. My contacts tell me they don't even want to make the first move by contacting the Americans. They're afraid of setting a bad precedent."

"Doesn't anyone ever take the initiative there?"

"Jack, right now examining the Japanese government's financial bureaucracy is a lot like watching a game of ping-pong. Any balls you'll see are small, light, and, if you blink, you'll miss them. Anyway, I'd have thought your Treasury would have seen what's going on here and tried to give the Bank of Myanmar a hand. It's not as if Washington was pleased by the kyat's collapse."

"Maybe they're asleep at the wheel. We'll see what happens as New York opens. I'm going into the office. I'll speak to you from there."

"Keep the faith."

Jack took a quick shower, threw on his suit, slipped his laptop in its case and shot out the door, grabbing a cab on CPW. The lights were just coming up over the city as Jack sped through the nearly empty streets. It had rained overnight, and the blue of clearing sky was reflected in the rain-filled potholes the car splashed through.

As he rode, the image of that hurricane-engendering butterfly returned to Jack's mind. It was one thing for the insect to whip up a typhoon with its flutters, quite another to try flapping the cyclone away. More than likely the insect would find itself flying into the wind and getting its wings torn off.

The cab pulled up in front of Stone's building at 6:20. The lobby's polished marble floor was slick with trekked-in rainwater, and Jack nearly slipped running through. When he got up to the trading floor, Caroline was already there, and the two traders split a bran muffin as they watched the kyat struggle against seemingly impenetrable resistance.

By 7:00, Hubie, Carl Rich and Peter Torrelli had joined them. With Ted and Caroline's assent, Jack had ordered Pete's trading desk moved over to those of the troika, a gesture not missed on the floor.

When Ted Harris arrived, he marshaled Stone's phalanx of bond salesmen, priming them to execute the Myanmarese bond sale that had been the price of his acquisition of the Colmedia stock. Jack heard Ted finishing his pep talk, ending with a jaunty "Good Luck!" As he looked down at the price of the kyat on his screen, he muttered, "At this rate you're gonna fucking need it."

"Hope you skipped breakfast this morning, 'cause it looks like we'll be eating a shitload of Myanmarese bonds," the physicist whispered as Ted sat down at his trading desk between Jack and Caroline. "And don't forget the side order of public humiliation."

"Hey, Jack, you know your whole Burma idea?" Ted made a double thumbs-up and flashed his toothiest grin. "Sucks! But hey, worst comes to worst, at least we picked up the Colmedia stock cheap. Look on the bright side- we're in business with Zane now."

Caroline exhaled with disgust, dropping a half-eaten croissant onto a plastic plate. "Ted, you've really got to stop ruining my digestion."

The partners sent Carl Rich in to run the morning trading meeting. They were too busy watching the kyat deal fall apart. By 9:00 it had slipped back down to forty-eight to the buck. Pete's phone rang, and he listened for a moment and leaned over to Jack.

"It's Ashcroft. He wants out."

"Get him to wait a little while. At least 'till we get down past sixty. He's not even in the red yet."

Pete spoke to Ashcroft for a moment and hung up. "He says he's out at fifty-nine no matter what."

They sat watching the kyat drift downward. By 11:00 it was trading at fifty on the interbank market. Ted's bond salesmen had taken to shooting rubber bands at each other.

Then the floor erupted as a story came across the room's hundreds of Bloomberg screens, tearing Jack from his kyat contemplations:

"Market sources report rumors that the Takamura bank has sustained losses so serious that they have been attempting to liquidate a large portion of their Treasury holdings... .The problems are said to be tied to the recent decline of the Myanmarese kyat...."

"Oh *shit*! " Caroline shouted as she grabbed her phone. "We're gonna get caught!"

U.S. Treasury bonds immediately began to drop, with the ten-year issue down twenty-eight ticks, or almost a percent in value. Jack's eye caught Nate Henckel's, looking up from a Reuters screen. The risk control officer mouthed a quote on the kyat: "Fifty-two." His face bore the expression of a man who'd just accidentally swallowed a bug.

Pete was back on the phone with Ashcroft. He covered the receiver and shouted to Jack. "He wants out now. What the hell can I tell him?"

Before Jack could answer, Hiro Yamada called him back. Jack stuck a finger in one ear as he held a receiver to the other, struggling to hear Hiro above the roar.

"Where the fuck did that come from, Hiro?"

"How the hell do I know? With all the shit that's been going on lately, someone must have figured it out and leaked it."

"Well, issue a fucking denial!"

"I don't think the market's going to buy it, Jack. We gotta get out while we still have something to sell."

Jack felt the huge room begin to swim around him. It was all slipping through his fingers, flying out of control. He held the phone away from his head and screamed in frustration:

"What the hell happened to the Fed? What kind of Treasury Secretary is James O'Connor? Is he completely out of his mind? We laid this thing out for him on a silver platter. I just wish I could ask him what his fucking problem is!"

Jack's outburst silenced the traders around him, and then Pete calmly asked, "Hubie, where did you say the Secretary is right now?"

Hubie folded his arms. "He said something about heading down to the Keys."

Jack was barely listening. "What...what about his keys?"

Hubie nodded. "O'Connor. The Secretary of the Treasury. My old boss, remember? Jim's got a winter place in the Florida Keys. He told me he might head down there this week and go after marlin."

"He told *you*?"

"Yeah. It's like I was telling Pete the other day..."

Pete leaned across his desk. "Go on, Hubie."

Hubie shrugged. "Well, you know back when he worked on the Street he used to be my boss. I traded on his desk. He lived out in Port Washington, and we took the train in together. We keep in touch. Last year I flew down and fished with him."

"You're kidding."

"Anyway, he doesn't like to be disturbed when he's on vacation. The guys on the Fed's foreign exchange desk probably wouldn't bug him without prior instructions." He laughed. "Not about the kyat, anyway. The Fed Chairman could call if he wanted, but he's probably not watching what's going on. This is the kyat, after all, not the yen. Now the Takamura thing is another story, but the news just broke so no one at the Fed or Treasury would have had time to digest it yet."

Jack tried to get his mind around what Hubie was saying. "So this whole deal's going to hell, and the only guy who could do anything about it is digging through a tackle box? That's just beautiful, Hubie. You know, you might have mentioned this earlier..."

Ted's voice was a growl. "Like before we got our balls in a sling."

"You didn't ask. What am I, a mind reader? Anyway, I told Pete..."

Jack screwed his eyes shut, attempting to control himself.

"Pete, you *knew*..." whispered Caroline. She whipped her head around and glared at Jack and Ted. "Pete and Ashcroft. Don't you get it, they're fucking us!"

Ted kicked his trading desk. "Goddamn, Pete, this is bullshit! This is..."

Pete began to laugh, looking at Jack and shaking his head. "You know, your pals here wouldn't know a life preserver from a manhole cover. I've met Jim O'Connor a few times but I don't know him that well. Of course if a friend were to contact him, someone he really trusts..."

Hubie spoke again, utterly nonplused. "Why? Would you've wanted me to talk to him about the kyat?"

Jack sighed. "Yeah, Hubie, that would have been swell."

"'Cause I could give him a call..."

The troika looked from Hubie to Pete in amazement.

"I've got his cell number. Like I said, I went fishing with him a couple of years back. I know he has screens down there, so he could see the situation for himself if I point it out to him."

Jack was still staring at Hubie. He wouldn't have believed a story like this from any other human being, but Hubie, for all his eccentricity, was entirely without artifice. Having this fruitcake call the most powerful finance minister on earth hardly seemed prudent, but Jack was a little short on options, and prudence went out the window with his sense of reality. He threw up his hands. "Sure, Hubie, what the fuck. Give him a call."

"And Hubie," said Pete, "Use your cell, not a recorded line. I don't think there's anything untoward here, but you never know who might think otherwise." He pulled Jack down into his chair. "What about Ashcroft?"

"Stall him for a minute."

Ted slumped over his desk. "You don't really think Hubie can get through to the Treasury Secretary?"

Hubie picked up his phone and a few seconds later spoke into the receiver. "Jim, it's Hubie. Yeah, some situation. No, I'm telling you, it's no good. Maybe you could've done something about it, but by the time it got to me it was hopeless..."

Caroline leaned over to Jack. "If that really is O'Connor on the other end of that line, then Hubie's killing us. Will you listen to that shit?"

Jack was listening, and to the amazement of his partners he was starting to smile. "Just give him a chance, guys." He put the phone in his hand up to his mouth. Hiro was still on the line.

"What the fuck's going on over there?"

"Hiro, issue the denial. The kyat's about to rally, and when the market sees that they'll start to believe your problems aren't that bad."

"How do you know?"

Jack kept looking at Hubie and grinning. "My friend, I just know."

Hubie continued to talk. "That's what I'm saying. It's never gonna get better. There's nothing you or anyone else on earth can do about it."

Ted reached out as if to pull the phone out of Hubie's hand, but Jack grabbed his arm. "Don't worry, man. They're just bonding."

"What are you talking about?"

"I think I'm finally starting to grasp the insanity..."

"What? Jack, don't lose it on me."

Jack began to laugh. "That's just it, you can't get it *unless* you lose it."

"Sounds like some lame lyric from one of your friend's tunes."

"You've got to understand, Ted, Hubie and James O'Connor have something between them deeper than normal friendship."

Hubie was getting increasingly excited. "Well, how do you think it makes me feel? Maybe you could get a seat in Port Washington, but by the time it rolls into Great Neck the only way I'm sitting down is if somebody keels over and dies."

"They're talking about the train?" Ted was incredulous.

"They've *commuted* together. It's kind of like two guys who've shared a foxhole."

Pete started to speak. "Jack, Ash says..."

"Tell that bastard that the Fed's about to buy kyat, and if he bails out now he'll look like the asshole he is in front of the whole fucking market." Jack yelled loudly enough to be heard on the other end of Pete's phone.

Hubie was leaning back in his chair. "Anyway, I just thought I'd call to ask you if the guys on your forex desk are watching the kyat. I know you weren't keen on what happened to Myanmar. Take a look at the price action and last few news items. The stuff about Takamura. I think you'll see you can create some stability here... Yeah, right. See ya."

The other traders stared at Hubie, their disbelief bottomless.

"What?" asked Hubie.

The silence was broken by Ted "There's your buddy Hiro's gas coming across the wire."

Jack looked at his screen.

"A spokesman for the Takamura bank categorically denied market rumors that the firm had been destabilized by the kyat's decline, and refuted reports that the firm was attempting a wholesale liquidation of its Treasury holdings...."

He checked T-bond prices. They were stabilizing but not rising. The market wasn't convinced, and if they didn't get reassurance soon...

The minutes ticked by. Caroline read off quotes on the kyat: "Fifty-three and a half, fifty-five point seven two, fifty-six-one point four.... what the fuck?"

Jack leaned over Caroline's shoulder. In what seemed like the blink of an eye, he watched the kyat rise to forty-three to the dollar.

"Is that quote right?" asked Jack.

"Is *that* one?" replied Caroline, breathless.

Jack blinked at the screen. The kyat was at thirty-seven point six. He looked over at Hubie, who shrugged.

Caroline stood up from her chair and shrieked:

"The Fed is in!"

Minutes later the story flashed across the news screens.

"Market participants reported massive purchases of kyat by the U.S. Federal Reserve, at the direction of the Treasury. Reports of coordinated buying by the Bank of Japan and the European Central Bank are also widespread..."

The noise in the room was reaching a deafening level. Previously indifferent salesmen and clerks were running to their screens. The floor shook violently beneath the traders' feet.

"It's turning into a short squeeze," observed Pete, speaking into the phone. "Ash, looks like this thing's a winner."

"Pete, we're not being taped, are we?" Simon Ashcroft's voice was an angry staccato, but he was not so furious as to forget the precaution he and Pete had taken for years.

"No."

"I believe we had an arrangement..."

"Like we said, Ash, if the trade somehow worked, that deal's off..."

"The only reason it's working is because you're *making* it work! We had an understanding...."

"Yeah, but you never said 'Simon says.'"

"I can't believe this. You mean to tell me you've actually bought into that fool's nonsense?"

"You know, Ash, you're not so hot at looking into another man's soul. That's understandable. So few people in this business have one."

"Fine. If you're going to do this, I'll keep my position and make my profit, but I've got to tell you, Pete, better to lose your soul than your sense, and that, mate, is what you've just done."

"Ash, it's been a long day and I'm older than I used to be. Things slip my mind. So just let me ask…did I forget to tell you to go fuck yourself?"

As Pete hung up, Ted nudged him and pointed at a screen.

"Look at the bastards run," laughed Ted as he watched the kyat rise. "T-bonds are coming back, too."

"Pete, what did Ashcroft have to say?" asked Jack.

"When we blew past thirty-five, he said he was willing to stick it out, seeing as it was for the good of humanity and all."

"Asshole."

"More like the whole lower G.I. tract, actually."

As the kyat rose above thirty-three to the dollar, the phones on the bond sales desks began to warble; a few at first, then enough to sound like a flock of geese. Yet they were barely audible above the traders themselves. Their bellows and shouts blended until the air rang with a sound Jack found incongruous amid the high-tech trappings of the trading floor. An ancient sound, a war cry. Ted emerged smiling from among the traders, and Jack gestured back toward them.

"I see the Golden Horde is triumphant again."

"You've got a problem with a little show of corporate enthusiasm?"

"Shit, Ted, they sold some bonds. They didn't sack a rival tribe's village."

"Just call me Genghis. So let me get this straight. The whole global financial system just got turned on its head because a couple of guys were pissed at the Long Island Rail Road?"

"Trust me on this. It's an event not without precedent." He glanced at Pete, who allowed a slight grin.

Ted turned to Hubie. "Talk to the Treasury Secretary often, Hubie?"

"Once in a while. Actually, I'm glad I gave him a call. I was kind of worried I offended him the last time we spoke. Jack here kept interrupting me about that kyat sale of his."

"Figures," Jack said, nodding and laughing. "Sure. Why not? Makes absolutely perfect sense."

Ted threw his arm around Jack's neck as they headed back over to the bond sales desk, where Caroline was talking intensely with Nate. "You know, Jack, we're gonna make a mint on this thing. The kyat's just shy of twenty-nine now and Caroline's slowly unwinding our position. The bond sale'll be over-subscribed. We're golden, man." Henckel looked over his shoulder at the approaching partners, and it hit Jack they'd never let the risk control officer in on what they were doing.

"Oh, Nate, hey, I'm sorry about us not keeping you in the loop on this thing..."

"Actually, I was just thanking Caroline for your consideration."

"I don't follow..."

"I've learned sometimes being in the loop just means having your head in a noose. If this thing went south, I could honestly say you kept me in the dark. Plausible deniability. But, uh, you should know I've been offered another position, and despite Caroline's efforts to persuade me to stay you'll excuse me if don't. With the crap you maniacs pull, it's not healthy to be known as the guy responsible for controlling your risk."

By mid-afternoon the kyat had slowly slid to thirty-two and a quarter to the dollar, and though Jack knew now that Takamura would be stabilized, he wasn't sure about Myanmar itself. When Stone had sold out its allotment of the bonds, the trader gave Hiro Yamada one last call.

"Feeling better?" asked Jack.

"Relieved."

"Stepping back from the brink will do that to you."

"Fuck the brink. My uncle just smiled at me."

"Congratulations."

"You don't understand. He *smiled.* I don't think he's done that before. Ever. I'd imagined that by now the muscles involved had atrophied into permanent scowl. Anyway, he's got a lot to smile about. BankBurma, McKenzie-Kent, and Perth should all be able to make their payments. We've been able to expand the size of the Bank of Myanmar's bond sale as well."

"That should give them the capital to jump-start their economy."

"Oh, I suppose after Myanmar's bureaucrats and their local tycoon cronies deposit their cuts in Swiss bank accounts, there might be a little left for that. Already the market's wising up – see how the kyat's starting to slide? It won't go to its lows, and between that and the money we raised with the bonds there'll be enough to pay us off – we get our commissions up front, after all. But Myanmar's still screwed; it'll be years before they come back and the place is gonna hurt. You know, we didn't create Myanmar's problems - that country's corrupt as hell. We exaggerated the problem, and now we've removed the exaggeration. Isolated an economic contagion. We succeeded in not making things worse, that's all. The fundamental problems are still in place. America's trade deficit and foreign debt, Japan's underwater banks and protectionism... the powder keg's still there, and some other spark might come along tomorrow and blow the whole thing up. We just avoided being the guys who lit the fuse. We did what we always do: saved our own asses."

Jack rubbed his eyes. The images from the "Year in Review" program Hubie called about had never really left him. He'd told himself this bailout could make it right, that it wasn't just self-interest, but now he realized it was more like self-delusion. His spirit sank, and in his moment of victory this realization was starting to piss him off.

"There just isn't... I mean, maybe we could help out with the restructuring here... reinvest some of our profits on terms favorable to Myanmar. After all, we had a lot to do with this crisis in the first place..."

Hiro was laughing. "Funny thing about Americans. For all your wealth, it's not enough; you need to believe you've done good by making it, as if getting rich were some moral imperative. Manifest Destiny, alive and well, in all its hypocrisy. In older places - Europe, Asia - we've had enough history to realize money and power justify themselves. Do you see Ashcroft or me agonizing over whether a winning trade is 'right'? We're just lucky we're getting out while we can. Everyone made a bundle on the kyat trade, we got our swaps bailed out, you got your Colmedia stake, the bonds are sold..."

Swaps and the Colmedia stake. Selling bonds. Something about these things set Jack's mind in motion, a wave of reason swamping his rage like ice water on a lit match. Colmedia sold records in many countries. That meant lots of currency risk. The kind of risk you'd hedge with swaps. Given the stake Takamura had held in Colmedia, it stood to reason they'd handle Colmedia's currency hedging business. Wouldn't they also handle currency hedging for independent labels distributed through Colmedia? Helen had said she'd issued her royalty bonds through a Japanese bank. And what was Hiro's remark about warning a few of his best clients about impending trouble?

"Oh, not *again*... you're fucking kidding me..." Jack whispered under his breath.

"About what?"

"Nothing, Hiro. Nothing at all." He made a mental note to stop this business of talking to himself, but he couldn't worry about it now. Jack watched his hands fly over the keys of his laptop. In seconds he'd punched up a summary screen on Anodyne Records' bonds, and found the lead underwriter: Takamura Securities, USA, the American investment banking subsidiary of the Takamura bank. He switched to the Web and pointed his browser at the site he'd viewed on New Year's Day. The bottom of the Web page bore the legend "Distributed by Colmedia." There was also, in glowing blue, an e-mail link for fan feedback, the "webshop" address he'd seen before.

Jack leaned back in his chair, looking out at the clear winter afternoon, and understood. The world isn't round, he thought – it's shaped like a cone stood on its open end, its point towards heaven. And as you rise to the top, the circle around the cone shrinks until you're amongst everyone else approaching the zenith, even those whose paths up were very different from your own.

He shook his head. It was insane, and the trick was to find the almost-rhythms of the lunacy, the strange attractors.

"Just another fish on the bus...."

"Hey, Jack, you're starting to frighten me, buddy."

The trader closed his eyes.

"Tell me something, Hiro. Got any clients who sing?"

Before he left that day, Jack went up to his office. Looking out across the city, he would have liked to see some sign, maybe a rainbow's arc over the towers and the park below. Some seal from on high, a promise that the storm would not return. Yet only a few wisps of cirrus graced a sky blue and empty.

The bottom line. That phrase everyone around him was so fond of. The bottom line was that things were no better than the day they'd screwed up and flattened a country. At best they'd kept things from getting worse, and then only for a while.

A comet of red curls bounded through his door – Jenny Murdoch, Stone's publicist, grasping a press release. "Jack, this is so awesome! Investment bank bails out Burma and makes a fortune doing it!"

"Jenny, it's a little more complicated than that."

"Spin's never complicated, Jack, that's why it works. What more could you ask for?"

"I'd...I'd like..." He looked at her, all bright blue eyes, freckles and smile. "Listen, Jen, just put out whatever you like."

"Great! And this time I'll get you guys the cover of Forbes!"

As she flew away, he realized he did need more out of this. Something tangible, positive, if not for redemption then just to prove more was possible in the world he lived in. An idea did come to him, and he was immediately embarrassed by its inadequacy. Absurdly insignificant in the face of the misery he'd helped to unleash. Silly and sad, really, but all he could think of.

Jack opened his desk drawer and pulled out the printout of the e-mail he'd received before New Year's, the one with the Shakespearean warning. He thought for a moment, then wrote a few words on the paper.

He dropped it in a Fed-Ex envelope and printed an address on the mailing slip, preparing to send it on his way out. Though bone tired, his exhaustion mixed with another feeling, that same one that hit him on the trading floor, talking to Hiro.

"Go figure..."

He heard a knock on the open door behind him and looked up to see Pete, Ted and Caroline standing there.

"So I see you guys found some common ground."

Pete smiled. "About a hundred million dollars' worth. Our 'common ground' is some very expensive real estate."

'We'll try to be a good neighbors, alright?" Ted put his hand on Pete's shoulder.

"Look, Pete, Ted and I want you to know...about what we said on the floor," Caroline bit her lower lip. " Obviously we had you all wrong...we were out of line, and we're, well, we're..."

"No need to finish the apology, Caroline. I wouldn't want you to sprain something. Anyway, I chose to keep you people in the dark. It was a lot more fun this way. The looks on your faces...just wish I'd had a camera."

Ted was in high spirits. "Truth is even I'd like to have seen that photograph. So, Doc, just got off the phone with Yamada... cleaned up the details of the Colmedia stock transfer. He was saying you're conscience won't let you wallow in glee like the rest of us swine."

"*My* conscience? I'd say in light of recent history that's truly an example of someone making a mountain from a molehill."

"Well, remember we didn't set this game up. We just learned how to win it."

"We just work here, huh?"

"That's the deal."

"Yeah..." He tapped the Fed-Ex envelope against his palm. "Listen, Ted, speaking of deals... about this Colmedia thing, specifically the *Manhattanite.*"

"What about it? This isn't gonna be more handwringing over the death of literary integrity, is it? Because I've already heard it from our friend here." Ted pointed his thumb at Caroline

"This is just business. Suppose I could find us a partner - someone who'd inject capital into the operation, and had the media and marketing know-how to turn the thing around."

"Now you're a turnaround artist, huh?" Ted laughed. "Hard to believe anybody'd put money into that loser, let alone be able to get it off life support."

"Can you give me some time?"

Ted looked at Caroline and shrugged. "We won't be in a position to do anything with that property for a couple of months..."

"Maybe I won't need that long."

"It would certainly make life easier with our resident poet. What the hell... give it a shot. Listen, we were thinking of taking Hubie and a few of the guys out for a little victory dinner..."

"Can we do it tomorrow? I've had about two hours of sleep in the last forty-eight. Come to think of it, I don't know what's holding Hubie up either..."

"Done."

As Ted and Caroline walked out Pete hung back, leaning against the doorframe. He smiled. "Nice work today."

"Pete... that thing with Hubie and O'Connor... how did you know..."

"I pulled the tape."

"Huh?"

"You said Hubie was on the phone when you gave him your kyat order, so I pulled his line's tape to see if I could make out your voice in the background."

"I should have thought of that."

"When I heard it, I knew you weren't shitting me. And I recognized the voice on the other end of the line, and talked to Hubie about him. So I knew about our ace in the hole, so to speak." He smiled. "You see, I make a point of knowing who I'm doing business with. Like Ted and Caroline, for example. I suppose you know they're about to get hitched."

"Didn't know it was that far along." Jack smiled. "Next they'll be having kids. Wonder what that'll be like."

"Ever seen *The Omen?*"

"Look, Pete, about Hubie, he really is..."

"A loon." Pete laughed. "A complete nutjob. But he's alright, properly supervised, I mean. You're O.K. too, by the way. What Ted said Yamada was talking about; it's not all true, not exactly. You really did keep the Japanese from puking those bonds onto the market, at least for a little while. Probably made things a little easier in Myanmar as well. That's not a small thing."

"Depends on how you look at it, and on what you had to do with starting all this in the first place."

"In a free market there's only so much control anyone has. That's what makes it free."

"It'd be nice to think it's possible to have a less ambiguous impact."

"You know, in the last century a lot of guys had an 'unambiguous impact.' Stalin, Mao, Hitler...from what I've seen when guys start talking 'unambiguous,' its time to head for the hills. That's the genius of our system – it acknowledges ambiguity is usually the best you can do."

"I'm just saying I'd like to do something I can feel good about."

"Yeah, well, that's the thing..." Pete stared at him, and Jack could feel the intelligence working behind his gaze.

"What?"

"Your idea with that magazine...not for nothing, but it's not going to work."

"You haven't even heard my plan."

"Like I said, I make a point of knowing the people I'm in business with."

"Yeah, but why...? "

Pete turned to leave, then looked back. He shook his head, and his grin faded.

"Because, son, your friend with the thing for tubers? She's a businesswoman."

Chapter 9: Consider the Lilies

"Hello, Ted?"

"Hey, Jack. Surprised to hear from you on a Sunday morning."

"Listen, a guy I know at Morgan just offered me two floor seats for the Knicks game tonight. Interested?"

"No can do, bud. I said I'd take Caroline out this evening. I don't feel like getting chewed out. It's Valentine's, you know."

"Yeah, well, not a big deal for me these days."

"I never did ask what happened with your musical friend."

"Haven't seen her since the New Year."

"Sorry, man. Not the most viable merger I've ever seen, anyway."

"Spoken with the wistful romanticism of an investment banker."

"Seriously man, you don't need that lunacy. Talk to you later."

"Sure." That's about right, Jack thought. Lunacy; from lunar, of the moon. And the moon is cool and remote, brilliant and fair. A queen of all midnights, even those she does not attend, for you know how bright they would be if she did.

He was standing on his terrace. The air was surprisingly warm, with what he thought was an early hint of spring. Later he might go to the office, look at a couple of prospective trades, but it seemed too nice a day to spend in an airtight glass tower. And he had business elsewhere.

He went downstairs and his doorman hailed him a cab. He slipped in the back and gave the driver his destination.

"You are originally from New York?" the driver asked in a thick accent Jack couldn't quite place.

"Long Island," said Jack. "You?"

"Iran. I was born and raised just outside of Teheran. I came to this country a few years ago."

"From what I see on the news, I gather that was a good move."

"Very definitely. The country is run by clerics. You cannot even breathe, believe me. "

"You like the freedom here, then."

The cabby, his face framed by a thick black beard, turned around and smiled. "It is, as you say, like a breath of fresh air. Truly. Here you have music, books, newspapers...Any idea can be expressed. Nothing is forbidden."

Jack liked this driver. It was nice to meet an idealist for a change. He worked among people who thought they had a God-given right to make seven figures a year, and this guy was just happy to be in a free country.

"You know, not enough people here appreciate that," said the trader.

"And your cinema, television, music," the cabby continued. "So free. Wonderful. Just the other day I was watching one of the music channels on cable, and they showed the tape of a concert by, ah, what is her name? Very popular. Anyway, right in the middle of her performance she made a physical gesture of love to a small potato."

Jack said nothing.

"Truly! I can see from your face you think I joke with you, but I am quite serious. Actually I don't think it was a potato, but rather one of those little things. You know, orange, sweet."

Jack sighed. "Yam."

The cabbie snapped his fingers. "Yes, that's it exactly. Now back home a woman might be stoned for such an act. Ah, but in this country, how do you say it? Anything goes."

"Uh, yeah."

The cab pulled up to Jack's destination.

"Let me tell you something, my friend," said the cabby, turning to face Jack. "Life without freedom is no life at all. You should never know such a life. In America you can think and do and be whatever you like. In such a country, anything is possible." The driver's voice conveyed genuine emotion. "In such a country, a woman may express her love for yams in any way she wishes." The cabby paused for a moment. "You know I like them too, though not so much as that."

Jack smiled as he got out of the cab and handed the driver a twenty for a six-fifty fare. "Keep it," he said. "I thank you, and the Republic thanks you."

Jack crossed the sidewalk and walked through the glass doors of the Museum of Modern Art. He paid the admission fee and proceeded through a turnstile. At a few minutes before noon, he entered a room in which hung Monet's famous triptych of water lilies on a pond.

The room contained a few cushioned benches and the huge panels were hung in an arc around them. A seated viewer felt surrounded by the painting's colors, gently vibrant under soft illumination. Those colors made Jack happy to be a member of the same species as their painter. Somehow from the chaos of nature emerged great beauty and peace, and it comforted him to know men existed who understood this. Beauty and peace seemed in short supply lately.

He sat amongst the Sunday visitors looking at the painting for a few minutes. Then he heard a voice next to him:

"Consider the lilies... Solomon in all his glory was not arrayed as one of these."

He looked up at a woman in a leather jacket and jeans, wearing sunglasses and a baseball cap.

"Actually that refers to lilies of the field," said Helen, "but you get the idea."

She sat down next to Jack and he stared at her for a moment.

"Happy Valentine's Day, Dr. Kline."

"Funny running into you here."

"Well, it was your idea." She reached into a pocket of her jacket and pulled out the e-mail printout Jack had sent her by Fed-Ex weeks earlier. Under the *Macbeth* quote, he had written a request for the present meeting; its time and place, and then a single line:

Now I will believe that there are unicorns...

"*The Tempest*, right? So what's that supposed to mean?"

"After what you did, now I'll believe anything. Anyway I figured I'd go with your Shakespeare theme...though apropos your ducks and falcons and Dickinson, I almost went with 'Hope is the thing with feathers.'"

"I'd have liked that. What changed your mind?"

"A smart man told me not to be so optimistic. Even if you are a rara avis."

She smiled, then glanced around the room. "Morbid, this thing you have about returning here on the fourteenth at noon." She looked at the painting "Though it's hard to be morbid, looking at this." As she spoke, she scratched at the back of her neck, a quick, nervous motion.

"It looks even better if you're not wearing shades."

"A necessity of my profession. Hey, I didn't bring any security in here, you know."

"I was wondering where the Seventh Army was. You really need that kind of muscle?"

"I capture people's imaginations, and that's a dangerous thing to do." She looked at him over the top of her glasses. "So how'd you know it was me?"

"I found out Anodyne distributed through Colmedia, and I figured if Takamura handled Colmedia's currency hedges, they probably handled yours as well. How'd you put it – you had foreign exchange exposure when I was still playing with protons? Then I discovered Takamura had underwritten your royalty bonds, so I knew they'd worked for you. Hiro Yamada told me he'd warned some of his best clients about impending trouble, though I doubt he told you the details..."

"He told me more after the fact. At the time he just sounded worried, and told me to make sure I limited my exposure to the global markets. When I asked him if he knew you, however, he mentioned the Myanmar thing and said something about your having started the whole damn mess."

"I see."

"Fact is, he normally wouldn't have told me anything. I'm a small client by his standards, but he likes me – people do celebrities favors for no apparent reason, even Hiro, and he's richer than God."

"I wouldn't know. I've never seen God's books. Interesting that Hiro never told me he knew you."

"We met when I played Paris a couple of years back; he was visiting, Junior was there and introduced us. His bank did a great job for me with my royalty bonds. And he knows how to keep his mouth shut – in contrast to Zane, whom I met with at Colmedia a day after I talked to Hiro. The little eel told me your firm was buying out Takamura's stake at a lowball price. I figured Hiro must have been up the creek to agree to that, and it stood to reason his problems were somehow tied to the warning he'd given me. It sounded like the whole thing started with your kyat adventure. Anyway, after meeting with Junior I went down to Colmedia's web group to look at the site they'd put up promoting my new album. I answered a few fans' e-mails, then I sent you my note."

"Very impressive. Why not just tell me yourself? For that matter, why warn me at all?"

"I knew you'd discover my alter ego sooner or later. I couldn't see you taking market advice from Æther; I mean, she probably doesn' read the *Economist* …"

"Look, I'm sorry about that..."

She waved her hand dismissively. "I'm not that sensitive."

Something told Jack she was indeed that sensitive. Helen went on: "The way Hiro was talking, this sounded like something very big and very bad. I just didn't want you to get hurt. I didn't think you'd try to do anything about it."

"You didn't think a 'carrion bird' would intervene? You know, the other day I looked up red-tailed hawks on the Internet. They're in the genus *Buteo*, along with various buzzards."

"I guess even buzzards have their moments." She grinned only a little, but the laughter in her eyes was the same as the day he met her.

"So since you're not so sensitive how come I didn't hear from you sooner? You didn't return my calls. Hell, I figured it was twenty-to-one against you showing today."

Her smile vanished. "I didn't say I'm numb."

"I was just caught off guard. I really didn't mean to put you down like that."

"How did you mean to put me down?"

"Helen, I'm just trying to apologize."

"Yeah, well...so am I. Look, it wasn't all your fault. I shouldn't have played with you like that."

They sat and said nothing for a while, until she asked: "So what's this business you wanted to discuss?"

"How much do you know about Stone's deal with Fred Colson Jr.?"

"Zane told me about the plans he has for the *Manhattanite*. He's a delightful young man, isn't he? You know he's working a whole new attitude."

"He mentioned that. Just knowing him has enhanced my life."

"Anyway, my guess is sooner or later Junior will drop the 'zine completely. Truth is he hates the thing. He'd rather stick to music."

"Exactly. That's why I think I could persuade him and my guys to sell the magazine."

"Who'd want it?"

"There's a new venture capital outfit that'd might be interested."

"Oh yeah, those kinds of guys love to save literary magazines."

"They'd come in with another investor. One with the expertise to turn the thing around."

"Who?"

"Anodyne."

"You've got to be kidding."

"I'm quite serious."

"Why would I be interested in owning a piece of a magazine?"

"I've studied your business. I think you're trying to build Anodyne into a true media company, not just a vehicle for your music."

"Maybe. One can't dance around in a sprayed-on costume forever, you know. But what makes you think I could get people to read anything literary?"

"You have a gift for influencing public taste. Remember a couple of years ago when you released that video with you wearing that ...whatdayacallit? That little hat with a tassel?"

"A fez."

"And for six months so many teenagers imitated you that every mall in the country looked like an adolescent Shriner convention."

She smiled. "I did get a kick out of that. Actually, I thought they looked cute. Sort of like Secret Squirrel's sidekick Morocco Mole – loved that cartoon when I was a kid. But it's a lot easier to get kids to dress like an animated garden pest than it is to get them to read."

"What I'm looking for is a way to save the *Manhattanite* while still preserving some of what the thing is."

"Uh-huh. Even assuming I had the slightest inclination to engage in something like this, which incidentally I don't, what so-called venture capital firm would want to spend actual money helping you fulfill this dream?"

"My own. I'm resigning from Stone. Cashing out of the partnership. I figure with my own money I can seed the fund, and I can think of a few investors who might come in. One of the Stone partners, for example, has some history with the magazine and might help. I'm planning to finance start-ups and turnarounds, and the *Manhattanite* certainly qualifies as the latter."

"Your pals at Stone know about this?"

"Not yet."

"That place is your personal cash geyser. Why would you leave?"

"You know your whole speech about how we've reconciled our talents with the realities of the marketplace?"

"Sure. And from this idea I can see you've missed that point completely."

"Well, that's just it, Helen. Exactly when do you *stop* compromising? My net worth is in eight figures, and you know something? I honestly think I can find some way to get by on that. And you've got how many times what I've got? Isn't it worth buying the chance *not* to compromise? At some point, isn't that the only thing worth buying?"

"Not if it means making a fool of yourself. You take that approach and, believe me, you won't have your money for long."

"That's where you come in. Making money is one thing - making it doing something you believe in is another."

"What you're suggesting is completely insane..." Again she began scratching the back of her neck, and Jack pointed at it.

"What's with that, anyway?"

"Damn body paint gives me a rash. I've got my makeup guy working on a new base..."

"Maybe it's time to find another shtick."

"Right after I finish promoting my new album...fifty million's worth a rash."

"Look, as it stands the *Manhattanite's* dead. We'll never find a buyer, and without some trick up our sleeves we won't pull in enough money to keep it afloat. You're the one person who could help me fix it, and might give enough of a shit to try. If Bowie could start an art journal, why can't you help save a lit mag?"

She thought for a moment, grinning. "I suppose there are a few things I could do..."

"Just so they don't involve pictures of you dressed like a hooker from Neptune."

She laughed. "See? You're already killing my business plan. And that's the point – after what I'd have to do to save it, it wouldn't be "it" anymore. Anyway, this all sounds really guilt-driven on your part. What is it, some kind of crush a country, save a magazine thing?"

"I'm just trying to find a way Stone can make money off the Colmedia breakup while preserving something of value. Have our cake and eat it too."

"Interesting expression - ever consider the only way to do that involves vomiting?"

"So it's a long shot. Someone's got to make those bets, find a way to make a few of them pay off. I'd like to help build something. What did you say about what one does when dreams are dying? Maybe I'd like to keep Zane from finishing this one off."

"You mean you'd stand in the way of his rolling out *Finnegan's Wake - The Video Game*?"

"He told you about that, huh? Anyway, at least Fred Colson Sr. could stay as editor..."

"Ah, for with thee is mercy, that thou mayest be feared..."

"That's the second time you've gotten biblical on me today."

"From a psalm...something like that, anyway." She looked at him as one might a patient whose fever had rendered him delusional. "Look, I know I made that speech and everything but I was just trying to show you how things are, that we made the right choices under the circumstances. Both of us. I didn't mean for you come up with a stratagem for bankrupting yourself, and, what's far worse, me. Even if Anodyne got involved, it wouldn't make much of a difference. We'd just do in print what we do in music. Maybe some of Colson's stuff could ride along, but that's not what people buy. I love art too, but this is business. Its one thing to make a charitable donation in support of arts no one will pay for, but when real money is on the table you need to be very smart about keeping your product very dumb."

"So what you're saying is you're prepared to spend your intelligence and talent and the rest of your life putting out stuff you consider idiotic? I mean, you don't see that as an incredibly depressing contradiction?"

"Jack, my business is popular culture. We put the moron in oxymoronic."

"So dumb is the new smart, huh?"

"I knew you'd catch on, with that Ph.D. and all."

He sighed. "Can we at least have a cup of coffee and talk about this?"

"No time – you'll have to settle for walking me out. I'm leaving for Australia this afternoon. I'm performing at this concert to raise money for environmental causes. They're calling it *Ecofest Down Under*."

"Sounds kinda granola to me..."

"The crunchiest and nuttiest."

"And suspiciously altruistic."

"I suppose it's a good cause. Besides, it's going to be the biggest concert ever held down there. Huge. I'll be there, so will 'Angst'..."

"And let me guess. 'The Cud Munchers'?"

"As a matter of fact they will. I'm surprised you've heard of them."

"Zane said he was going to sign them."

"He didn't sign them."

"First good thing I've heard about the guy."

"They signed with me."

"Ah...you must feel like a Medici."

"I'm reworking their image – got them to spell their name with a 'k' and a backwards 'r' ....you know, in my business everything's cooler when it's misspelled."

"So I'm told."

"You really need to broaden your horizons. I'll send you their new CD. It's got their number one hit, *Grazing*..."

"You're very kind. Now I can see why my proposal wouldn't interest you. Backing musical ungulates would fulfill anyone's creative impulses..."

As they exited the museum, Jack saw Helen's driver open the door of her Mercedes.

"Jack, I need to ask you something."

"Sure."

"See, I'm donating my services for this *Ecofest* thing, but the increased publicity will drive my Australian album sales through the roof."

"Good for you."

"So I'll have a lot of exposure to the Australian dollar..."

"The last time I checked the Aussies looked pretty solid."

"What I mean is, you're not planning to *do* anything to Australia, are you? Because I have this mental image of you seeing a few numbers on that screen of yours, and picking up the phone, and the next thing you know impoverished Australian children are wandering the wilderness hunting Koala bears for food..."

"O.K. ..."

She lowered her sunglasses and made her eyes large in mock innocence. "I realize you have limited compassion for humans, but even you wouldn't hurt Koala bears, would you? I mean, they're so fuzzy, and they have those cute little noses..."

He rolled his eyes skyward. "Nice, very nice..."

"Oh, so you can give me shit but I can't return the favor?"

"Helen... never mind."

She sighed. "Hey, don't take it so hard. I'll think about your idea and give you a call when I get back."

"Thanks. I always find sarcasm goes down better with a chaser of condescension."

"Jack, I wish I could do things like you're talking about, but it's a slippery slope back to artist's garrets and your friend's tower with the bats. What do you want me to say? I don't know how to sell what no one wants to buy, or make people hear when no one is listening. Like I said, I learned the hard way. And I don't have your inner need to go broke. So you're not thrilled with the way things are. You can't seriously want to throw away your comparatively small fortune in some misguided, pathetic attempt to balance a ledger only you can see. I mean, are you really that lost?"

"Yeah, Helen, so if a tornado should come along and drop a house on you, can I have your ruby slippers so I can find my way home?"

She spun around to face him, and the grace of her motion reminded him of her turn that night on the sidewalk. "You know you'll miss me, with only the money munchkins to play with."

He touched her cheek. "I already do."

She looked down at her shoes. "Prada doesn't do ruby. You want a lift instead?"

"No, thanks. I think I'll walk to my office, check on a few things."

"Yeah…listen, take care of yourself, O.K.? Don't do anything I wouldn't do." She smiled. "And certainly don't do some of the things I would." She kissed him, and he turned to walk away.

"Jack."

He looked back and she was standing behind the door of her car, holding it like a shield, and he saw her as he had before, small and vulnerable.

"If you find your math isn't doing it for you, try dancing. It doesn't cost anything, and it works for me. Most of the time, anyway."

Jack watched her drive away. He began to walk to the Stone building, but found he'd forgotten why he'd wanted to go. He looked up at the towers above Sixth Avenue, his and the others, shining in the sun. They once gleamed in steely permanence, but now seemed oddly delicate, just glass and tin, a part of something fragile.

As he stared at them he thought of her words, her "particular kind of cynicism." He didn't have to buy it. Maybe he'd come up with something else.

"Like the man said, anything is possible."

He might have worried he was talking to himself again, but, he figured, no one was listening.

ABOUT THE AUTHOR

Jeffrey J. Trester holds an S.B. in physics from the Massachusetts Institute of Technology. He attended Yale University for doctoral studies in physics, and the Wharton School of the University of Pennsylvania, from which he received his Ph.D. in financial economics. His scholarly writings have been published in the Physical Review, the Astrophysical Journal, the American Journal of Physics, the Journal of Banking and Finance, the Journal of Economic Behavior and Organization, European Financial Management and the Journal of Portfolio Management. He is co-founder and co-CEO of PriceSCAN.com, the pioneering Web consumer portal, and president of the economic consultancy and venture capital firm that bears his name. He has served on the Business Council of the Federal Reserve Bank of Philadelphia, and has been interviewed by Forbes, Bloomberg, CNBC and other national media.